Tin Man Nuptials

JP Wright

To my husband, without whom my dreams may never have been realised

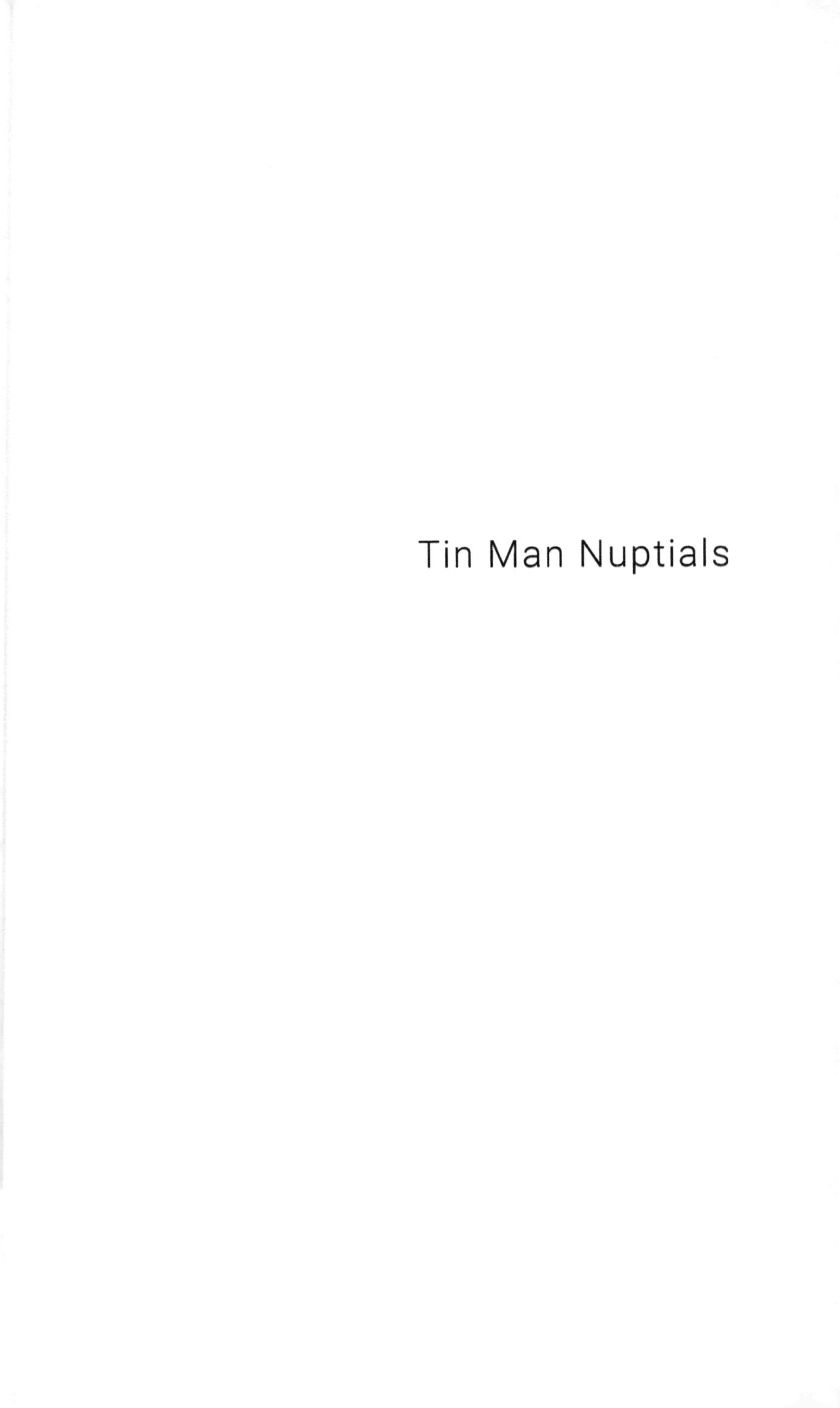

Tin Man Nuptials

ISBN: 978-1-7636967-0-9 (print)
ISBN: 978-1-7636967-1-6 (ebook)

First Printing, 2024

Edited by Sam Cooney
Cover art by @topcreativemind, Fiverr.com

Published by Joel Peter Murray
Tambooroora House,
Bunya Creek, QLD, 4655

1

Chapter 1

Gerald couldn't find James, and Charlotte was being absolutely no help. She was a mess, to be honest. Runny nose, white-girl wasted and barely able to string two thoughts together. She must have had at least a whole bag to herself to be that drunk and still standing. Gerald's bag was only half-full itself, and as he gets curt and short-tempered when he's on, he definitely wasn't in the mood for her bullshit right now.

The night had been going well by anyone's standards, but Gerald just didn't feel right, like something was missing. He'd successfully been able to push that feeling deep down so far, busying himself with hosting duties, drugs and liquor to keep unwanted feelings at bay, and right now he had other things on his mind.

As he peered through the sea of bodies heaving inside the venue, his caught sight of the lilacs that had started to slimp in their clear, plastic vase beside where he and Charlotte stood. 'It's all too much,' the flowers seemed to be saying.

It was just the sweltering heat making them act this way, Gerald thought to himself. Everything that had felt fresh and new about today now felt stifling. The venue they were confined within was a polished brick and concrete function room that they'd gussied up to look like a wedding venue. They'd done their best, but it still looked like a generic, empty function room playing a part it couldn't really live up to. Gerald didn't feel his thumb unconsciously touching the ring that had been on his finger only a few short hours, but he did feel a pang in his chest at the thought of tit not matching up to expectations though. He couldn't escape that, even with all the revelry surrounding him, he he felt as deflated and the neglected lump of cheese that lay sweating on the table beside him.

His damp shirt clung to his body, encouraging more sweat to build up and trickle down his torso. He huffed, rueing the decision he and James had made to hold their wedding in the middle of summer. If only they'd chosen a different venue, one that looked like it was ready for a wedding, instead of one that looked like they were trying to make it into something it simply wasn't.

Sweat was beading on his upper lip. His father's departure was imminent, and he bristled with anticipation to finally be rid of him. The whole day had been a triumph. He'd proven how wrong his dad had been when he'd left Gerald all those years ago. He needed air, but he also needed to find James. All the planning, the discussions about which chairs to hire, which food and drinks options to choose, where the reception would be held, how they would look, all were in part in pursuit of this very moment. This would be the bookending of their achievement in being married.

He took a swig of bubbles and plonked his glass on the lonely cheese table. He was glad at least that they didn't waste too much money on a sit-down dinner. Typical gays watching their figures for when the shirts inevitably either came off or unbuttoned themselves enough to show the appropriate amount of skin. He knew he needed to send his father home before things got completely messy.

Charlotte was now blabbering about wanting to convert one of James's friends after the reception. Gerald left her there and went tunnelling his way through the crowd, in search of his new husband.

Six months ago, weaving his way through a gathering this dense might have seemed unthinkable, not to mention the ability to dance and sing at a wedding. But the spectre that was the Covid-19 pandemic, and the heavy restrictions that accompanied it, now seemed like a distant memory. The new-found sense of freedom didn't seem at all lost on this crowd. They'd all received their two shots, after all, and having fulfilled their service to the state, they were ready to forget everything they'd all collectively been through. No one was wearing face masks. No one needed to "show their papers" to prove their vaccination status. They didn't even need to scan QR codes to get into the venue. Gerald could only imagine how different his wedding might have been under the draconian restrictions of the last year and a half since the Covid pandemic arrived in Australia. Capacity limits. Singing and dancing outlawed at weddings, pubs and clubs. Even standing while drinking had been illegal at indoor venues. But that was all over. Covid was now like a forgotten dream. They were ready to pretend it had never happened.

He brushed past guests on the dance floor. He flicked them the snippet of an insincere smile as he passed, totally unaware of how razor-sharp and caustic his features turned when he was no longer in the mood to play the good host. Moving felt good, though. It would help push back these unwanted feelings that were fighting to make themselves known. Perhaps they would dissipate after he'd gotten rid of his father. That would surely change everything. He pushed all such thoughts to the pit of his stomach and focussed on the task at hand.

As he slid his way through the congratulatory eyebrow raises eyebrows and back-pats, he heard James's familiar voice slur its way over the music. He turned to see James draped over Benny's shoulder, a watermelon cruiser in his hand and eyelids draped so far over his eyes they were nearly shut. He also couldn't help but notice that Benny was helping James stay upright with a hand around his left butt cheek, rather than his waist.

'James!' Gerald called out.

James's eyes to slowly track their way to where Gerald was standing.

'Hey! I wondered whether you'd gone wandering . . .' James managed to say, even though he didn't seem to be making any effort to find him.

Gerald might have found this sight amusing if he weren't so intent on fulfilling his final objective for the night.

'You need a bump,' he said, grabbing James around the waist and carting him off to the bathroom to sober up.

As they stumbled away from Benny's clutches, Gerald didn't look back. But he felt that if he did, he would have seen Benny looking like someone had just stolen his lunch. While this annoyed Gerald, he would have to leave it for now. He could only tackle one task at a time. His problems with Benny would have to wait.

Getting James to the appropriate bathroom to jointly have a line was going to be the tricky part. With more than 160 guests — at least forty of whom were part of the Sanders clan (James's family and extended family) — and only two toilet blocks on this level, they needed to be discreet. Luckily, this venue they'd hired was one portion of a larger venue that had three levels: this big function area they were in, the smaller one downstairs, and a restaurant on the ground floor. Gerald just needed to get James down the steps and into the downstairs function area's bathroom. Thankfully, the concern some people in the community still had about large group gatherings and the threat of Covid meant the downstairs section wasn't booked this evening. It should be empty and free.

'Congratulations!' their friend Gavin yelled at them as they tried to pass. He threw his arms out wildly and landed on them with a clumsy hug.

'Thanks, babe!' Gerald called out, stumbling to stay upright. 'Just going to get this one a little sobered up,' he added in a lower voice, millimetres from Gavin's ear.

'Say no more,' Gavin said with a smile, retracting himself and helping gently bulldozed a way through the bodies on the dance floor until they reached the staircase.

Gerald couldn't help but think they didn't really need to invite so many randoms to their wedding. It cost way more than it should have, but he was very glad to have such an amazing party. Everyone seemed to be having a good time, whether they were dancing and partaking in the wilder side of life, or sitting on chairs and chatting, as James's grandparents, extended relatives, and some of their quieter straight friends were doing.

Gerald wondered how much longer it would be until the family members went home and they could live it up a little. He didn't like his worlds clashing so obviously. Family time with the Sanders was always a wholesome affair, and while it made Gerald feel a little awkward, he enjoyed his time with them all the same. They were what Gerald always imagined a family unit to look like. Very welcoming. Yet, as inclusive as they were, he always felt slightly disconnected – a rigid out-sider, standing in the corner, with easy familial interactions so rusty to him that his mere presence seemed to scream out the need for an oil can. The Sanders always smiled a little too warmly when they greeted him, maybe to make up for the fact that he was such a cold fish, possibly in an attempt to warm him up. Gerald couldn't help feeling like damaged goods they were trying their best to mend.

His stomach sank at this thought. He wanted to be better, to be worthy of this seemingly unconditional love or whatever it was James's family gave him merely for being James's partner, but he knew he didn't deserve it. Not with all his faults. His secret proclivities. His inability to be honest about who he was. Their world was a far cry from the world he knew. He wanted so desperately to fit in, but he also needed to keep the worlds separate, to keep one part of his life unspoilt.

They were making their way down the steps; the music had started to become distant. Pauline, one of James's co-workers Gerald had only met once, came tip-toeing up the stairs and gave them a conspiratorial grin. Gerald's face flushed at the idea that the spare bathroom was being used willy-nilly by every Tom, Dick, and Harry wanting to "sober up." His chagrin heightened when he saw a queue of tweaking bodies giggling naughtily in the dimly lit space outside this bathroom. Obviously, word was out that this was the place to go freshen up.

'Come on,' he said to James, remembering that there was no such queue outside the upstairs bathroom. *Fuck it,* he thought, *it will have to do,* and dragged James back upstairs.

They made it into the upstairs bathroom without anybody else stopping them. Then, as James lifted his head away from the toilet seat, rolled note still in his hand, he blurted out, 'Let's fuck.'

They were in the bathroom alone. This toilet block, situated just off the dance floor, was at that moment abandoned. Everyone who wanted to dance was popping off downstairs when they needed to use the facilities, and the other toilet block was closer to the food table, meaning the teetotaller crowd was using that one.

'Not here!' Gerald replied, still painfully aware that this toilet's current state of abandonment surely couldn't last long. Someone was bound to walk in at any moment. Besides, Gerelad reminded himself, time was of the essence. They needed to send Gerald's father on his way. Together, as a couple.

'It's our wedding night! We can do whatever the fuck we want!'

James's hands fumbled past Gerald's cummerbund and were unzipping his fly and unbuttoning his pants before Gerald even grabbed James's wrists in protest. James could barely stand, but the way his slutty little fingers were still able to find their way around a man's zipper was a major turn-on. *Perhaps we can,* he thought, *just for a moment.* A little fun on their wedding night wouldn't hurt. As long as it didn't last too long.

Soon enough he let go of James's hands. The pretence of prudishness abandoned, and he was looking at the ceiling as James's mouth started to work its magic. *James is right,* he thought as his breathing became heavy, *it is our wedding.* They could conduct it however they saw fit.

'Have you douched?' he whispered.

'Mmhmm,' James responded over the sound of the bathroom door opening in the background. Gerald noted the sound but ignored it. In fact, it kind of heightened the experience. They would have to be quick. Quiet. So whoever was entering the bathroom right now wouldn't hear them. This was so wrong, so hot. They could be caught at any moment. It was as if the bouncer had walked in on one of their trysts at Arq or at some dance party. It only added to the tension. James would have to take his dick with silent moans and muffled whimpers, but he was good at that. He loved hearing a bottom struggle to control themselves against his thrusts.

Gerald watched as his husband's head slid backwards, slowly revealing Gerald's rock-hard cock. James took some small packets of lube out of his pockets with his lips and tongue still teasing Gerald's head. What a good, prepared boy scout of a husband James was. He'd get his dirty little reward. Gerald fumbled around as quietly as he could to slide his pants lower, failing miserably at maintaining the conspicuousness of their closed bathroom stall from the outside. James was no less silent in unbuttoning his own pants from his position kneeling on the floor.

Abandoning the idea that they could do this with any modicum of secrecy, Gerald let out a deep, gutteral sigh as James slid his mouth off Gerald's shaft and then smeared lube from the now-broken packet over his hole. Who cares if they got caught? Their guests wouldn't care. They'd probably be proud more than anything. Consummating their marriage in a manner befitting their reputation only made it hotter.

'Gerald?' the other figure in the bathroom called out. 'Are you in here?'

Gerald and James both nearly leapt out of their skin. James collapsed back onto the toilet seat and Gerald's arms flew outwards, hitting the walls of their stall. Of all the people to come into the bathroom, it had to be his father. It had to be *Patrick*. Why couldn't he have one moment of peace without his father ruining everything? This wasn't how it was supposed to go down. He quickly chastised himself while looking down at James, who was smirking unhelpfully.

'Yes! I'll be out in a second!' Gerald called out, trying with difficulty to manoeuvre himself back into his now-tight underwear and zip up his pants while James looked on. He frowned down at James and motioned for him to pull himself together. *This wasn't supposed to happen.*

This couldn't be happening. Of all the people to come into the bathroom, it had to be his *Patrick*. Why couldn't he have one moment of peace without his father ruining everything?

'Okay, we'll be going soon,' his father called out into the ether of the room, a thinly veiled reminder that they'd been wanting to go now for probably over half an hour. The voice echoed over different parts of the bathroom, as though he was looking around at the different corners of the room, pretending he didn't know both James and Gerald were in there together. This pretence annoyed him even more.

'Yep, coming!'

Gerald tucked his shirt back into his cummerbund furiously while James stumbled to his feet and started sliding his shirt back into his pants. His father's imminent departure was the whole reason he went to find James in the first place. James had distracted him. He'd forgotten they hadn't even said goodbye. The night wasn't yet theirs to enjoy.

Music blasted briefly into the bathroom as the outside door opened then closed on its squeaky hinges, indicating that his father had left them to tidy up. Gerald opened the cubicle door and marched to the mirror to make sure everything was in place. James giggled from behind him, apparently thinking getting caught in the act by a parent particularly amusing. Gerald wasn't in the mood. He'd literally been caught with his pants down when this was supposed to be the moment of reckoning. Being caught like this wasn't what he wanted his father to remember about tonight. It's not why his father was there.

James stumbled over to join his husband at the sink and Gerald stared at their reflections in the mirror. James was a mess and Gerald wasn't much better, though. Their matching white jackets had been discarded hours earlier, after their first dance, and they now stood looking in the mirrow in matching tuxedo tops. The crispness of their shirts had long ago melted away with sweat from the steamy dance floor. Gerald's now-almost-see-through white top lay clinging to his muscular frame and his his bow tie slumped in its place. He manoeuvred his wavy black hair to where it fell damply to the right side of his face, framing his angular features and large lips in a more flattering way. Gerald hated his pale skin and the sharp contours of his face. His Mick-Jaggeresque lips and his one crooked tooth were also sources of consternation, but his mother had always said he was beautiful just the way he was. While he didn't believe a word of it, he refused to change his appearance, in memory of her. Instead, he chose to focus on his physique and hair to take focus off what he considered his less appealing mug. Of course, his lips were quite a normal size, and some would even say beautifully luscious, but young minds have a way of magnifying elements they don't like about themselves, labelling them monstrous rather than unique. This was especially true in a world that idolised youth and boyishness over more angular, mature looks.

James, on the other hand, was classically attractive: blonde with a mix of manly and boyish features, the kind that look youthful now but should also age well. His athletic build was visible beneath the clothes that hung dishevelled upon his slender frame. His bow tie was missing – probably lying dead and being trampled by countless people's shoes on the dance floor. His buttons were undone halfway down his chest, and even though Gerald had seen him tucking it in, his shirt still lay half outside of his cummerbund, which sat twisted upon his waist. His beautifully tanned skin somehow still found a way to be pasty and blotchy. Poor James always showed the signs of his excess.

Was this how they were supposed to act as a newly married gay couple – fucking in cubicles like it was just another night out at Arq? Everyone had been so proud of them at the ceremony, but Gerald couldn't figure out whether they'd been proud of Gerald and James as people for taking this big step, or just so proud that they were finally attending their first gay wedding. He felt like a fraud. There was so much pressure on them to be a symbol of the modern gay couple, of marriage equality. But what was gay marriage supposed to look like? He hated feeling this way. He felt every bit as unable to live up to the task as the venue they'd hired could look like a proper wedding venue. It really was the perfect choice in that regard; the venue and Gerald both trying to live up to something they're not. Gerald was no good at playing happy families, but what could he do? All the eyes watching them walking down the makeshift aisle of brown carpet in the Botanical Gardens earlier that day had added to the gravity of the moment, magnifying the pressure he felt for them to make this marriage work.

He remembered the day that marriage equality legislation had passed. He'd received the notification on his phone at work – one of those little updates from the Guardian Australia app, then from Apple News. Then in the break room when he got up to get some water (or more correctly, stretch his legs and read the article in peace, away from his desk and the prying eyes of bosses) there was a reporter on Channel Nine breaking the news. Visuals of Magda Szubanski screaming and cheering in a white Equality t-shirt were spliced between the reporter's live coverage. Everyone was talking about how good this would be for the young gay community. They would no longer be second-class citizens, denied the opportunity to love. It would reduce teen suicide by normalising same-sex love, and remove the "otherness" of same-sex attraction. It would change everything.

Now that it was an option, though, it almost felt like there was a duty to take part in it – that every gay couple should make honest men and women of each other. A flurry of wedding chatter and activity occurred over social media as eyes turned in friendship groups all over the country towards couples who were in the kind of relationship others might want to celebrate. Gerald couldn't help but feel a little pressure to take the next step – or was it excitement at the prospect, rather than pressure? In any case, that was back when he was still with Steve, which is probably part of what contributed to their break-up. The concept of a relationship being permanent was made so much more real, and heightened the flaws in their flimsy union.

Yes, today was a moment of catharsis for his friends. Tears were being shed, Gerald knew, not only for him and James, but for what this day meant to the guests. Their long struggle for acceptance, in some cases over whole lifetimes. Gerald and James were the pretty young lightning rods that crystallised the culmination of their activism and struggles, and Gerald was more than acutely aware of the hopes and dreams that were being layered onto their union. But he also felt this wasn't quite fair to them as people to be deified like this.

Gerald finally pushed this line of thinking out of his mind and looked back into the bathroom mirror. More pressing things to consider. He shrugged it off and focussed on James, arranging his garments and hair for him because there was little he could do about his drooping eyes and blotchy skin.

'There we go. Perfect,' he lied.

It was imperative they both looked somewhat presentable, at least until Patrick left. This momentary lapse into debauchery had been a massive setback to the message he was trying to send his father, but he hoped this would all be rectified before his dad finally pissed off.

2 |

Chapter 2

Gerald and James's relationship had hardly existed outside the Covid timeline, so it was almost unimaginable that they'd be here in this venue after the tumultuous period the whole of New South Wales had experienced since they'd met in February 2020.

Gerald had spotted James a week before they 'officially met' at the Mardi Gras after-party. James had been swanning around the Ivy pool deck with his pert ass almost bursting out of a tiny pair of light-blue speedos, his soft lips nursing the straws of different-coloured daiquiris. Gerald sported bright-red speedos of his own, which he knew was a brave move with his pale colouring, but he also knew the contrasting colours would garner him attention, and he liked how his manhood was showcased through the slutty nylon fabric. He was rather proud of the way he filled a pair of speedos. From the way James's eyes glanced over to Gerald, then down at Gerald's package, then back to his friends at several times throughout the day, James appeared to feel the same way.

It was when Gerald had gone to the bathroom to empty his bladder that they had their first tryst. He'd been chuckling to himself as he heard an audible sniffle come from one of the cubicles behind him. When the door opened, he cheated a glance backwards to get a look at who it was, only to find the the hot tart in light-blue swimmers emerge like a tanned prince. He was even more handsome up close.

From the corner of his eye, Gerald saw James giving him a look, so he exaggerated the gesture of shaking himself clean before stuffing his meat back into his speedos. He stalked over to the sink then sidled up beside James, making sure James could see him check his ass out as they both washed their hands.

'Columbian cold?' Gerald asked with a cheeky grin.

'Just something to keep the energy levels up,' James responded, adding, 'Nice speedos.'

'Glad you think so,' Gerald replied honestly, keeping his body turned sideways to play coy.

'I'd be happier to see what's inside,' James said, which was more than enough for Gerald to stop acting coy.

'I'd be happy to oblige,' he said, turning towards him.

Gerald looked into James's eyes and felt electric charges seem to buzz all around them as they moved towards each other. Their lips opened and their tongues pressed against one another as Gerald's hand made its way to James's ass and James's hand caressed the outline growing in Gerald's speedos. Gerald's body pulsed as they stumbled into the cubicle and slammed the door shut. Without looking, James locked the door with one hand and relieved Gerald of his speedos with the other. When Gerald had been undressing James with his eyes out on the pool deck, he'd imagined himself as a brutish hunter that might take and devour his prey with animal instincts. Instead, he felt like a hapless piece of meat beneath James's skillful touch.

He suddenly felt James's lips leave his own, and could only watch as that same mouth slid down and engulfed his shaft.

'Fuck,' he whimpered.

James's left hand gently fingered his lower back, drawing it towards him. Gerald leaned back on the cubicle, allowing his body to arch towards James's seemingly endless oesophagus.

'Wait, you're gonna make me cum,' Gerald said after a few minutes. He didn't want to blow. Not yet. He'd surely want to fuck something or someone later in the night, and he hoped that someone would be James. But James didn't care. His greedy mouth continued to work despite Gerald's protestations, sending him over the edge. Gerald cried out, and in spite of himself, his body convulsed and emptied his balls deep into James's throat. The feeling of James's throat contracting as he swallowed made him spasm at the ongoing stimulation.

James finally pulled away and stood back up.

'That was so hot,' he said with a smile. 'Thanks.'

Then he opened the cubical and was gone, leaving Gerald to tuck himself back in sheepishly and head back into the party. The rest of the day, James barely looked back at him, but he was all Gerald could think about. What a perfect specimen. If only he'd been able to fuck him.

They officially met the following week when a mutual acquaintance, Doug, saw Gerald at the Official Mardi Gras Afterparty at the Horden Pavilion and tried to introduce them to each other.

'I know you!' James said before Doug could say anything. His eyes were the size of saucers and he was dressed as a slutty gay gladiator.

'Oh, really?' Doug said.

'Only in the biblical sense,' James answered, and Gerald felt himself twitch downstairs at the memory of being so thoroughly used.

'I'm Gerald,' he said.

'James,' was the answer. 'Who are you supposed to be? Lucifer?'

Gerald always chose his outfits to highlight his best assets, those being his body and his package. Tonight, he was in black Tom of Finland bike-short-style trunks, plus a black harness with wings combo. He hated the wings, but his friend Jerry had convinced him to wear matching outfits. Had Gerald known Jerry would be disappearing for such large chunks of the night he would have declined, but what was done was now done.

'Something like that,' he responded. 'I'm supposed to be matching with my friend, but he's wandered off.'

'Hang with us, then,' James offered, adding, 'Want one of these?' He motioned to the Chupa Chup he'd been sucking on. Gerald could suddenly feel how tightly his mouth was drawing his cheeks inwards, and wondered how large his own pupils looked. 'I can see you're having a good night,' James said cheekily as he fished a spare lollipop out of his bum bag, confirming Gerald's private suspicions regarding the current state of his appearance.

'Thanks,' he said sheepishly, hoping it was early enough in the night that he looked sexy rather than like a walking dead.

'We were just going to get a drink, wanna come?'

'Sure.'

James's overall demeanour seemed like an obvious sign that Gerald had been relegated to the friend zone, but he was happy to be saved from standing by himself again. And Doug was always fun.

'So where'd you two meet, Grindr?' Doug asked while they were waiting in line.

'Pool party,' James replied.

'Ha, figures.'

Gerald spent the rest of the night with James and Doug and a host of other friends who came and went at different intervals. Since Gerald looked so messy, and since he and James had been to the bathroom several times together to sprinkle their drinks without any lude incidents occurring, he was convinced they would now be nothing more than friends. He decided he could live with that. James was conversant and fun. Sure, they grinded against each other numerous times on the dance floor, but they both grinded against several other people that night too, including Doug and Jerry (when he'd finally reared his treacherous head again).

Gerald was quite taken aback, then, when at 6:30, an hour and a half before the party was set to shut down, James sidled up to him, pressed his crotch against Gerald's, and said in his ear, 'So, are we going to fuck tonight or what?'

After the amount of party favours he'd had that night, Gerald was also surprised to feel himself instantly stiffen up at James's suggestion. James slid his mouth towards Gerald's and they their lips connected. They pashed heatedly, the kind of heated kiss that only comes from drugs and a slew of disgusting bodies surrounding you on a dance floor. The world seemed to melt into darkness, leaving touch and the feeling of James's tongue as Gerald's only senses. He could barely hear the music blasting as they pulled each other close like they were trying to meld their bodies into something new. Their lips gnashed against each other like two rats fighting over the same block of cheese. Gerald was obliquely aware of Doug and Jerry's bemused looks, but he didn't care; all he could see, feel, and taste was James. It was only when Gerald's hand slid up James's gladiator skirt and his finger slid into James's hole that their friends finally took their leave and they were alone in the sea of strangers. They kept going like this for what seemed like an eternity before James finally suggested they take it back to his place.

The rest of the night, from the silent cab ride back to James's, to the jittery trip up the elevator, the walk down the brightly lit corridor in their tattered costumes, the jangle of keys and the creeping walk to the bedroom, before Gerald finally got to destroy James's hole: it was all like a dream. James was perfection. He was electric. That he could go from funny and friendly to whorish seductress within the span of a breath caught Gerald's imagination like nothing else.

When Gerald finally came, he knew the drugs were starting to wear off. He kept playing with James's hole until James blew too, believing that without having blown, there was no connection, and Gerald desperately wanted to establish a connection with him. Of course, Gerald's friends had tried to tell him that this preposterous views on ejaculation and affection betrayed an overall relationship between sex and love that he'd failed to work through, but this didn't matter. The important thing was that he got James to cum. They were bonded now.

'What are you doing later?' James asked, walking back into the room. He'd just finished aborting Gerald's babies in the bathroom, leaving Gerald to sit uncomfortably on the bed, not knowing what would happen next.

'I've got Bero,' Gerald said, referring to the Laneway party that happened every year as Mardi Gras' official after-after party.

'Same here,' James said. 'Maybe we could go together?'

'Sure, that'd be great.'

'Let's get some sleep first. Sleep here for a bit if you want.'

Gerald needed no convincing – he just wanted to spend more time with this enigmatic creature. They curled up in each other's arms and fell asleep.

Gerald awoke in the afternoon to James prodding his shoulder.

'It's three o'clock,' was all James said. 'Wanna get some food?'

Gerald's stomach screamed at the mere mention of it. They exchanged numbers and agreed to meet at Lumier, a trendy Sydney coffee house and morning-after establishment for the Darlinghurst gays. Then Gerald did the walk of shame back to his place several blocks away on Darlinghurst Road.

Showered and dressed in the Beresford uniform of tight shorts and a tight t-shirt, Gerald walked past headlines in newsagency windows scrutinising who knew what regarding the unloading of passengers with Covid from the Ruby Princess cruise ship and the widespread panic gripping the entire world. A lot of his friends had had trouble getting outfits from AliExpress and other such online shopping outlets due to the supply chain disruptions caused by the lockdowns in China, not to mention the troubles going on elsewhere. Things were looking worrying for Sydney, too, but thus far everything, including Australia's borders, had stayed open.

Gerald tried not to think about the news as he dragged his exhausted body along Bourke Street towards Lumier. He hoped there were no sniffer dogs on the streets or at the entrance to the party, deciding not to shelve the two caps he was bringing and instead stuffing them in his wallet. After last night, they might not even do anything, but any extra help for today's event would be welcome.

Over their late lunch, Gerald discovered that James was an architect, had a brother and a sister, was the baby (which explained his entitled and bossy bottom energy), and grew up in the Northern Beaches. He didn't have a favourite pop diva, preferring jungle beats and house mixes. This surprised Gerald to no end, especially since some of his deepest conversations with his friends were about which pop girl was contributing the most to pop culture at any given time. Luckily, James was still able to discuss the topic eloquently when the eggs Benny arrived. James went on to talk about his family and how close they were. As someone from a broken home, Gerald thought they couldn't have been more different, but he rather liked that about James.

They spent so long talking at lunch that they didn't get to Laneway until after 7pm, and even then spent the whole party together. Regardless of the lateness of their arrival, Gerald burned through both of the caps he'd stuffed into his wallet and downed several drinks before going back to James's place and doing it all again.

It was early Monday morning when Gerald stumbled home to shower, then he crumbled into his desk at work, looking and feeling like a dog's regurgitated breakfast. The first thing he did was text James to let him know he'd actually made it in, something James said he wouldn't believe until he saw it. James had planned ahead and taken the Monday and Tuesday off, which Gerald now sorely wished he'd done. Not only was he jealous that James had time and space to recover, but Gerald also felt that James's ability to live his life according to his own truth was truly admirable. To take these days off after Mardi Gras, James would have needed to request the time off, letting his whole office know that he'd be over-indulging over the weekend. It would have required that he be open and upfront about what he wanted — just as he had been in his interactions with Gerald — and to have left himself open to judgment on everything from his personal life to how his managers viewed his dedication to his performance at work. This kind of bravery was something that Gerald could only hope to aspire to. To be such an open book. James was everything he wished he could be.

Now they were married. James was his, and he was James's. He should have been the happiest man on earth, but somehow, something was still missing. That gnawing feeling that had been nagging him all night, eating away at his happiness, was still there. Perhaps after his dad left, this would all change. He hoped he was right.

3 |

Chapter 3

Gerald pushed the door open and was startled to find Patrick and his girlfriend Jennifer standing only paces from the bathroom door. Patrick was looking as dowdy as ever, standing awkwardly just on the edge of the dance floor. He was actually quite handsome. Great skin for a 52-year-old public servant, and he still had a good body, with no paunch in sight. But his brown hair was always a little messy, his clothing drab, and his shoulders stooped slightly inwards. Gerald always thought this posture made him look sneaky and untrustworthy, like he had something to hide. This assessment was only confirmed by Patrick's past behaviour. Tonight, he was dressed in a standard-issue dark-brown suit, while Jennifer stood beside him, radiant in a red dress and black heels. Jennifer was a total glamazon. Immaculate skin — the kind that money buys — and impeccable makeup to go with her one-shouldered gown. Jennifer exuded self-made-business-woman vibes. She was clearly the alpha in their relationship. *Typical that Patrick would find someone to sponge off,* was Gerald's long-held view on their situation.

He huffed internally at the sight of them, but tried his best to adopt a pleasant demeanour. You'd think that, even though they were ready to go, Patrick could maybe paint the beginnings of a smile on his face, at least to avoid wrecking everyone else's mood. *Unless this is a power play,* Gerald thought, *and Patrick's showing us he never wanted to be here, anyway.* There had to be something going on with him. He'd been particularly unenthusiastic the majority of his time there, skulking around and not saying much to anyone. At least Jennifer looked like she'd had a good time. What she was doing with his dad, Gerald could not fathom. She was nice. Gerald would like her if she wasn't Patrick's girlfriend.

'All finished up?' his dad asked, either making fun of Gerald or trying to be okay with his lifestyle – Gerald couldn't decide. In any case, he batted away the innuendo.

'Yeah, all good. James was feeling a little queasy,' Gerald replied, thinking it rather a good save of face. 'Too much alcohol.'

'Is that what that sound was?' Patrick replied with a smirk.

Gerald's face burned. This line of musing seemed a little too familiar for his tastes. Besides, what they did in the bathroom was their business. It didn't make them a joke for some nosy parker to be smirking at. *How dare he not just take the statement at face value?*

'Gerry always knows how to make me feel better,' James chimed in with an unhelpfully knowing smile and a rub of Gerald's arm.

Gerald broiled even more. He couldn't tell whether it was the plastic smile that was beginning to freeze itself onto his face or the daggers shooting from his eyes that gave him away, but he could tell his mask was slipping.

'Well, thanks for coming,' he said, hoping it didn't sound as blunt as it felt when it came out. At this point, he couldn't hide the encompassing sulk his body was going through. It was time for them to go.

'Our pleasure,' his dad said, which was obviously a lie since he showed no signs of enjoyment the whole day.

'Yes!' Jen said. 'We're so happy for you!'

Ergh, Jen. She really does try to overcompensate for Patrick's total lack of personality.

'Thanks for having us,' Patrick chimed in again. 'Your mum would've been so proud.'

A knot caught in Gerald's throat at this statement and the room was suddenly sweltering. He had been priming for this goodbye, buzzing in the lead-up to his head-to-head with his father, but he hadn't expected him to bring up his mother out of the blue like this.

He could hear Jennifer saying something about how great they looked, but all he could think about was what his mother, Annie, might say if she was really here. He imagined her standing in front of him, straight blonde hair draped past her shoulders and a fringe framing her eyebrows. She'd probably be wearing something strapless to show off her slender shoulders. Surely she'd be smiling, with a subtle lipstick being maybe her only bit of makeup, perhaps also wearing a worried expression? The same kind of expression she'd give when Gerald had been at gymnastics tournaments and he'd fumbled the landing or his arms had been sloppy. Concerned support.

The question was: why would she be concerned? Which part of this wedding thing did Gerald think she'd be concerned about? He didn't want the answer to these questions. He wiped his brow and the room began to spin.

He wrenched himself back into the room and focussed on the laughter he could hear from the people around him. James had made some quip about how, now they were married, they wouldn't keep looking good for much longer. Gerald almost sighed. He just wished the two of them would fuck off already.

The laughter died down and Patrick congratulated them again.

'I'm sure you two will make a better go of it than your mum and I did,' he said.

Gerald bristled. *What was that supposed to mean?* He imagined his face must be turning crimson by now, but he barely had time to scrunch his face up at Patrick's comment before the goodbyes started.

Patrick shook Gerald's hand awkwardly, then moved on to hug James as Jennifer came careening in to hug both of them at once. She obviously seemed to think the night had been a success. Jennifer gave Gerald two big kisses, then laughed and wiped the marks off his cheeks. He smiled and played as best he could before they finally turned and made their way through the crowd. Although he was seething at some slight he was sure his father had just thrown his way, he considered from Jen's response that perhaps he hadn't been quite as blunt and dismissive with them as he felt he'd been.

Watching them walk away, Gerald reflected that this encounter with Patrick had not yielded the results he'd wanted. Patrick was supposed to have been wowed by how much happier Gerald was than him. Instead he'd skulked around the whole time and then made some pithy slight about his deceased mother. Patrick had to have meant something negative with his parting statements. In bringing up Annie like that. In saying he and James would *make a better go of things.* What did Patrick know? He'd been out of Gerald's life longer than he was in it.

'That was nice,' James said encouragingly.

Gerald didn't agree. His father had definitely engaged in some kind of sniper attack. He was sure of it. He just couldn't figure out what it was yet. Still, all Gerald could manage through an insincere smile was, 'Yeah.'

He looked around the venue. It was already starting to look like a nightclub in here. Raggedy shirts were halfway unbuttoned and women in bare feet stomped to the music. Would his mother really have been proud? If only the lights were dimmer it wouldn't look so tragic. Maybe if the music was louder. He needed to wipe that last interaction from his mind. He needed a distraction.

'Come on,' James whispered at shouting volume over the music. 'Let's go finish what we started. Let's make some babies.'

The room turned from hot to sweltering. He thought he'd gotten over it, that he'd pushed past the guilt of his parents' divorce and the feeling of being unlovable, but it all came rushing to the surface. Annie told him it wasn't his fault, but she'd never given him a real reason, just that his dad *had faults*. But Patrick was always weird around Gerald. And when he left, all Gerald got after that were some Christmas presents and birthday gifts, and a few awkward and irregular catch-ups. And since his mum was amazing, he couldn't see any other reason why his father would leave.

As his mind ticked over, he could feel his breath quicken, like something was bubbling inside of him. For so long, Gerald had pushed down the idea that Patrick never loved him, that it was his fault his mother had such a hard life as a single parent, that there was something wrong with him. That he was unlovable, that he didn't deserve love. He always felt, deep down, that it must have been because of him. And now here Patrick was, at Gerald's wedding, seemingly confirming all his fears. How could it be anything else? He didn't know James from a bar of soap. And as far as he knew, Gerald and James's relationship wasn't any different from anyone else's, except that they were gay. They wouldn't spontaneously have a baby come along and fuck up their relationship. Gerald had anticipated Patrick throwing a grenade at him. Surely, this had to be it. It all fit.

He was furious, or hurt. He could figure that much out, but he didn't want to think about it either. He needed a drink. Fuck it, he needed a line. His father was gone; he could finally let his hair down.

James hugged him from the side, gently pressing his crotch into Gerald's thigh, but Gerald wasn't ready for human contact. Not yet. He smiled and hugged James back, but it felt like he was at the other end of the venue.

'I just need another drink first,' Gerald said.

'Okay.'

'I'll be back.'

He broke away and strode through the gauntlet of bodies that barely avoided colliding with each other on the dance floor until he got to the bar. He grabbed one of the pre-poured champagne flutes from the counter and plonked it straight onto his lips. When he kissed the bubbles he immediately felt better. It was like there was a nerve at the roof of his mouth that attached directly to his diaphragm and relaxed it. The cool liquid caressed his throat in quick, gentle gushes, and he savoured the feeling of safety it brought. *Maybe Mum would have been happy about tonight*, he thought. *She wouldn't have been concerned. Would she?* That question could only be further explored after a line. He downed the rest of his drink, grabbed another, and made his way to the bathroom.

The day had started out so nicely – all sweetness and innocence and good intentions. They'd decided not to see each other from the night before to the time they walked down the "aisle." This was a logistical nightmare, as the aisle was a long brown carpet they'd placed in an alcove of the Botanical Gardens. They not only needed to stay hidden from each other, but also hidden from the guests that would begin assembling on either side of the carpet. They chose a spot where they could hide behind two different clusters of trees and shrubs, shielding them from people's eyes, as long as the guests followed the directions on the invitations. Unfortunately, some know-it-alls chose to make their own way, ruining the surprise for themselves, and forcing either James's or Gerald's team to wave them to the other side of the shrubbery. Gerald faked smiles at them while inwardly cursing the whole idea of them doing this in such an uncontrolled environment. Getting permission had been a nightmare, and he knew people would do their own thing. Not only that, but people who weren't guests were walking past, eyeing them with levels of interest Gerald didn't appreciate. He'd advocated for a simpler wedding space, but of course his voice of reason was ignored. If James enjoyed being gawked at by strangers and allowing their big entrance to be ruined by the meandering entrance of the guests, that was on him.

Julie, the celebrant, was fantastic. She'd manoeuvred attendees to the appropriate positions like a fabulous shepherd. Her makeup alone was enough to grant her a place within the drag community. Blue eye shadow, pinkish-red lippy, big brown hair with blonde streaks, and dressed in a tight-fitting light-blue satin number. It was like her taste level peaked in the late nineties or early naughties and hadn't changed since then. Between that and her bubbly, motherly tone, she was the perfect choice, really making the ceremony fun and festive. From behind the bush, Gerald could hear her doing her thing, and it helped to calm his frustration at things not going exactly as he would have liked them.

Diana Ross and Lionel Richie's version of 'Endless Love' started playing, and Gerald's entire groomal party almost leapt out of their skins. This was the cue for the grooms' people to start emerging from their respective hiding places. Gerald stood next to his groomsmaid-of-honour, Charlotte—Charlie for short—feeling butterflies fluttering around his stomach. Gasps, oohs and aahs could be heard from guests all intent on having as much of an emotional reaction to their gay wedding as possible; a first for many of them. Gerald looked at his grandmother, Nanna Tomlin, who would be walking him down the aisle in the place of his mother. Nanna Tomlin's moist eyes were shining bright, and Gerald decided this is what happiness must feel like. The jitteriness, the sense of something new beginning. It was so exciting. He usually liked to keep his emotions safely at arm's length, relying on analysis to make sense of a situation. As such, he couldn't feel happiness in the same uncontrolled way many people do. But whatever it was he was feeling, Charlie was feeling it too. She squeezed his forearm as he hugged his grandmother and mimed a scream.

Charlie was the first one to knock on the door that morning, sporting a sluggish shorts and t-shirt combo, a face full of makeup done professionally at DJs, her hair in tatters.

'Aaaahhh!' she'd screamed, throwing her hands in the air. In one hand was a bottle of Veuve and in the other was her yellow floral dress in a black plastic carry bag. The deformed bulb dangling awkwardly at the bottom of the bag must have been her heels. His two other groomspeople, Davey and Hannah, arrived within five minutes of each other. Davey was his bestie from London and Hannah was his oldest childhood friend. They all managed to get along like a house on fire. Once Hannah arrived, Charlie popped the bottle of Veuve open.

"I've been sober long enough today!" Charlie cried out, popping the the champers within moments of Hannah's arrival and pouring everyone a glass.

They cheered the lucky groom and took elegant sips while the the mobile hairdresser set up her station in Gerald and James's one-bedder. James was getting wedding at his parents, leaving their pad as Gerald's home base.

By the time the hairdresser was finished making them wedding-ready, Gerald and Davey's hair had been lacquered so firmly in place it was like they were wearing helmets. Meanwhile Charlie and Hannah looked like elegant Dallas Vixens with hair nearly as wide as their shoulders. Even Nanna Tomlin's short hair was puffed up like a frightened chook. Davey seemed particularly bemused, and slightly worried by how tizzied he was, but there was apparently nothing else for it. The entire grooms party must be completely wind-resistant and outdoor proof.

As Diana's dulcet tones filled their small section of the Gardens, Hannah stepped away first as Gerald's oldest friend, and was joined by James's brother Andrew. Hannah was already a mum, which Gerald thought must explain her more subdued excitement. Perhaps she was always tired, or saw everything from a supportive mother's perspective. Who knows. Davey went next, paired up with Jessica, James's sister. Davey was such a hands-on friend. He'd been giving Gerald hugs and pats all day. He made Gerald feel grounded. Now that he was gone, there was nothing but the crazy, nervous energy of Charlie as she worked herself up into a froth, and with

Nanna Tomlin trying to match the excitement Charlie was dreaming up, Gerald was starting to feel decidedly unhinged.

When Charlie finally stepped away, Gerald took Nanna Tomlin's hand and squeezed it. She squeezed back, and Gerald wished he could hold onto this jittery feeling forever. This feeling of excitement and hope.

But here he was, once again, bent over a toilet seat in a white cubical, chasing a continued euphoria, trying to ignore the burning questions this wedding was pushing him to ask, refusing to address the feelings of emptiness churning inside of him.

As the white powder slid its way up his nasal passage, he wrenched his head back, closed his eyes, and flicked his nose. Just what he needed, a little kick. He wondered whether it was just the excited energy he was chasing, or whether this was the only way he could feel happiness. Perhaps that's why quiet drinkies so often ended in a call to someone's dealer and a bigger night than they'd anticipated. Maybe there was just something about the way "friends of Dorothy," as Gerald's older friend Paul, who speaks the language of the yester-gay would say, were made up. Like they couldn't keep from destroying innocence and seeking out debauchery. Was there something missing from all of them that made them feel hollow, in need of something to fill the void inside?

He took another swig from the champagne glass sitting on the tiles beside him. The bubbles were a help. He would forget. One more swig and he was ready to face the world again.

Out on the dance floor, Charlie was dry-humping Benny, and Sam was dry-humping her. James's parents were still here, and Geoffrey, James's dad, was observing the trio with an amused look. It's obvious where James got his sense of humour from. James's parents were impossibly nice. They were at ease about the gay thing, James's lifestyle choices, and even about Gerald. They seemed to like Gerald straight off the bat, no questions asked. This had always made Gerald feel squeamish. *If only they knew the full story,* he thought, but pushed that down again for the time being. He would turn over a new leaf, as of tonight.

He felt an almighty slap on his behind.

'Argh!' he screamed, and spun round to see Paul's bright-eyed smile beaming at him. Gerald didn't actually know Paul's real age. He wondered whether he had always been so wide-eyed, or whether his skin had just been pulled so tight from all the work he'd had done that he now looked permanently surprised. In any case, there seemed to be a few more lumps in his cheeks than when Gerald had last seen him two weeks ago. Gerald thought it was nice of him to make sure he was looking extra "youthful" for the occasion.

'I'm so proud of you guys!' he cried out over the noise of Megan Thee Stallion's verse in 'WAP'. Gerald was glad they'd hired a gay DJ. By now, a straight one would definitely have started playing 'Groove Is in the Heart' or some other stock-standard wedding "classic."

'Thanks, Paul,' Gerald replied as Paul went in for the hug and started slow dancing with him. Paul's cap was clearly kicking in.

'I love you guys,' Paul continued. 'You're so beautiful. I'm so proud of you. I'm so glad you guys get to do this, and I think you guys really deserve it.'

Paul kissed Gerald's neck, then continued to wrap himself around Gerald like a harmless boa-constrictor as they shuffled on the spot.

'Thank you,' Gerald said, patting his back. What more can you say to someone who's peaking and on their appreciation spin cycle?

It wasn't so much Paul's slow dancing that bothered Gerald, but the weight of expectation hanging on his and James's marriage. Like the whole world was watching them, expecting them to be the perfect example of what gay marriage should look like. Though maybe this extra scrutiny could be a good thing, he reasoned. Perhaps it would help to reign in his extra-curricular proclivities.

Gerald could now feel Paul's crotch pressing against his as the hug became tighter. Paul often got handsy when he was high, so this was basically to be expected. Gerald rolled his eyes and reciprocated, pressing his crotch forwards to create the friction Paul needed. Paul was a good friend, very generous and very caring. This fleeting moment would last long enough for Paul to see some other shiny object he could bestow his appreciation on, or until he needed another drink. Gerald merely had to wait it out, and hope this diversion into being static with one person, in one location, didn't leave him too much time to dwell on other thoughts.

4 |

Chapter 4

The night Gerald proposed to James, he was the most excited he'd been in a long time. He was home early from work with butterflies fluttering around his stomach. He'd picked out a really tasteful ring. Plain. Platinum. Very masculine, but also rich-looking. Classic. He couldn't wait to see it on James's finger. He knew James would cream himself. They'd kiss and fuck, then go to dinner, or lie on the couch and get takeaway. Maybe even go out for drinks after James told his friends. The possibilities were endless.

'When do you finish?' he'd texted James. 'Can you come home early?'

'I don't think I'll be back till 6. Everything okay?'

'Yeah, all good. Just home already. See you then.'

Bugger, he thought. It was only 2pm. Such a long wait.

He got up and paced around the apartment. He needed to do something. To calm himself down. He decided to give himself a bump. Just to "calm the nerves."

4 hours to go.

He still felt restless. Like the walls of this tiny apartment were staring back at him as he sat on the couch, waiting. The apartment seemed to be getting smaller with every passing minute he was stuck in here. He needed to feel active. He couldn't stay cooped up like this for hours. He had to stretch his legs. Get some air. Let off some steam.

As soon as the thought flicked into his mind, he couldn't stop it.

Steam.

Sauna.

Sydney Sauna.

A quick trip, just to calm the nerves, he'd told himself. *It's not like I'll do anything.*

Sydney Sauna was a gay bathhouse just across the road from the fashionable Monument Apartments where he and James were living. The Monument was a block of units that looked like a big white toaster, smack bang in the middle of Oxford Street. Gerald moved in there with James nearly a year beforehand. But their 12-month lease was nearly up. And they were about to move into the Horizon Building in Kings Cross.

The Horizon Building was a dream for Gerald. It was iconic. Another white building, but this one was a massive block that grew resplendent and tall out of the steep hill leading up William Street, elegantly looking down on the tiny buildings surrounding it, with uninterrupted views. It was definitely an upgrade. He'd always longed to be one of "those gays" who could sit in on the balcony and overlook the whole of Sydney and the harbour. Covid's effect on the rental market had made this dream a reality. Their application had been approved a week earlier, and Gerald was excited to be moving in soon. *This will be our wedding pad*, he thought, *if James says yes.* It would prove their relationship was on the up and up.

There was no guarantee of anything, though. The thought occurred to him that maybe James didn't feel that way about him. Or maybe Gerard was jumping the gun a little. Might James say no?

He couldn't sit still with these thoughts any longer. The butterflies were starting to flap a little too intensely in his stomach. He had to move. He grabbed his keys off the kitchen counter and headed for the door.

As his legs carried him to the lifts and outside the apartment block, he knew Sydney Sauna wasn't where he should be going, but he couldn't stop himself. It was so close, and he really couldn't stay sitting staring blankly at the walls at home. Besides, he was going more out of interest than anything else, he told himself. *Just passing the time till James gets home.* Nothing would happen. He was firm in that conviction. He was really only going to observe. His intentions were truly innocent. He wasn't going to do anything with anyone, just stalk the corridors for a bit. No harm. As his mind worked through the justifications, his body was powering him forward, moving of its own accord.

After a rushed trip down Oxford Street, he slipped stealthily up the stairs, passed the admission counter and into the change room. Once he was firmly inside the dimly lit maze, with the standard-issue red towel hugging his waist and an elastic band holding a key to his ankle, he relaxed. He hadn't been seen.

He hadn't anticipated other factors, though. For instance, that temptation was lurking around every corner. The particular temptation Gerald found as he turned one random corner was the sight of a muscled older gent with a thick but solid waist, nice chunky legs, and come-fuck-me eyes walking wantonly towards him. The moment Gerald locked eyes with him, the daddy yanked the towel from his waist and kept walking towards him, allowing his cock to dangle like a metronome between his legs. Gerald stopped in his tracks. They locked eyes again. The daddy walked slowly past him; pheromones were flying and tension was building in Gerald's nether regions. The daddy wanted him, and despite himself, Gerald couldn't stop from being turned on.

As Gerald watched him walk slowly away, he could see the man had a beautiful and obviously needy butt. Gerald was heating up. He could barely breathe. The man slipped into an empty cubicle just a few paces away, and Gerald told himself he shouldn't move. He followed anyway.

The older man was waiting, seated right near the edge of the black pleather bed, reclining with his hands behind him and his cock dangling between his spread legs. Gerald shouldn't be here. He should walk out, move on. He had a marriage to propose and a fiancé to make. But again he couldn't stop himself. He stepped forward, got down to his knees, and took the dangling meat in his mouth.

As he swallowed, he became hungry to show this man how good he could be with his throat. He felt like he was trying to prove something. *Naughty Daddy,* as Gerald had ironically started to think of him, since Gerald was the one being naughty for being here, grew inside his mouth. Gerald became even more eager. He loved knowing he could turn a guy on. He got off on the appreciation. He felt the Naughty Daddy's hand slide through his hair, then the hand took Gerald's hand off the pleather bed and slid it gently along his thigh towards his butt. Gerald knew what the daddy wanted. Naughty Daddy wanted to show Gerald what a good boy he was. He wanted Gerald to teach him a lesson for being so naughty. He wanted Gerald to punish that hole.

Gerald slid a digit inside. The daddy was already wet; either he'd been used once already today or he'd pre-lubed himself. Gerald didn't care which. He coaxed a second finger in as the daddy lifted his leg and leaned back on the black pleather bench to give Gerald better access. Gerald kept his fingers in there as he freed his mouth and stood over him. The daddy's legs sprawled in anticipation. Naughty Daddy placed his legs onto Gerald's shoulders. *That's right,* Gerald thought to himself, *that's where they should be.* Just one pump of the lube dispenser that sat waiting on the wall beside them and Gerald slid his way in.

He watched the daddy's eyes roll around in his head as he moaned. Gerald was completely overcome by a need – a need to prove something. He wanted Naughty Daddy to know how good a fuck he was. He started slow, but gradually became more and more ruthless, watching the daddy's head lull back and forth, his mouth open in delight or surprise, maybe discomfort, or maybe a mix of everything. He slid the daddy closer until his butt lifted itself higher, for better access, then started pounding down on him. The daddy's legs twitched and his moans grew louder, letting Gerald know how much he was enjoying it. Gerald felt worthy. He knew the daddy was loving it. He wanted the daddy to see what he'd been missing his whole life. He'd make daddy want him again after all this was over.

'You need that dick, don't you?' Gerard said.

'Yes, sir.'

'You love that dick, don't you? You've been waiting your whole life for it.'

'Oh, yes, sir, yes.'

'You'd never think of giving it up, would you?'

'Fuck no.'

'Come on, I want you to cum. Show me how much you love me fucking you.'

Naughty Daddy wouldn't be seeking out anyone else for the afternoon when he was finished, Gerald wanted to be sure of that. He wanted him to be satisfied. Satisfied by Gerald. Satisfied with Gerald.

Salty sweat trickled down Gerald's eyebrows and stung his eyes. The vinyl beds and stuffy air made his entire body slippery with sweat. His fingers, well-developed from all the bodyweight exercises he did in the gym, gripped the daddy's hips harder to gain traction as he kept thrusting.

Finally, the daddy blew his load, but Gerald didn't stop. Not until he'd cum, too. It was watching the daddy toggle between loving the sensation of being used and it starting to hurt—of not being able to say no but kind of wishing it would stop, of Gerard having that control—that sent him over the edge.

When he finally blew, his body convulsed, and he cried out in a mix of ecstasy and sorrow. The realisation that he shouldn't be here came back down on him like a tonne of bricks. *What the fuck.* He was due to propose to his boyfriend in a matter of hours. This was so wrong.

'That was awesome,' the daddy said, but Gerald was already in his own head, consumed with regret and self-admonishment.

He couldn't respond. He flicked a false at the daddy and slid himself slowly out. The daddy looked on as he wiped himself down.

'Let me know whether you'd like to do this again,' the daddy added.

'I shouldn't, actually,' was all Gerald could manage as he threw the towel around him and slid out the door, closing it behind him to give the daddy his privacy, then slinked back to the change room without showering. He just wanted to be home. He'd shower and wash his clothes when he got back, then wait for James like he should have been doing this whole time.

It was three o'clock now. Another three hours of swallowing guilty feelings and promising he'd never do something like this again. His gut was twisting as he pulled his jeans on. Why would he do something like this? He promised himself he wasn't going to when he came in. He shook his head, slid on his t-shirt, wrenched on his shoes, and ran down the steps, stuffing his socks and underwear into his jean pockets.

Once in the light of day again, walking past the cafés, buses and cars all going about their business, he thought about the champagne that was waiting in the fridge and the exciting night he had planned for James. He decided to forget this latest blip had ever happened.

***

Something about the darkened lights in the wedding venue, and the way Paul's crotch was pressing against and seeking out Gerald's package as they swayed on the dance floor, reminded Gerald of that night, and a lump formed in his throat. He wanted to forget, but he couldn't. It hadn't always been like this in his relationship with James. He actually thought James had cured him, but he hadn't. Perhaps it was more the circumstances surrounding their courtship, rather than their courtship itself, that made Gerald feel as though he'd turned over a new leaf.

Their relationship was intimately intertwined with the events of the Covid-19 pandemic. When lockdown first happened, two weeks after Mardi Gras 2020, Gerald and James had known each other just three weeks (and that's only if you count their tryst in the Ivy Pool Party toilets). And while there was already a connection there, if anything, Covid deepened their connection. It provided them with the means to be monogamous through the implementation of the "bubble buddies" policy. They'd been in constant contact since Mardi Gras, and had gone out together two weekends in a row. They could genuinely claim they were dating, and could at a stretch claim they were in a relationship. And because they were both lucky enough to be able to work from home, it meant they could go for long walks together around the deserted streets of the Pink Triangle suburbs of Darlinghurst, Surry Hills, and Potts Point. They chose a different path each time, ensuring the view never got boring, even if their conversation didn't always flow as easily as it could. Being bubble buddies also meant that they could have sex with someone without the worry of catching Covid, and could watch Netflix and relax on the couch afterwards without feeling lonely.

The couch in question would of course always be James's. James lived in a one-bedroom apartment in the aforementioned Monument Building. Gerald, on the other hand, lived in a shitty studio apartment in The Westbury, an old Art Deco block on Darlinghurst Road, right near the Coke sign. Not only was James's apartment a better choice because it was the type of thing an aspiring finance bro like Gerald wanted to see himself in one day, but Gerald's own apartment was so tiny that his living space was also his office space, which meant his ability to switch off after work was severely limited. Especially since, before lockdown, Gerald never had any need for a television (where would he put it, anyway?). Unwinding from work during lockdown would essentially mean lying on his bed and watch something on his laptop, which was also his work computer. Far from ideal. James, though, also had a sunroom. By turning the sunroom into a home office, he was able to separate the lounge room from his workspace. This was yet another thing Gerald admired about James in those first weeks.

In the manufactured, idyllic haze that the Covid lockdown created, Gerald felt his constant need for reassurance and sexual exploitations make way for wanting quiet nights at home with his new partner. He found himself sneaking glances at his mobile phone during working hours, as it sat taunting him on the desk he'd hoicked up beside the bed. He'd stare at the clock on the top of his work laptop, waiting like a domesticated puppy for James to text for lunchtime walkies or to tell him he was all done for the day. Almost as soon as the text came through, he'd be walking down the large corridors and granite staircase of his apartment block, pushing the hefty front gate and barrelling down towards Taylor Square with no thoughts other than James.

This phenomenon was new for him. He'd so often found his eyes wandering, somehow never feeling truly settled. He wasn't even phased when he heard reports of private parties being broken up by the cops, with hefty $10,000 fines being issued to the criminal participants. Nor when his friends had been telling him about their escapades in Sydney Sauna, which remarkably had managed to stay open throughout the whole of lockdown. These stories would ordinarily have filled Gerald with FOMO, but it seemed as though James was the epiphany he'd been searching for his whole life.

Epiphanies so rarely last, though. And if change does occur, it usually does so only in small increments. It's easy not to be distracted by the next shiny body when the streets are deserted and options for eye candy have been withdrawn by order of the state. When lockdown eased again, people started heading out to meet friends for drinks. The streets filled up with boys, and attention once again started flowing Gerald's way. It was only fair that he should reciprocate flirtatious glances and advances. Just an eye here and a wink there, which is all you could do with everyone still wearing masks most of the time. Those twinkles in the eyes were all harmless fun, of course. Until they weren't. Gerald didn't understand why he couldn't temper his compulsions to act on the allure of extra-curricular encounters. What was the deep well he was trying to fill?

Yes, promiscuity was rampant and normalised within the gay community, but surely it wasn't just that Gerald was a product of his environment. He continuously promised himself he'd never do it again. And even while going through with many of his devious trysts, he could sense that he was doing the wrong thing, but felt powerless to stop himself. But why was Gerald thinking about any of this? He wrenched his mind back to thinking about Patrick.

Patrick's departure was supposed to bookend a major victory in Gerald's life. Everything had been designed specifically to throw Gerald's success in Patrick's face. Hell, apart from James's insistence that family was so important, the only reason Gerald agreed to invite Patrick was so he could prove what a success he was compared to his old man. They'd done a good job, too. They'd put on a great wedding, with so many memorable moments, and everyone congratulating them. Patrick should have been left in no doubt that Gerald was wanted, loved, and needed by his friends, James's family, and his grandparents. But Gerald didn't feel like he'd won. Not yet.

Paul's fingers caressed Gerald's ribs, distracting him. The pit of his stomach squirmed as he was brought back into the room. Flushed faces swirled around him, betraying his own frenzied thoughts. He pushed his father out of his mind and decided that, whatever Patrick meant by his comment earlier, Gerald was going to prove him wrong.

Paul wasn't ready to let him go yet, so Gerald sighed and gazed out onto the scene. Benny was chatting up the DJ, who was humouring him but obviously not interested. Poor Benny. He was handsome enough, but his continual scatter-gun approach was so desperate it was a turn-off to almost everyone. Gerald's cousin Franny was sitting with his Aunt Bethany, eating some more of the wedding cake – they were two of the few guests allowing themselves to indulge in carbs tonight. Everyone else knew shirts would be off within the next hour, so were saving their waistlines. James's co-worker Rebecca was grinding against her husband, Tim, as though 'Pony' by Genuine was playing and Tim was Channing Tatum. Everyone seemed to be having a good time. So why wasn't he? He didn't like the idea that there might be something wrong with him, that he couldn't be happy or couldn't be loved, but he also didn't like the fact that he seemed to keep sabotaging things with James. After all, people only self-sabotage when they secretly don't want what they're getting. Did that mean this wasn't what he really wanted?

Paul's hands were now tracing the line of Gerald's spine that sat in the valley of muscle of his back and lats. It was time to ease out. He'd been static too long; it wasn't helping to have all these thoughts swirling around.

He tapped Paul on the back a couple of times.

'Hey, I'm just going to get another drink,' he lied.

'Sure!'

Paul recoiled his arms and started pumping and stomping like a little toy soldier marching to the music. Gerald left him sucking on his cheeks, promising himself that if he found someone with gum or Chupa Chups he would send them Paul's way. But right now he just needed air. A change of scenery. The night had been so messy. It needed order. He had to shake off Patrick and the grenade he'd thrown. He had to forget the insinuation that he'd spoiled his parents' love. But he couldn't. He wanted to prove him wrong. He had to take back control.

5 |

Chapter 5

As Gerald stalked his way through the crowd, leaving Paul to his own devices, he caught a glimpse of James. His "hubby," as he'd decided he was going to refer to him from now on, was looking more sober now. The bump had done him good. He was grinding with Benny. Benny's right hand was molesting his left butt cheek. Edwina was shouting something at them, egging them on. *He'd make a good dad,* Gerald thought to himself. He walked over and grinded on James from behind, who looked and felt good as the meat in a Gerald and Benny sandwich. Benny's hand went around Gerald's waist as James's butt pressed against Gerald's crotch. This felt right. This felt nice and slutty, like Gerald could have another bump and fuck James in the bathroom again. Gerald grabbed James's hips and pressed his hard-on against the seam of James's pants. James arched his back and craned his head backwards so it rested on Gerald's shoulder.

'Are you thinking what I'm thinking?' he whispered in Gerald's ear, giving him a *Let's finish what we started* look.

'Definitely.'

They excused themselves from Benny, who again looked like he'd had his lunch stolen, then conspicuously made their way towards the bathroom. Benny's reaction actually pissed Gerald off this time. Harmless flirtation and dry-humping with your friends are one thing, but Benny seemed to think James was really going to sleep with him – and that their wedding night was the night to make it happen. Gerald's indignation stormed inside him as he followed James's staggering footsteps through the dance floor. Far be it for him to tell James who he could be friends with, but he would have to find the right time to bring up Benny seemingly trying to take advantage of James while he was heavily under the influence.

'We should have kids,' he blurted into James's ear, and they both came to a standstill.

'Huh?'

James had obviously heard him, but didn't seem to comprehend why he was being greeted with this statement at this moment.

'I think you'd make a good dad,' Gerald said.

'Okay . . .'

James 's stunned and confused look should have said it all – that it wasn't the best time and place to bring it up, but took the look as dismissive. As a refusal.

'What's that look for?' he asked James, in answer to which James asked what the question was about.

Gerald considered the segue quite obvious. In the time it had taken him to leave Paul and find James, he'd followed the logical path in his mind. 'Let's go make some babies,' James had suggested. Since then, Gerald had weighed up the question of whether they should have children or not, and decided they should. Especially since Patrick seemed to think they couldn't handle it. This was the part where James was supposed to say yes. Gerald didn't understand where this attitude was coming from, especially on top to his annoyance about Benny.

'Don't you want kids?' he shouted over the music, feeling his features becoming harder.

'What are you talking about?' James called back, but was only met with silence and an indignant expression from Gerald. 'I don't know. Not right now,' James continued to shout over the music. 'Who'd take the time off? Who'd carry the baby? What would that look like?' There were obviously no easy answers to these questions, and Gerald's dumb and stumbling expression led James to add, 'It's just a weird thing to all of a sudden bring up. Come on.'

Gerald continued to let himself be led to the bathroom by James, but his lustre had waned. Why hadn't they discussed having children before they decided to get married? This was such a big decision. They hadn't even brought it up. Gerald sniffled. His nose was running on empty and his face had turned sullen. Had he just made the biggest mistake of his life? Was marrying James not the right decision? Without having children, how would they ever know whether they were a better match than Patrick and his mum were for each other?

They burst through the bathroom door and into the harsh overhead lighting. They both looked slightly deformed, the way people do when they're high. Pasty and weather worn. It reminded Gerald of a time when he'd been out clubbing with his ex, Steve. It was midway through the night and Gerald looked just as mutilated as he did now. Steve, though, still looked normal. The night's proceedings hadn't affected his appearance the way they did everyone else because Steve was more of a stoner who used to joke that he'd been born in the wrong time. If he could have been a hippy, he would have been. They had been so different, Steve and Gerald. That was a big part of the reason they eventually broke up, but looking at his mutilated appearance in the mirror right now, Gerald couldn't help but think that maybe if things had kept going with Steve, he would have been a calming influence, rather than enabling his addiction like James seemed to. *Steve had always wanted kids, too.*

This, of course, was the real reason Gerald's mind was drifting back to his ex. If he was with Steve right now, they might be having a real conversation about how to make kids happen, instead of winding up in the same old place, doing the same old thing, and expecting happiness to somehow materialise out of thin air.

Gerald always thought that getting married would make him feel settled, that it would change him, but he still felt the same, like he was chasing something – anything – that could truly make him happy. And now he wanting to discuss having kids, something that might actually make him happy, and his husband didn't want a bar of it. James almost seemed obstinate. What would their future look like? Gerald was pushing thirty. Would they still be looking at their dishevelled, zombie-like appearance in bathroom mirrors when they were fifty, or however old Paul was? James was being so unfair to rebuff the discussion out of hand.

'You shouldn't hang around Benny so much,' Gerald said tersely.

'What the fuck?' was all James responded.

'He obviously wants you.'

'He's a friend.'

'I've seen the way he looks at you.'

'Yes, the same way your friends look at you.'

'My friends don't actually want to sleep with me.'

'Gerald! Of course they do!'

Gerald was flabbergasted. He couldn't believe that the harmless flirting he did with his friends was anything like what he saw from Benny towards James. Besides, Gerald didn't sleep with friends. Of that, at least, he could be proud.

'Anyway, do you think you own me?' James continued. 'What, do I have absolutely no agency in your eyes? You're obviously pissy because I said no about discussing kids just now.'

Gerald scrunched his face up as though James had said something completely out of left field, but James wasn't having a bar of it.

'Of course you are! I could feel your hand turn into a jellyfish and your feet turn into logs as soon as I dismissed the idea. It was like I was leading an elephant to water. So where did that even come from? One minute we're on the way to the bathroom, and then suddenly you're asking about having kids, when you've never brought it up before as something you're even interested in. And the logistics of us being able to have kids isn't the easiest thing in the world to sort out.

Who'd be the donor, who'd carry it – have you thought about that? And what would her role be, how involved would she be, what would be our rights? This is what you wanna discuss on the way to the bathroom to fuck? Debt's a real turn-on of yours all of a sudden, is it?'

James arcing up like this was not what Gerald had expected. Having kids was obviously so far off his agenda that he was just being aggressive to start a fight. In that moment, Gerald couldn't see how he could ever bring it up again. Could it be that James really wasn't the one he'd ever have children with, to start a family with? Could his dad have been right?

'Okay,' was all he could manage. He could feel himself sliding more and more inward, retreating from the white walls and tiles of the bathroom stalls surrounding him, creeping into a mental hole to hide and think.

James sighed and put his hand out. 'Come here,' he said, and Gerald dutifully walked into his embrace. 'Let's talk about it tomorrow.'

The hug was nice, but useless. He couldn't believe he'd been shot down so harshly just for wanting to talk about their future together, just for bringing up the idea of kids. Was Gerald to have no say in how they'd live the rest of their lives? James's hand traced its way down Gerald's back as his hips pressed forward. How anyone could think of sexy time at a moment like this, Gerald couldn't fathom. His father was winning and he didn't know how to get the upper hand back. Gerald and James probably would last longer, if for no other reason than they'd never be properly tested. They'd never have their love strained by the difficulty of waking up in the middle of the night with a crying baby or stressing over school fees. Their biggest concerns would probably remain which parties to attend and how they'd sneak into bathrooms to have fun. He looked at his own sullen eyes in the mirror from over James's shoulder as these intrusive thoughts continued. James's hands were sliding through Gerald's underwear, down his butt, which made it harder for him to think. James's slender back was visible through the white tuxedo shirt, wet with sweat from the dance floor, his shoulder blades sliding over his ribs as he fondled Gerald. In spite of himself, he found himself kissing James's neck.

'Good boy,' James said, which made Gerald stand to attention.

He soon found himself stumbling backwards into the cubicle that had been waiting with its door ajar like the face of Luna Park, inviting them in to play. The overhead lighting bore down on them. The tiles squelched with ecstasy against their shoes. Everything was telling them to fuck.

Gerald's hands quickly attacked the buttons on James's shirt. He wanted to see his sweet husband bent beautifully over the toilet seat, to watch James's muscles twitched and those shoulder blades squirm as Gerald fed him what he needed. James would bury his face in his hands, moaning from the sensation of being tunnelled like the good little slut he was. Gerald could resist his advances no longer.

Soon enough, James's pants lay crumpled around his ankles. His hands held the tiled shelf above the toilet seat while Gerald ripped open a small pack of lube he'd stashed away from their earlier liaison that night, then slid in. James let out a moan, as though on cue, then arched his back. Gerald pulled on James's hips, allowing James to support himself with one hand and stroke himself with the other. Somehow, this all felt like it had been done before.

'You like that, don't you?' Gerald asked reductively.

'Yeah, baby,' was the equally reductive answer.

Gerald told himself how exciting this was. This felt good. Better than fighting. *Why can't James always be so accommodating?* Fuck his dad. James was getting more vocal as Gerald pumped harder. *Give in, slut.* Gerald felt powerful. James felt amazing. Gerald was lucky. He would forget about his dad. Forget it all. This is all they needed.

The sounds of James's moans echoing off the cubicle walls were rudely interrupted by the sound of the bathroom doors swinging open, silencing James and the thoughts in Gerald's head. They froze, panting, sweltering inside the tiny space. Gerald's sticky hands still held James's bare, sweaty hips. They were both out of breath but trying to remain silent. James cheated a look over his shoulder with Gerald still inside him and giggled silently. Gerald reciprocated the gesture, but his heart wasn't in it. He was crouched forwards, awkwardly frozen, waiting to see what would happen next.

Footsteps—male footsteps—clunked towards them on the tiles outside, and Gerald and James could tell they were going to one of the cubicles. This man was making a full pit stop, not just a trip to the urinals. They drew away from each other, realising that this would have to wait. *Yet another interruption.* Gerald probably couldn't cum right now anyway, he reasoned. He was too high.

James silently put his shirt back on as Gerald quietly drew some toilet paper from the roll to wipe himself off. The footsteps stopped and the couple froze with a start, unable to breathe. Had they been found out? When the footsteps proceeded to the stall beside them, they realised whoever it was had simply been checking themselves out in the mirror. Gerald zipped up his pants and waited for the man's cubicle door lock to flick shut. Gerald looked at James, James at Gerald. They were an absolute mess. Gerald hoped James would fix his shirt a little better than that when he came out. His parents were still here, and even though they weren't the judgemental kind, it still wasn't a good look.

After waiting till the person in the stall beside them had flopped their own pants down to the floor and plonked themselves onto the seat, Gerald carefully and quietly unlocked their door and slipped stealthily out, allowing James to click it shut again and wipe himself down. Gerald thought the guy beside them must be able to see or at least hear his pair of shoes swishing away from the second pair of shoes, but the man politely huffed and fidgeted with his phone, allowing them to maintain the fantasy that they hadn't been caught.

Gerald took a quick glance at the mirror—dishevelled, horrible—before quietly pulling the door open and walking out, all thoughts of a quiet escape quashed as the music burst in from the dance floor outside.

Chapter 6

Gerald knew that James had once seen his parents fighting in the car on the way to Dreamworld. They were pissy at each other the whole way from the parking lot to the front gates, and they were still fuming while they walked around the park huffing at the different attractions. It lasted until James and his two siblings were put on a ride. By the time the ride was over, his parents were laughing and everything was fine again. Since then, James's coping mechanism when it comes to disagreements has always been to give it space, after which everything would have settled back down and everyone could happily move on with their lives. James obviously assumed that would occur now. He and Gerald had had a disagreement; they'd made up. Everything was fine.

Gerald, on the other hand, was catastrophising on the edge of the dance floor, a fresh drink in his hand and a stormy expression that matched his mood. *They'd gotten married too soon. They didn't really know each other. James didn't want to be a father. James just didn't want to be a father with Gerald. He didn't trust Gerald. He didn't think Gerald was capable of being a parent. Or a good parent.* On and on the catastrophising thoughts went, ticking over in Gerald's brain. He'd been momentarily distracted by James's playful-yet-unfulfilled advances, and insecurities once again rushed to the surface. They were happy for now, but what about the future, and the greater issue of their long-term compatibility? Surely every fight or disagreement couldn't be settled with a trip through James's back alley.

At the ceremony, after James had made his little joke about Gerald's *endowments as a husband*, Gerald had stood like a statue watching as James's voice crack and falter with emotions as he tried to get through the 'I do' part of his vows. And when it was time to say his vows, Gerald had looked into his partner's watery eyes with nary a tear on the horizon. He'd just put his lack of tears, and the clarity with which he was able to speak, down to his usual emotional frigidity, but maybe it was more than that. They hadn't even discussed children before marriage. What else hadn't they thought about? What other barriers might James put up as deal-breakers when Gerald made suggestions? They'd only been dating for a year and a half before getting engaged, and now, six months later, here they were. It had all been so fast, like they'd been swept up in the unreality caused by Covid's major impact on their lives. What if it could all fall apart at any moment?

Gerald looked out across the room for an escape from his personal rain cloud. Charlie was talking to James's parents just off the dance floor. Geoffrey, James's dad, saw Gerald and gave him a big, excited wave. Maureen saw him next and waved him over in a comedic over-the-top gesture. He had to play happy families, regardless of how he was feeling.

'Jimmy's always been a character,' he could hear Geoffrey telling Charlotte as he approached them.

'Gerry!' Maureen called out, giving him a big hug. 'Welcome to the family.'

Gerald hugged her back, but felt awkward as always with the brimming and uncensored emotions displayed by James's family. Geoffrey then joined in, making it a three-way hug. He tried his best not to shrink away from the outrageous reception.

'You're one of us, now,' Geoffrey added. 'You can't escape.'

'Thanks, guys,' he said.

'For better or worse, as they say,' Maureen quipped. 'Bet you didn't think we'd be part of the equation when you said those words today, did you?'

They both let go and Gerald felt he could relax again. At the best of times, pretending to be an emotionally open book was one of the more awkward social interactions he ever had to perform. He usually preferred to play the part of the intellectual friend - loyal, supportive, and more interested in helping his friends solve their problems that discussing his own. People wouldn't be interested in his problems anyway. Sidelining his feelings was a better operational method for him. As such, these massive displays of affection were completely out of his comfort zone. Besides, he hoped to the god he didn't believe in that James's parents couldn't smell the musky scent of sex on him.

'Didn't Charlotte do an amazing job with the decorations?' he offered as a way to deflect some of the attention that had been thrust upon him.

'Oh, yes, it's wonderful,' Maureen replied.

'Thank you,' Charlie said, oozing with insincere modesty.

This was her time to shine, and it set up a conversation about the ins and outs of the wedding planning. She really had done an amazing job, and she was never one to shy away from tooting her own horn when she'd done something well.

As she started talking about where she sourced all the material from and how she was able to hang the palm leaves from the ceiling, Gerald looked out across the exposed-brick function room that was 238 Castlereagh. It was just an industrial shell that Charlie and co had zhooshed up with mountains of flowers and large palm-leaf fixtures dangling from the ceiling, making it look like a fantastic Arabian palace or a preloved Aztec monument between mountain vegetation that had only just been discovered. It was the perfect backdrop to the bright colours and sleek lines of the guests' formal attire. They looked like hedonistic colonial explorers as they swayed to the music the DJ was pumping through the venue or sat at the tables to the side of the dance floor with crisp white tablecloths adorned with yet more flowers, candles, wine bottles and a few nibblies remaining just in case any guests got hungry.

'The Botanical Gardens was me and Julie,' she continued.

They'd purposely chosen a spot in the gardens with two massive tree clusters either side, so Gerald or James couldn't see each other as they waited for their big entrance. The drama had been palpable.

Gerald had stood stiff-kneed with nerves, sipping a glass of Veuve in his white tuxedo, bow tie around his neck, with a fitted shirt and pants hugging his legs. He felt like a million bucks. The groomspeople were dressed uniformly: all the boys in light-blue pastel jackets and white pants, the women in long, floral, yellow dresses, bought on the cheap from The Iconic since they'd never be worn again. These light and bright colours added visual spectacle to Gerald and James's white outfits, and made the whole groomal party look like a bouquet of flowers against the outdoor greenery.

When 'Endless Love'— the cue for the grooms-people to start entering at 30 second intervals—began playing, Gerald's heart leapt. Charlie, Davey, and Hannah, all starting to jump on the spot, miming squeals. Nanna Tomlin, next to him, putting her hands to her mouth and bobbing up and down as though she too were jumping (her knees). Hannah quickly composed herself, re-setting her fringe and stepped in a semi-robotic fashion out into the view of the other guests. Next, of course, went Davey, by which time Gerald's breathing had quickened to an almost panting pace. Charlie wrenched the bottle of Veuve out of the esky beside them, filled Gerald's glass and told him to skull. She watched him finish the glass like a mother ensuring their child had taken their medicine, then turned and walked out just in time for her line: 'And I . . . I want to share . . .'

As the volume on the groomspeople's song faded, Gerald gingerly placed the glass into the esky, careful to avoid making any sound, then Elvis Presley's 'Can't Help Falling in Love' started to play. Nanna Tomlin took Gerald's arm, gave it an excited squeeze, and they slowly stepped out from the bushes to see James and his dad walking out from behind theirs.

James looked amazing. He and Geoffrey were walking arm in arm. Geoffrey wore a standard-issue black tux and James sported his white jacket tuxedo to match Gerald's. When he saw Gerald, James's smile broadened, and Gerald couldn't help joining in. The mood was infectious. All four of them walked down the brown bamboo mat that led up to Julie, who stood in front of a tacky white arch with bouquets of flowers either side that looked cheesy but absolutely perfect. They looked a little like Dorothy, Tin Man, Scarecrow and the Cowardly Lion on their way to Oz. Although Gerald usually felt like the emotional frigid of the group, today he felt like Dorothy. James would of course have to be the Scarecrow – not because he didn't have a brain, but because his public persona was that of the fool, someone who didn't really seem to have an analytic brain behind those doe eyes, when in fact he was rather switched on.

Julie wiped a performative tear away, as though this wasn't just another regular day for her. Gerald loved that about her. She was so nice, such a glamour girl – she would definitely have been one of the girls who'd partied at Mardi Gras back in the nineties.

As they walked along the brown mat, guests smiled at them from behind iPhones that were capturing the event either through video or photo. He managed to see Patrick's sullen face in the crowd – of course he couldn't crack a smile.

What was his problem this time? That gays shouldn't be getting married? Gerald wondered which way he'd voted in the marriage plebiscite, or whether he'd voted at all. Then he wondered whether Patrick was just there out of obligation. In any case, Gerald would show him. This wedding would be amazing. Patrick would rue the day he left. Gerald felt his mouth curling at the thought, as though he'd just licked the juice off a lemon. He was no longer paying attention to the smiling faces he was passing on the way to join his groomspeople. Nanna Tomlin squeezed his arm again in excitement, which brought him out of his funk and reinvigorated his absent smile.

They'd reached the end of the line; their respective crews closed in on them. Nanna Tomlin hugged him and gave him a kiss. While James's dad hugged James, Gerald noticed him whispering something (probably supportive) to him. Gerald wondered what it might have been that a father would say to a son as he watched from over his nanna's shoulder. Then both Geoffrey and Nanna Tomlin headed into the crowd, leaving Gerald and James standing like schoolchildren at assembly in front of the principal.

Julie did a great job with the ceremony. She was an absolute pro, inflecting her voice with light tones then dropping it down with emphatic gravity, and even included a few polite jokes that weren't that funny, but everyone laughed because of the mood. The perfect type of joke for such an occasion. All of this put Gerald at ease.

Once they'd spoken their vows and slipped on the rings, they had a final kiss – which James made last longer than was appropriate, forcing Gerald to pull away, garnering another big laugh from the crowd. Gerald and James had invited Julie to the party after signing the marriage certificate, but she had yet another ceremony to officiate. Very much in demand – or maybe she just never mixed business with the personal.

***

As he stood on outskirts of the dance floor with Maureen, Geoffrey, and Charlie, silently reminiscing about these earlier events, Gerald realised he'd been fiddling with his ring. It didn't quite feel real on his finger yet. He wasn't the type to wear jewellery, so his thumb kept touching it and sliding it around. Like it was something his body felt shouldn't be there. Even though he'd clearly been excited about marrying James, he definitely wasn't feeling the way he thought he should, the way a groom should feel on his wedding day. He wasn't settled.

He took another sip and looked around the venue. With Charlotte's monologue still going strong, he could appreciate that this empty, exposed-brick space had been decorated sublimely. Earlier in the night he'd picked apart his surroundings as basically a cold, brick shell, like an old warehouse with wooden floorboards, the remnants of some classic old building long forgotten, but he really did admire Charlie's work. She was able to make it look awe-inspiring, with the massive palm leaves dangling precariously from the ceiling, the large flower bouquets at each corner of the room, and the tables and chairs surrounding the dance floor. It was still just an industrial shell at the end of the day, but Charlie had made it look wonderfully festive.

The cold shell giving the appearance of something it wasn't is exactly how Gerald had been feeling as the night wore on. It was like he was decorated in wedding mode, with all the outward enjoyment that came with the ceremony and being married to a wonderful man, but somehow underneath he still felt slightly sterile, like he was putting emotions on top of a person who remained as cold and empty as the brick façade he was staring at.

Leading up to this moment, Gerald was convinced that marrying James would complete him. That the ring that sat like a foreign body on his finger right now was going to be a symbol of Gerald finally achieving peace. Or wholeness. It bugged him that he felt the opposite. All the time and effort he'd put into this event, and the result was being snatched away from him. The worst part was that, in the back of his mind, he couldn't quench the one question: Did James even like Gerald?

He had to wonder, especially after the joke James had made during his vows about Gerald's "endowments" as a good husband. Yes, Gerald liked to promote his physical attributes, but it seemed as though that was all James cared about, that this was all James saw in him. The thought that not even James liked him for anything but his size downstairs was almost too much to bear. Maybe he really was unlovable.

He tried to take another swig from his champagne glass. It touched his lips but only a drop fell out. *Fuck.* It was empty. Charlie was still talking about the decorations and where they'd sourced materials and ideas. Luckily, Geoffrey had seen him take a swig from his empty glass and given him a smirk. Gerald smiled back and shook his glass, giving him a sign that he was going to get another drink. Geoffrey winked at him. Gerald mimed an empty offer to get him one too, which Geoffrey thankfully turned down. Gerald wanted out of this conversation once and for all. He broke free from that particular episode of playing happy families and headed to the bar.

7

Chapter 7

Charlotte was now up to the part of her story where the tablecloths had been cancelled last minute because the company they were buying them from couldn't get their order through from China, which was still experiencing shipping issues due to its ongoing Covid Zero policies, and how they had to instead shop locally, which was way more expensive, but they still matched the Tiffany chairs James and Gerald had been arguing about, and Charlie managed to get them a great deal, 'So it all worked out for the best, anyway.' As he left her blabbering to Maureen and Geoffrey about the decorations, Gerald marvelled at how different James's family was from his.

He'd met James's parents after the first Covid lockdown lifted. They lived in Avalon in Sydney's Northern Beaches area, so during that first big, national lockdown, it was impossible for James and his parents to see each other due to the fact that they were more than five kilometres away, putting them outside the legal travel distance for non-work purposes. Gerald wouldn't have been able to meet them anyway, as social gatherings had been restricted to two people (or household inhabitants and one extra person). This effectively meant that during the first lockdown, Gerald and James were a gathering. They couldn't legally include either of James's parents into a catch-up, let alone both. And while this turn of events was very upsetting for James, Gerald couldn't help but feel quietly relieved at avoiding family interactions over this period.

This relief continued into Christmas and New Year's, when Gerald was supposed to attend his first big Sanders family Christmas lunch but was saved again from that fate the Northern Beaches outbreak and its subsequent lockdown, making that one area of Sydney essentially trapped over the holiday season. Gerald had only caught up with James's parents twice leading up to this moment, and he'd never met either James's sister, who was apparently a real kook, or brother, who was a doctor and had been busy and overworked since the start of the pandemic.

'Oh no! I was looking forward to that,' Gerald lied when James told him the news.

Gerald had been secretly dreading the baptism of fire of moving from lunch dates with two other people to a sprawling and noisy Christmas mess with James's immediate and extended families.

'I'm sorry, babe. We'll do something nice to make up for it,' Gerald offered as a consolation prize.

To say that he was relieved by this sudden turn of events was an understatement. Gerald felt like he deserved an award for how indignantly upset he pretended to be for having to miss out on the big event.

What these circumstances did do was to provide an opportunity for James to participate in an orphan's Christmas, which was much more within Gerald's wheelhouse. His grandparents had moved to Queensland years ago, and since he had no desire to see his father, his Christmas tradition consisted of catching up with other friends who also didn't have families to celebrate with. That year was hosted by Juan, who was excited that they could make it but also sad at the circumstances behind the happy news. As someone from a very Catholic Columbian family, Juan made a big deal of Christmas. His studio flat was decked out in a mix of tinsel, baubles, Christmas tree stuff, and religious iconography. This included a large picture of "the virgin" Mary, dressed in blue, and a nativity scene. His soundtrack for the day consisted of a mix of bopping secular Christmas standards and 'O Little Town of Bethlehem' style numbers. While all the religious stuff made Gerald's eyes roll nearly to the back of his skull, he found it sweet that Juan cared so much about something, and it made the whole day a wonderful replacement for James's family Christmas. The sweetness created by Juan's endearing sincerity (atypical within the gay community, Gerald thought), and the fact that ten people were stuffed inside Juan's tiny apartment, sitting on the couch, bed, and floor while eating off paper plates with plastic cutlery, created a closeness that provided yet another wholesome Covid-related core moment for Gerald and James's relationship.

By the time the next Christmas rolled around, Gerald had met James's parents several more times, had met the siblings individually and as part of a group catch-up, had celebrated

James's birthday at a family dinner and at James's birthday party. James's sister Jessica (who was also a party girl, when she could get a baby-sitter and when it was a big occasion) had come to Gerald's birthday party, too. Gerald was much more prepared when they finally made the trip to Avalon as fiancés on Christmas Day in 2021.

Maureen and Geoffrey were in good form as they opened the door, with Christmas hats already on their heads from some shitty Woolies Christmas crackers they'd popped earlier. Jessica's kids were screaming down the hallway; she was telling them to sit still or they'd be going home without any sweets (an obviously empty threat). James's brother Andrew's kid was sitting in the lounge room, putting a puzzle together. Everyone suspected he was somewhere along the spectrum, but no diagnosis had as yet been sought.

'Well, I'm not getting tested again,' James's sister Jessica was saying. She was a yoga instructor, and quite vocal about her displeasure with the amount of money the on-again-off-again restrictions had cost her business. 'I still can't believe they forced us to get the vaccines, but what can you do? It is for the *greater good*, I guess.'

'At least you didn't get trapped overseas,' Andrew chimed in. He'd been on holidays in India when the Delta strand hit. They'd been on a well-deserved holiday, on the cusp of returning home, when the Morrison government decided to effectively make them stateless by refusing to allow them back into the country. Needless to say, he was shocked. And while there was some minor outrage in certain parts of the media, he was surprised by how willingly his fellow Australians accepted their country negating a citizen's passport, once again, for the *greater good*. His young family had to scramble to find a place to stay, which wasn't so hard considering they had money, but the big problem was that they had no idea when they might be returning home. This posed difficulties for their spectrumy kid, Sebastian. 'I'm never voting for this government again,' Andrew continued indignantly.

Gerald found it amusing that conservatives only cared about injustice when it directly affected them. Even though he considered himself a free-market boy, he'd never vote conservative because they were always so backwards on social issues. Plus, they demonised Centrelink recipients (something he'd grown up being) as lazy dole-bludgers, as *leaners* rather than *lifters*.

'I don't like the alternative much, though,' Andrew said finally, which Gerald took to mean that, regardless of how badly the ruling conservative party had treated Andrew and his family, he couldn't bring himself to vote for the Labor Party.

Gerald flushed a little. He was glad not to be part of this conversation, otherwise he'd have pushed back against this foolish sentiment. *Rich people are rich regardless of who is in power*, he'd have argued. *It's really only the poor who suffer when governments change.*

'Well, I'm happy I got my vaccines and the government's keeping us safe!' Geoffrey said.

This comment led to a shift in the conversations to lighter topics. Although Geoffrey had partially bankrolled the lot of them during at least some point in their life, it wasn't as though they weren't above arguing with him about his political preferences or the rights and wrongs of the government's actions. It was just too early in the day to start such arguments. Even so, Gerald couldn't help but notice how sullen both Jennifer and Andrew's faces turned at this last comment. They gave each other a suspicious look, like they were dropping the subject for now, but were merely biding their time for when they'd push back. Apparently, your father choosing the good of other people, the status quo in this case, over you, was universally upsetting. Gerald couldn't help but feel a kinship with Andrew at that moment, considering his own father's inability to show any care for his well-being. James said Andrew always had a major case of middle-child syndrome, which was also apparent in his sulking manner from then on.

Gerald wondered whether the last comment Andrew had made about not liking the alternative was more of a placatory statement than an actual intention to change his vote. In the car on the way home, James told him it was probably the latter, as all the Sanders kids talked about their voting preferences, and Andrew had switched his allegiances long before the India incident.

Jessica, on the other hand, had become totally nuts since becoming a yogi. She'd adopted raw-food diets, and no one was sure whether she really got vaccinated against Covid or if she was just lying about it. Her penchant for conspiracy theories and fake news were influencing her voting decisions. She now liked fringe-dwelling parties like Palmer United, which, like its more abhorrently racist alternative, One Nation, presented itself as a challenge to the supposed status quo maintained by the two major parties, yet the policy solutions they offered actively encouraged maintenance of the status quo. There was no convincing her of anything else, though, so they just left it alone.

James said the biggest fight Jessica and Andrew got into as adults was when Jessica intimated to Andrew that the reason his kid was on the spectrum was because of the normal childhood vaccines Sebastian received as an infant. Andrew completely lost it. This was offensive to him on so many levels (one of which was that he was a junior doctor who knew better than the memes she'd been consulting on Facebook). Despite his upset, they made up at Andrew's 25th birthday a few years ago when they were both drunk and high on ecstasy. Since then, she'd kept her anti-vax talk to Facebook and Instagram, where her insistence on reposting bullshit to her feed meant Andrew had muted her on both. The fact that she managed to put shitty chemicals and alcohol into her body on big occasions and then insist on raw food diets and purity of living in other areas of her life showed just how deep her cognitive dissonance ran.

Despite the landmines that existed between the lot of them, Gerald was surprised that the rest of Christmas lunch went surprisingly well. Andrew's wife Miyuki handled alcohol extremely badly. She was already slightly slurring her words when Gerald and James arrived, and was busily discussing how hot it had been this summer with Anwar, Jessica's husband.

Poor Anwar didn't drink, and Gerald could see that, despite his nodding and expressive reactions to Miyuki's slurring conversation, he was silently wishing he could teleport himself away from the situation.

After Gerald received hugs from each family member individually, with Jessica's and Anwar's kids running up to hug Uncle James and "Uncle Gerald," and Andrew and Miyuki's son giving them a brief wave, Gerald stepped in to save one in-law from the other. In truth, he was happy to escape the huggy nature of the Sanders clan. He preferred the cooler tempered in-laws.

And while Gerald was actively creating a distance between James's family and himself, the experience wasn't as painful as it might have been if he'd come a year ago, when he and James were less than a year into their relationship. James was so at home with his family. Despite their differences, they obviously loved each other, and joked and laughed about almost anything. The conversation flowed easily, and although all three siblings had screamed at their father when the conversation finally came back to politics, they were all laughing moments later about some story from their childhood. Even Miyuki entered the fray on a number of occasions, while Anwar and Gerald sat like cold fish observing the mess in front of them.

Their manner had shown Gerald that they considered him one of the family that day, but Gerald still felt a distance between them, like he was a visitor to their closeness. This only made him feel worse, as he knew that this inability to connect was totally on him.

As Gerald drove James home later that evening, he replayed moments from the day in his head while James drifted in and out of a drunken stupor. The emotional openness James and his family displayed was something totally foreign to him, but something he aspired to. That a family could openly discuss their differences of opinions with a seeming lack of consequence was so different from his mother's emotional volatility, his grandparents' stoicism, and whatever the hell Patrick had going on. It was yet another thing that Gerald admired about his husband. It seemed to confirm for him that this is the future he wanted for his life.

So how come James had been so dismissive of him when he'd brought up children? How could he reject him so out-of-hand like that? Did Gerald really want James, or did he just long for that type of life? Perhaps he'd mistaken admiration for love, and perhaps he and James weren't the match he'd been telling himself they were.

Out on the dance floor, Paul was now sniffing around James's friend Darrel, which brought a smirk to Gerald's otherwise sullen features. Darrel couldn't stand Paul, but weddings are one of those rare occasions where everybody has to play nice. Darrel saw Gerald and waved like some poor, drowning tourist at Bondi, desperate for help from the lifeguard, but Gerald simply nodded, pointed to his glass as though to say, "I'll come save you after I get a top-up," then left him there to drown. He really shouldn't be so petty, but he had the distinct impression Darrel had tried his hardest to one-up the grooms by being the hottest one at the wedding. Well, now he'd have to live with the consequences.

Gerald was still giggling to himself when he saw Hannah sitting by herself at one of the tables on the other side of the large room.

'Hey babe, are you okay?' he asked her after he'd crossed the floor.

'Oh, yeah,' she said. 'Just having a little time-out. Been a long day. I don't know how you have the energy.'

Gerald's eyes darted awkwardly and a silence hung in the air around them. Hannah was one of Gerald's school friends, and wasn't the type to use extraneous substances to lift her energy levels. Gerald never discussed his drug use with or around her. As far as he was concerned, she didn't know about his proclivities. Hannah was one of his pre-London friends. He kept the two groups mostly separate, as though they were from two different worlds – the pre-orphan world and the post-orphan world. Hannah was there at Annie's funeral with him, and dropped him at the airport when he decided he was going to London because there was 'nothing left for me in Sydney anymore.'

'It's just the excitement for me, I guess,' he lied.

'Are you happy?'

She smiled as she asked it, and it was such a simple question, but it landed in Gerald's stomach like a loaded bomb. Of all the people at the wedding, Hannah was one of the people that knew him best. She saw the way he'd started to withdraw after Patrick left. She knew the feelings of helplessness he'd had and the self-blaming he'd done. He'd never talked about it with her, though. Too scared to bring up how he felt in case someone confirmed his worse fears. Even still, she'd seen the change in him – from mostly fun and outgoing to withdrawn and detached, as though he was living his life from behind a screen. There, but never fully accessible. This was one of the reasons Gerald loved drugs so much – they let him step out from behind the screen a little. With drugs it was more like there was merely a thin invisible film between him and his surroundings, rather than a thick plastic separator. It set him free.

He'd started using in London when his friend, Matt, offered him a pill.

'I've never done it before,' he told Matt.

'Oh, shit. Stick with me then, mate,' Matt said.

Matt looked after him the whole night, talking him through everything to make sure he felt safe and supported. When it kicked in, it was like Gerald had stepped into heaven. He finally felt what love must feel like. He hugged people and danced with reckless abandon, all under the careful supervision of Matt, his guardian angel. All of Gerald's defences came down completely. The next day at coffee, when the serotonin was still living large in his system, he decided he never wanted not to have that feeling again. This is what life should feel like.

Of course, nothing lasts forever, and chasing the feeling of the first time was all just par for the course nowadays. Nothing ever feels the way it did the first time. It becomes a habit, and drugs had simply become a way of adding some MSG to social situations. Making them just a little livelier. The problem was, he kept needing a little more MSG each time to feel that spark.

Standing in front of Hannah now, as the new and improved version of the person she used to know, he felt extremely vulnerable. He was scared stiff of letting slip that he was a *user*. He didn't want her judging him, and he thought, of anyone, she'd know it was a band-aid for something that wouldn't heal from outside influences. When she asked if he was happy, he knew how much history that question had.

'Yeah, I am,' he answered, hoping it sounded convincing, but angry that he couldn't fully mean it.

He watched from behind that plastic screen as Hannah answered, 'That's good. I'm happy for you.'

'Thanks, babe,' Gerald smiled, and the interaction was so strained now that he pushed the eject button, adding, 'I'm just going to get another one. Are you good?'

She nodded. He left.

Poor Hannah had taken a back seat to his new friends when he got back from overseas. The new friends liked what he liked, and didn't know the damaged little boy he'd been when he left. They didn't remind him of one of the darkest times in his life. He knew it wasn't fair, but tonight wasn't the night for making amends. He needed to feel better again. He decided on going to the bathroom instead of getting the drink. It would have to wait. He needed to take the edge off.

8

Chapter 8

As he knelt over the bathroom seat, Gerald had gone back to fuming about Patrick for putting a dampener on things. He knew it was crazy to give him so much of his bandwidth, but the interaction with Hannah just now reminded him just how much he just absolutely hated the asshole, that it was in large part his fault that everything seemed to be going so wrong. *How dare he draw that parallel between his relationship with Annie and Gerald's relationship with James.* He wasn't going crazy. Surely it had to be a swipe at the fact that they couldn't have kids.

Gerald's hands were shaking as he fiddled with the baggie and tipped some clumps onto the toilet seat. He tried to imagine what the fuck would make Patrick think he wouldn't be a good father. Patrick didn't even know Gerald, because Gerald had done his best to distance himself from his father his entire life. The idea that he could make *any* judgement value on the success rate of Gerald's marriage incensed him.

He chopped frantically with his credit card as he processed the other implication of his comment: that without kids,

James and Gerald's relationship wouldn't suffer the same fate as Patrick and Annie's. As though Gerald had been the problem. As though he was the reason everything went pear-shaped. Fuck Patrick, he thought, rolling up a twenty-dollar note. At least Gerald would be able to teach his kid about right and wrong. *At least I'll be there.*

His crumpled body pulsed as he hunched over the toilet seat. He just wanted one more, just to cope with tonight a little better. As the rolled-up plastic note slid along the toilet seat like a Dyson without its head, he pushed any thoughts of Patrick's relationship with his mother from his thoughts and instead focussed on considering all the ways he wasn't like his father. He was there for people, and despite his occasional proclivities of the nocturnal variety, he was a considerate partner. He also felt bad every time he cheated o James. He felt horrible, in fact. Surely that meant something. Surely that showed a conscience and desire to be better...

He also made sure he thought about people's feelings before he spoke, because he knew how much people needed to feel safe. He was a good friend in that way, and always there for people when they were going through a crisis, rarely burdening them with his fears and troubles. Maybe he wished he could open up a little more, but the time was just never right. He wasn't selfish like Patrick.

And besides, he was actually successful in his career! Patrick was a useless council clerk. His dad was *poor*. He was withdrawn and shifty. God knows how he scored Jen, who was an outgoing and fun businesswoman. Gerald was certain that anything Patrick had failed at, he could easily succeed in.

He'd just gotten married, which is more than poor Jen will ever have. And if he wanted to have kids, he'd be able to; nothing would stop him. He could easily show his dad who the better man was if he wanted to. He'd just have to figure out how.

He flicked his nose a few times to make sure it was all clean. He had to find James. Or Charlie. Either would do.

He pulled himself together, swiped his finger along the toilet seat lid to collect the remaining powder and then rubbed his teeth with it. *That was* so *unhygienic,* he realised a little too late, but hoped a bit of Veuve would sterilise it.

He burst through the doors of the toilet stalls like a fully charged racehorse and made a beeline towards to the bar, grabbing one of the pre-poured champagne flutes but only tipping a little down his throat. He needed to be clear-headed. He couldn't waste any of this expensive buzz on a downer like alcohol.

'Hey, honey!' he heard Charlotte call from over his shoulder, slithering her way onto the bar beside him like a plane crash-landing onto a rough paddock. 'Are you happy?'

'Yeah,' he lied as a way of moving on to more pressing topics. That question was coming thick and fast tonight, which seemed strange, but annoyingly uninteresting at this present moment. 'Hey, do you think I'd be a good father?' he asked.

'Of course you would!'

Charlie was fiddling around with her fascinator, which was pretty much ready for the bin at this point. She hadn't been wearing it since she grabbed the microphone and made her impromptu "speech" earlier that evening. Obviously, she'd found it again, and decided it'd be a good idea to put the wretched thing back on.

'You'd be such a good dad. Why, are you and James thinking about it?'

'Maybe,' he answered shiftily. 'I think my dad doesn't think I can do it.'

'Of course you could!'

The feeling was building up in Gerald's chest. He could be a good father. Fuck his dad for not believing in him. He could have a child by the time he was 31, according to the calculations he was doing in his head while watching people around them stomp like equestrian horses to the beat blaring through the speakers. Charlie could probably carry the baby, or he could pay someone in America to do it, like some of their friends had done. He just needed James to get on board. And James would do it. He was more the homebody of the relationship, anyway. Gerald would also stop sleeping around on James if he had a kid, which would be a bonus. In fact, rather than ruin their relationship, it'd probably make them stronger. He just needed to find James to figure out all the details. He was glad he found Charlie first. She'd given him the confirmation he needed. She was still talking, but he wasn't really listening again. He caught the tail end of her sentence, though.

'. . . are so cute together.'

'Thanks, babe.'

'Come on, have a dance with me!'

'I need to find James.'

'Poo! Okay, give him a big kiss for me.'

Charlie turned to the barman and started flirting—poor thing—and Gerald saw James with his two siblings, Andrew and Jessica, who were dressed in their groomsperson attire. Jessica's husband, Anwar, was with them, standing stiffly, like an out-of-place statue among the increasingly unruly revelry. Andrew's wife, Miyuki, was a few metres away, talking drunkenly to Maureen and Geoffrey. Gerald made a beeline straight towards the Sanders siblings. So many beelines, so little time.

'Hey, fam, can I borrow my husband for a moment?' he asked, and they excused themselves.

'Hello,' James said as Gerald put one arm around his waist, held James's hand with the other, and started slow dancing with him.

'You know what I've been thinking?' Gerald said. 'I think you'd make a great dad.' He could kind of tell he was being intense, but that wouldn't stop him. Not when there was so much on the line. He was going to make one final pitch to James. James was going to say 'yes' this time. He just had to show James he meant it. 'I'm serious, I think we should have kids. Maybe Charlie could carry the baby. Or we could pay someone in America to do it. I think it's a really good idea. We could make it happen within two years, I reckon. It could be your sperm or mine, either way.' Gerald realised after saying it that this was a lie. He definitely wanted it to be his child, the first one at least. After that, they could have one with James's sperm. 'We both earn enough to pay for it. We'd have to get a place that's big enough for the three of us, but we could make that work. What do you think?'

James was still allowing himself to be led side to side, but he wore a bemused and slightly exasperated expression.

'I think you're high,' was all he responded.

'James, come on, I'm serious.' Gerald tried to push aside his resentment at James's belittling dismissal, but could feel his movements become more and more agitated. 'I think we should do this.'

'We can talk about it in the morning.'

Gerald was gob-smacked.

James's answer was so condescending he could barely see straight. So what if he was high? *James* was high. And drunk too. This was such a non-answer. Like he was trying manage Gerald. Who the fuck waits till the morning to discuss something unless the answer is no? His mind went back to how quickly they'd done everything. They'd only been dating six months before moving in together, and had been together only one-and-a-half years before Gerald popped the question. He knew friends who'd been together more than three years and were only just now deciding whether they wanted to take the giant leap to combine households. Yet only six months after his proposal, here they were, married. It had been a lightning-bolt pace trying to organise the wedding, and that was one of the main reasons they'd chosen this god-forsaken shit-hole as their wedding venue. It had been second-best, good enough. And second-best is exactly how James's refusal to talk seriously was making Gerald feel right now. Maybe he could always sense that James didn't truly love him. Maybe that's why Gerald sought stolen moments with outside participants.

He could feel himself mentally retreat behind his plastic shell again, but he still danced arm in arm with his husband to maintain the appearance that everything was okay.

'Ugh, for fuck's sake!' James said out of the blue, breaking Gerald's focus.

'What?'

'Nothing,' he replied curtly. 'You do you. I'm going to get a drink.'

Gerald was absolutely bewildered by James's outburst. He liked to think he could disguise how he was feeling quite well. As he stood on the dance floor watching James walk off in a huff, he thought, *James must have stormed off because he was upset about the conversation we just had.* Gerald's body coursed with nervous energy and his mouth was pulled tighter than a cat's behind. No matter how much he wanted to create the family environment he'd experienced with James's family, James clearly didn't want that. He wouldn't even hear Gerald out, that's how little he cared.

Steve wanted kids, Gerald thought to himself, sulkily. *He would have said yes.*

Chapter 9

Until James, Steve had been Gerald's longest relationship. They were together for just over two years, though they failed to achieve even half the milestones he'd achieved with James. They never moved in together, and Gerald never met Steve's parents. Steve had actually met Patrick on a few occasions, mostly because Gerald felt like he needed the moral support to help him through the catch-ups and didn't want to be alone with his father. Steve was good for that, at least, but in almost every other aspect, they'd butted heads. Either his time with Steve had been more drawn-out, or his time with James had been unusually accelerated. It was probably both, Gerald admitted to himself. In any case, Steve's insistence on identifying himself as 'more of a stoner than a party boy' spoke volumes about their different approaches to life.

Steve was two years older than Gerald, but he'd let his career at Transport for NSW stall. He seemed happy to coast as a government employee, rather than being a 'slave to the capitalist agenda' (as Steve would put it) like Gerald apparently was. Steve would say that Gerald was 'obsessed with the accumulation of wealth,' while Gerald consistently bemoaned what a drag Steve was being on him achieving his goals. But being a stick in the mud was Steve, through and through.

'Fast fashion is killing the planet!' he exclaimed wildly when Gerald received yet another parcel from Shein. This time, it was a gorgeous floral chemise, with white flowers supported by sheer, almost-translucent panels. The panels were held in place by white fabric borders, buttons, collars, and cuffs. Like a male version of the sheer, white, floral dress Beyonce wore to the 2014 Grammys, only more sheer. It gave the impression that the flowers were merely hanging, suspended against the wearer's torso, showing off the lines of the wearer's muscles. You'd surely only buy this garment if you had the body to pull it off, which Gerald did. Why not show it off since he worked so damned hard for it?

This detour into climate urgentism frustrated Gerald, whose view was that if celebrities could wear an outfit once and enjoy themselves by looking and feeling fabulous, why shouldn't regular folks working at ANZ (where he was working at the time, after leaving Macquarie)?

'Don't be such a drama queen,' Gerald responded.

This, of course, set Steve off into one of his activist rants. Apart from hating being called a queen, there were important social issues to consider. Between the box and plastic packaging, the fuel required through postage, the return journey of garments that weren't wanted because they either didn't fit or just weren't right because the buyer couldn't try them on, and the increased waste in landfills from cheap, shitty garments that lost their shape after two or three washes. It all added up to one thing: toxic capitalism!

'Just because a market can sell things cheaper doesn't mean they should be allowed to,' Steve argued.

Gerald rolled his eyes at Steve's emphatic conviction, as though this was the first time he was lecturing Gerald about the issue.

Steve would go on and on about wanting a 'minor revolution,' whatever that meant. He would describe it as not a full-blown revolution towards total communism (which might take away ambition and agency), but a revolution that brought us back to a time when the rich paid their fair share and companies couldn't skip out on taxes by setting themselves up as multinationals, sending overhead costs off to their head office in tax havens to avoid making profits locally.

This was pie in the sky thinking, according to Gerald, who just wanted to make use of the easier access to things technology had provided them with.

'I suppose you just want to get as many eyes on you as possible with that shirt next time you're at the Beresford or Columbian. And then what's the end goal?' There was accusation in his tone which Gerald didn't appreciate. Steve wasn't a subtle character and this seemed to be alluding to other issues Gerald didn't want to discuss.

'Oh my god, Beyonce didn't want to fuck everyone in sight when she wore a sheer outfit to the Grammys!'

Gerald considered this retort rather clever, because to Steve and Gerald's generation, Beyonce was somewhat of a deity. Using her as a shield felt like an effective tool against further attacks.

It was telling that Steve brought up the Beresford, since this was such a sore spot for him. Steve hated the way people in Sydney (and possibly any big city, really) would stand there talking to you while their eyes were scanning the room (or outdoor courtyard, in the Beresford's case) looking for the next-best option. Steve always thought it particularly rude, and put it down to a paradox of choice, where there are so many other options out there that you can never be happy with the choice of person with whom you're stuck talking. There might be someone else even better that will make you even happier.

What Steve didn't realise was that if he wasn't such a wet blanket, and didn't use these social outings as yet another forum to discuss the appalling state of the world, his audience's eyes might be less inclined to wander. Luckily for him, he had beautifully thick Latin lips, courtesy of his Mexican background, and captivating almond eyes. And although he believed himself better than the average gay, who only cared about superficial things like appearance and sex, he too ensured his naturally muscular body always looked defined. He convinced himself he worked out for health reasons, but none of us are totally immune to societal pressures when it comes to body image. His physical attractiveness meant his audience always had something nice with which to distract themselves while he was sermonising about the social evils we must fight against. This distraction could only last so long, though. Eventually, the eyes inevitably needed to wander.

Gerald always found it kind of odd that someone who worked in communications really didn't understand the right time and place for certain conversations. *He works for the state government, though,* Gerald would reason, *so how good at his job could he really be?*

As a response to Steve's assertions that working for the government was allowing him to make the world a better place, Gerald would often wonder aloud, 'When was the last time anyone actively sought out the social media activities of the government?'

Steve would say he was ensuring people knew their rights, the availabilities of getting around easier, and the benefits of public transport, both environmentally and in terms of saving time and money on parking. Gerald considered this last point a furphy that had some statistical backing when you twisted certain statistics to fit the narrative, but to Steve, it was all important work that allowed people who had less to do just as much as those who had more.

As politically idealistic as Steve might be, though, he was no fool. Yes, of course Gerald enjoyed showing off his body and being seen as eye candy. The problem was that Steve inherently knew that, should the mood strike, Gerald might let them unwrap and sample the candy. He had no proof of this, of course, and sometimes he just put it down to his own insecurities, but something in Gerald's manner prompted the idea that his wandering eye might just be the tip of a much larger iceberg.

'So, you think what Beyonce really wants you to do is destroy the planet to emulate her. As though there aren't already enough white, gay men appropriating the identities and mannerisms of African-American women.'

'For fuck's sake, Steve, can you give it a rest? How is that even the issue now?'

This was the big problem with activists. They spend so much time thinking about what's wrong with the world they have no time to enjoy the good things in life. Unless getting off on guilt was your thing, in which case you're living your best life. Gerald didn't want to think about all the people who had it so tough, since he grew up with nothing and was very much enjoying not being poor anymore. So what if that made him a slave to the capitalist agenda? They lived in a capitalist society!

'It's because you do too much coke,' Steve explained to him one day. 'That's why we should all do more weed. Coke is the greedy man's drug, always pushing us to want more, more, more. Weed is the great leveller. If we all just did weed, the world would be a better place, and I reckon the environment would start getting better again, too.'

As this philosophical gem was the only social solution Steve hadn't ripped out of a book, article, or online discussion forum, it betrayed the fact that he wasn't as great a thinker as he imagined himself to be. It simply showed his bias: Steve was a homebody and a pot head. Naturally, he thought the world should operate in the way that he considered optimal.

'Okay, babe, remind me of that when you want a line tonight,' was Gerald's reply.

It was a Friday. Steve had slept over at Gerald's place, and they were getting ready for work. This comeback from Gerald pissed Steve off, because it was true that he did coke when he was out with Gerald's friends. But the truth was that he found Gerald's friends so fucking boring and dim-witted that it was the only way he could make it through the evening with them. Rather than responding thus, Steve opted for the silent treatment and a sulking strop-face as his answer. This way, Gerald could claim a victory, but it would be a bitter win. The kind of victory that made nobody happy.

After having walked down the steps of Gerald's apartment block in silence, Gerald said, 'Okay, bye then,' to which Steve replied, 'Yep, bye.'

As they walked their separate ways, Gerald reflected that for someone who believed so much in community—where the common good outranks personal preferences—and who longed for a stronger sense of community, Steve certainly didn't act like someone who was willing set aside personal differences for the good of others.

At first, their differences were cute. It's what made them unique and interesting. But once the initial sexual attraction wore off, Gerald found them tiresome. Steve was becoming a boring fuddy-duddy who just wanted to settle down and spend nights on the couch. Gerald wasn't ready to be a senior citizen just yet. He was only 26 at that point, but the two-and-a-half-year age gap can't have been completely responsible for the divergence of life goals. Gerald was far too ambitious, and too ready to live new experiences, to see himself fitting into the dinner-and-TV-in-front-of-the-couch life Steve seemed ready for.

It was only a month after the fight over the Shein shirt that things ended. Steve liked to say they'd broken up over the cashless welfare card, which was true in a way, but also an exaggerated punch line.

The cashless welfare card was something that was trialled as an alternative to the direct deposit of funds into a welfare recipient's bank account. The card could only be used at locations where certain items (like food) could be purchased, and couldn't be used at liquor stores or for cigarettes, nor could a recipient take money out of an ATM like they could with traditional welfare payments. It was a way of ensuring government funds weren't going towards drinks, smokes, or illicit substances.

Steve had been bemoaning the government's implementation of the card as paternalistic, offensive, and demeaning to those on the dole, because the government was dictating where their money could be spent. Gerald, while not a conservative voter by any means, defended it, because 'Why should they be allowed to buy booze and cigarettes, among other things, where they're on the government tit?'

'You're kidding me, right?' Steve asked, to which Gerald responded he of course wasn't. 'But you've been on Centrelink, when you were a student right? And when your mum was bringing you up as a solo parent?'

'Yes, of course.'

Gerald's cheeks flushed. He didn't like people using his mother in an argument, especially when he knew where this line of question was leading and that his argument would soon be derailed.

'So, you're telling me you never once went to a bar and bought a drink or to the bottle-o when you were at uni.'

'And what's your point?'

'My point is that you can't see the rank hypocrisy in what you just said?'

'I would've got better grades if I couldn't drink,' he replied, knowing full well he was in the wrong.

Of course he would have found it annoying not to be allowed to have a social life just because his parents couldn't afford to give him spending money or he didn't have a job while he was studying. He would have been up in arms about it. But he was already in this argument for a penny, so thought he'd keep going for the pound.

This was the straw that broke the camel's back for Steve. Gerald had been distant for the previous couple of weeks, with less time for catch-ups, fewer texts, and less words in each message. Steve was feeling neglected and hurt, and rather than bring any of this up, he instead went on a tirade about dishonesty. Corporations making all this money without paying tax, and all these rich people getting great accountants to avoid tax and rort the super scheme, investment properties that price people out of the market, all selfish people crying to the government to implement policies that make them more money while telling poor people they're lazy and deserve to be bossed around by the same government they want out of their own business. Gerald, of course, was not one of those people, even though his role as a financial analyst made him a cog in a large wheel.

'No, Steve, it's not the poor who are lazy – it's you. You've got absolutely no ambition. You just seem to want to lie around on the couch, ignore the real world, and imagine you're part of some revolution that'll set the world right from behind your phone screen.'

This was around the time that Steve had been talking of wanting to start a family, and the pressure was getting to Gerald.

'If that's what you think of me,' Steve answered, 'why don't we just break up.'

'Okay,' was the response that came back, so matter-of-fact that it seemed to wallop Steve in the pit of his stomach.

Steve finally let out a flabbergasted chuckle and said, 'Okay. Fine.' He stood up, refusing to look at Gerald, grabbed his phone, keys, and wallet, and headed for the door. He didn't slow down to wait for Gerald to stop him, that would look desperate, but he was waiting emotionally, mentally begging Gerald to take it back as his quick strides moved him towards the door. He turned the door handle and said, 'Bye,' without turning back. He headed towards the stairs as Gerald's apartment door closed automatically behind him, echoing down the corridor.

It was only when he was out on the street that the reality hit him. He couldn't believe they were broken up. It felt like some weird dream. It took a few weeks of random texts and arranging to collect the few things he'd left at Gerald's place, hoping each time that a reconciliation would follow, for the truth to set in, as well as the anger – the "healthy" kind of anger we use to mask the pain of losing access to something that, for the most part, made us happier than it made us unhappy. He never saw their relationship as being on thin ice, and truly could see himself raising a family with Gerald. For all his bitching about Gerald's priorities, he knew he'd be a good provider, financially speaking. It wasn't to be, though. He told himself it was no big deal and he'd just have to start again with someone new.

At 29, one might consider this easy enough, and Steve definitely did. He had a view that the universe provides when the need arises. But that was then, and things had changed. Since then, he had weathered a pandemic as a single man, one who took his role with the government seriously enough to strictly comply with the practice of abstinence in the name of social distancing, only going to his best friend Billy's place (who lived with his boyfriend Raf) as part of his bubble, and subsisting on walks outside with other friends as his only source of socialisation – when he wasn't updating the latest figures of deaths and infections on the government's social media. He was now 32. The pandemic and the time lost because of it had made him much more willing to compromise, and far less laissez-faire about his love life.

Despite their differences, he missed Gerald, mostly because he longed for closeness and Gerald was his most recent relationship. Now when he turns on Grindr—at home, at the gym, and on the walk to work—it's always the same old faces. He's either been with all the men he sees online, or rejected them, or they'd rejected him. At this point of his life, one of the only solutions he could see was moving cities; he'd become that desperate.

His views on relationships had hardened, too. He used to believe in playing above board, respecting relationships, putting all the information out there from the get-go, being a stand-up guy. Now he saw couples as fair game. He didn't view it as cheating if someone was partnered – instead, it was a sharing of resources. And if one half of a couple was sniffing around for something, Steve was happy to help them search for an alternative. He used to view this way of thinking as selfish, but now decided it was actually self-preservation.

All of this is to say that, if he had no fear of rejection or looking totally pathetic, Steve would immediately text Gerald and ask him to come back. He'd say he was prepared to be ambitious and work towards a common goal. He knew this way of thinking was weak, but loneliness can be a cruel mistress. If he had the chance again, he'd take it. Yes, it was weak, but he just didn't care.

10

Chapter 10

As Gerald stood on the dance floor, gazing stroppily across the room with his mouth receding dryly into itself, he realised that Steve's lack of ambition—his nurturing, placid personality and his convictions about making the world a better place—were exactly the type of qualities that would make him a good father. Perhaps all the arguments they'd had about the way the world should work were signs of a healthy relationship. And maybe Gerald just hadn't understood that at the time. Especially given his upbringing. Certainly, it had to be better than the way he'd just been dismissed outright by James.

'Hey,' he found himself typing into his phone, as the alcohol and drugs pushed him forwards like a shark, unable to take a step back and consider things from arm's length. 'You up?'

As he pressed send and watched the text pop into the blue speech bubble on his iPhone screen, instant regret gripped his body. *I shouldn't have sent that.* Texting Steve after almost three and a half years was a ludicrous move. No matter how annoyed Gerald was, that was clearly the wrong thing to do. But he'd been on autopilot. He wanted to take it back, delete the message, but he'd foolishly sent it through iMessage instead of WhatsApp. It was too late. He snuck his phone into his pocket and told himself he wouldn't look at it again for the rest of the evening. He had to forget about it. He had to lift his mood. Ignore his dad, kids, Steve. He pushed it all out of his mind and scanned the room.

Benny and Tim were gyrating in front of him on the dance floor. Tim was one of those friend of friends that you make just from being gay, and he worked in marketing, which Gerald thought was cool. Gerald really didn't like Benny, but he did like Tim, so he sidled up to them, pressed himself against them, and hugged them both. Benny's hand moved down the small of Gerald's back, slutty fingers caressing him like an insipid spider weaving a desperate web. Gerald took Benny's hand and guided it to his shoulder in more of a friendship posture. *Seriously! Benny was up for anyone tonight.* He was always like this, though. Gerald couldn't figure out why he and James were such good friends. Benny was always so handsy and desperate, whereas James was usually just out for to have a good time, which Gerald found adorable, even when he was a hot mess, which was often.

Out of the corner of his eye, Gerald could see Hannah still sitting at a table, so he broke away from the two boys and shuffled in her direction, shimmying and caressing himself seductively at her. She giggled, and he took her hand and guided her to the dance floor. He twirled her, and they two-stepped around the dance floor a little. 'Every Little Step' by Bobby

Brown was playing. Obviously the DJ had decided it was time to inject some of the "classics" into his rotation. Gerald hoped this wouldn't last long, but made the most of the opportunity to dance to something a little more innocent with his more-PG friend. He knew Hannah wouldn't be able to stay much longer. She was a mother of two, so tripping the light fantastic wasn't her speed, and never really had been. She'd done well to last this long. Gerald couldn't let all that effort be ignored, be wasted on sitting in a corner of the dance floor.

'Thanks so much for being here,' he said.

'Oh, it's my pleasure,' she responded. Such a beautiful and sincere personality.

'I love you,' he said, hugging her. They two-stepped in each other's arms for a bit.

It's much easier to be an open book when there's no danger of rejection. Hannah was as open a book as you could get, and didn't question Gerald the way others might. It allowed him not to have to worry.

'Such a beautiful day,' Hannah said as they swayed together. 'I can't wait to see the photos. You both looked soooo good.'

'It was,' Gerald replied hesitantly, trying to keep an undertone from his voice. 'Do you think I'd be a good dad?' he asked her, knowing this question was in spite of the promise he'd made only moments ago of forgetting everything.

Hannah's eyes flickered like she was trying to wake herself up from a dream. When she realised she hadn't imagined the question and that Gerald was serious, she answered, 'Umm, yeah, of course. Where's this come from?'

'My dad said to me, "I'm sure you'll make a better go of your marriage than I did," and I think he meant that because we don't have kids, we wouldn't get divorced. Which is bull-shit, right?'

'Of course! I mean, there's so much to unpack from that statement, like, the whole way you've interpreted it, but yes, you'd make a *great* dad.'

Hannah was right, he realised. There really was so much more to unpack from that statement, and Gerald wondered what other barbs might have been lurking in the undertone that he hadn't thought about.

For her part, Hannah had no idea where to begin in deconstructing all the different aspects that needed addressing. She was bamboozled about whether to first tackle the way he'd taken the implication of his dad's statement, or the suggestion that having children leads to divorce. She was distracted by their continued movement and unable to think strategically. Plus, she didn't have time anyway, as Gerald's response came quickly.

'Anyway, I wanna make it happen.'

'What about James?' she asked astutely.

'Yeah,' he nodded shiftily to *imply* that James was on board without saying that he hadn't committed, not knowing he looked even less convincing than he felt.

'Then I think it's a great idea,' she offered diplomatically, with a smile, avoiding pushing the point, but making it clear from her tone that she didn't quite believe her statement but would support him no matter what.

A silence fell between them. Gerald could tell that Hannah knew he wasn't being totally honest, so it seemed they both preferred just to enjoy the time they had together than play the insincere-statement game. After a few more awkward moments, where Gerald kept thinking back to James's lack of agreement, he told Hannah he was off to find his hubby.

'Okay, babe, love you.'

Gerald wished the sense of motherly worry wasn't so obvious in her voice. She was making it clear she knew Gerald was up to something he shouldn't be, but he ignored her warnings and pulled his phone out of his pocket once his back was turned.

'Hey stranger,' the response from Steve said, causing Gerald's stomach to leap to his throat. 'Good to hear from you. What's up?'

He knew he shouldn't respond. Contacting Steve had been a mistake that he instantly regretted. But Steve would know he'd read it, so it would be rude to leave it on read. He responded diplomatically with, 'Just at a wedding, wbu?'

He was hunched over his phone as he typed, knowing this wasn't a text chain that should exist, let alone be seen by anyone. Steve would probably know he was high, but Gerald didn't care. If Steve decided to be a bitch about it, it was no loss. In fact, he secretly hoped Steve would be a bitch about it. He didn't even know why he was texting him.

He put the phone away again and made his way to the bar to grab another drink. James was now elsewhere. Gerald looked out over the venue. Benny and Tim were making out now. *Good for Benny*, Gerald thought to himself. *Persistence really does pay.* They kind of looked like two dogs eating out of the same bowl. Surely they could go somewhere a little more private if their make-out session was going to be that intense? Gerald took his eyes away from Benny's tongue trying to impregnate the back of Tim's throat and pulled his phone back out to get a hold of James.

Steve had already texted back: 'I'm just at home. Wanna come over?'

Gerald's stomach leapt again. This wasn't the answer he'd expected. After the way they'd left things, he half expected either no response, or some cranky "Why are you texting me?" text. Instead, he'd received an open invitation.

He stared at the message, unable to make a decision on what to do now. James had openly shot down any discussion of having kids. Twice Gerald had tried to talk to him, and both times he'd been completely dismissed. Kids had to happen, though. He hated the idea of his dad sneering down his nose at his relationships, at his "lifestyle." People were always deriding the capacity for gay relationships to be fulfilling, for such couples to experience the fullness of straight relationships, including what comes from raising a child. He never wanted to be considered lesser, especially not by his dad. And his conversations with Charlotte and Hannah both made it clear that it absolutely should happen. The way James had acted, though! He'd completely shot down the possibility of ever having kids, as though Gerald was just supposed to accept it and move on, as though he had no say in his future. It was always James's way or the highway.

Steve had never shut down conversations. He was naturally a homebody, and his total lack of ambition career-wise made him the perfect candidate to be the carer. He had even shown himself willing to subjugate his ego by responding so affirmatively to Gerald's text just now. Things had been left on such a sour note, Gerald knew, that for Steve to forgive and forget so easily meant that Gerald was sure to be able to have a say in which direction things might go. The thought that maybe he could quickly sneak out and see how they both still got along with each other briefly crossed his mind.

He snapped out of it. It was his wedding night, for god's sake. It was unthinkable for him to leave the venue for one of his dalliances, and with his ex of all people. Everything could wait till the morning, till after the dust had settled and he'd had the chance to discuss it all with James. Yet he'd given James two chances to discuss the issue, and there was no guarantee that a third attempt would garner any better results in the morning. For all he knew, Gerald had received his answer, and he absolutely had to know, right now, whether children might be able to be in his future. He had to know whether there was even the slightest possibility of rubbing his fucking father's snotty nose in it by having kids and proving him wrong.

As the bile at this thought continued to build, he found himself typing 'Sure' in response to Steve's invitation. *Fuck Patrick,* he thought. *This'll show him.* No one was going to sneer at him and tell him he couldn't do something. Besides, it wasn't like he'd do anything bad. He'd just be going there to talk, to explore options. *More out of interest than anything else.* He told himself that nothing would happen. Yes, he had always enjoyed sleeping with Steve, which was unsurprising, considering Gerald assumed people rarely end up in a relationship with partners they find incompatible in the bedroom. Even so, he was just going to test the waters.

His train of thought was interrupted as Charlie came bounding towards him like a whirlwind, swaying to the music. Gerald whipped the phone into his pocket, straightened himself up, and flashed her a smile. Charlie crash-landed into him and they both broke out in laughter as they stumbled around "dancing." Gerald was all smiles as he worked hard to make sure she didn't trip over her gown. He had to keep any perception of a guilty conscience or underhanded communication with Steve off her radar. Deep down, he knew it was a stupid idea, and that even Charlie would rail against it. She'd possibly even confiscate his phone. He needed to keep it quiet.

He tried to maintain a calm appearance, like he was some elegant swan gliding across the lake in the Botanical Gardens while its legs worked overtime under the surface. Unlike a swan, though, his attempt at calmness was his usual level of intensity. His eyes darted with the racing of his mind, and his frustrations with the weighing up of options wore on his face. Luckily, he always wore an intense expression, so this looked kind of normal. There was a root cause for his current concern, though. Even before Patrick said what he'd said, Gerald felt something was missing. Maybe Steve had the answer. He had to know.

'Is that a wedding scroll in your pocket or are you just happy to see me?' Charlotte screamed at him with drag-queen expressions of shock, intrigue, enticement, and matronly judgement, then rubbed her breasts all over his chest, adding, 'Naughty!'

'You know I'm always happy to see you, babe!'

'I can feel it. Lucky James!'

They both laughed, but Gerald's laugh was mixed with a pang of regret. Had he made a mistake? He was so confused.

'So, you two love birds are off to South America, right?'

'Yeah, now that Mardi Gras and the wedding is done and dusted, we're escaping the Sydney rat race.'

'Honey, from what I heard, you *are* the rat. Scurrying around late night from Columbian to Universal, nibbling your face off with eyes as big as the moon. Let's just hope you get a bit of detoxing done while you're there.'

'Not if I accidentally catch the Columbian cold, love!'

Gerald made a big sniffing sound, and they both howled with obnoxious laughter at what any onlookers might have considered the none-too-subtle and rather tired joke.

'Babe, today was absolutely fucking gorgeous. I'm so happy for you.'

'Thanks, babe,' Gerald replied.

'You should be thanking me with all the shit I did to make it happen! Plus, the rest, but that's for later tonight.'

'What do you mean?'

'Tsk tsk, my pretty! You'll find out!'

Gerald felt content at this point. Being here with Charlotte in this moment was his happy place. He would push the idea of Steve from his mind. He meant it this time.

The moment was broken, though, when the sound of Davey's thick British accent came blasting in from behind them.

'What do we have here, then?' he shouted, whacking Gerald's butt and then sliding his finger to the fabric covering his hole.

Gerald's cheeks clenched and his body jolted upright. What was it about Gerald's butt that had everyone wanting to molest it tonight? He supposed it was a complement to the tuxedo pants he'd painstakingly chosen specifically to accentuate his sculpted contours.

'Top only! Top only!' he shouted back.

'I've heard that before,' Davey replied.

'I mean it, though.'

'Okay, maybe you could prove it to me, then.'

'Are you hitting on me at my own wedding?'

'If not now, when?'

'Yeah, you're right, totally appropriate.'

'I know someone you can top, honey!' Charlotte shouted as Britney's 'Gimme More' started playing. Her hips started gyrating in time with the beat, and a seductive look burned across her features. Gerald smiled at this. She really was a total ham.

'Ooh baby, come here!' Davey shouted back.

The way Davey and Charlotte started grinding on each other made Gerald wonder how much of the contours of each other's genitalia they now had intimate knowledge of. Only then did he notice how sheer the groomsmaid's floral dresses were.

Charlotte's hair was draping in a large clump over to the right side of her head, bouncing up and down in a heap. Her fascinator had been discarded once again and the lashings of hair spray worked overtime against the sweat and heat to keep her hair in some kind of shape. Davey's shirt was completely unbuttoned, giving Charlotte's breasts a chiselled chest to rub against.

Gerald was touched that Davey had come all the way from England for the wedding. Luckily, the Australian borders had opened in November after almost two years of remaining closed to non-citizens and residents, only allowing a small portion of actual citizens to return at any one time. Even the lucky ones that could afford the hefty price tags for flights home and were able to get themselves a ticket would have to rot in the hotel quarantine system for two weeks – which they had to pay for the privilege of. Davey missed all of that, and was able to kill two birds with one stone by doing Mardi Gras two weeks beforehand, which Gerald remembered was one of the main reasons he and James had chosen the middle of summer to get married. It allowed their international guests to combine their wedding with the "Gay Christmas" season, giving them more bang for their buck.

Gerald hadn't seen Davey since he lived in Vauxhall, where Davey was basically a part of the apartment furniture, but they'd been all over each other's social media ever since. Davey had always claimed he was bi, but he created an absolute scandal when he met and ended up marrying a woman by the name of Evelyn. Even when Gerald knew him, Davey had gone out to straight clubs and pubs about as much as he'd visit G.A.Y. with Gerald and his mates, but Gerald always assumed (from the number of boys he let take him home) that the gay side would win over. Evelyn blindsided almost everyone. In a world as binary as the gay community, it really does come as a shock when people break with norms, even within an "abnormal" community.

Davey had got with Evelyn about three months before Gerald left London. While Evelyn was lovely, Gerald really did expect Davey to break her heart when he eventually got over his "straight phase." Gerald put the whole affair down to Davey having a quarter-life crisis, temporarily settling for the greater commitment women are famous for when compared to men, especially gay men. But when they finally married in 2021, Gerald had long since accepted their situation (and Davey's status as a real bisexual) as genuine. He could only attend their wedding through a screen, with likes and comments on Facebook and Instagram the only interaction between them, as he was stuck inside the closed borders of Australia's harsh global isolation.

At that point in time, a person could only leave the country to attend the funeral of a family member or other special circumstances, and that was only through successful application to the government. This was followed by two weeks of harsh hotel quarantine upon their return, where meals were delivered by a knock on the door, the prisoner needing to wait 30 seconds before opening the door to retrieve their meal, and all in-person interaction forbidden. Covid tests upon arrival and departure were also required before freedom into the community was granted. Gerald would have done it, though, in order to attend his friend's wedding. Instead, all he could do was sit at home in the Morrison government's national penitentiary and watch from afar as the world moved on.

'What a naughty girl you are,' Davey was saying as Charlotte's hand grasped his butt cheek and thrust his hips deeper into her pelvis.

'What, are you gonna tame me?'

'I might have to.'

'I might have to tame you first.'

Gerald wondered where Evelyn was at that moment, as Davey and Charlotte continued "flirting" with each other. He wasn't sure that flirting was the right word to use when they were basically fucking on the dance floor, but it would have to do.

The last time he met Evelyn was June 2019, when he and Steve done a trip through Europe together. They'd all caught up for dinner, very tame compared to Davey and Gerald's life when they'd lived in the same city, but Steve was in his element that night. He was way more of a dinner and drinks kind of guy than a party boy. He loved talking conceptually, and he and Evelyn spent a large part of the dinner discussing colonialism and social construction from an Anglo-specific framework, leaving Gerald completely out of his depth. When he wondered openly what the economic implications of breaking the current social framework apart would be, he was met with cries of imperialism and institutional inequality. Even Davey was able to contribute to the conversation with clearly thought-out arguments and propositions on potential steps that could be taken. Gerald was left feeling like an audience member. He wondered now whether such moments with Steve could have actually led to moments of growth, rather than being seen as insurmountable differences in their interests. Could Steve have pushed him to be a better man somehow?

Even though he told himself that he and Steve had broken up on mutual terms, Gerald knew this was a slight colouration of the truth. They'd met on Grindr, with Steve's smiling and fully clothed face pic messaging Gerald's chiselled headless torso a 'Hi,' quickly followed by naughty pics. Steve had a great physique, which Gerald later found out was due to his indoor rock-climbing (the gym was a little too conventional for Steve). Gerald responded likewise with face pics and junk shots, resulting in Steve practically begging him to come over and treat him like a human fleshlight. Being a fan of feeling wanted, Gerald kindly capitulated. It wasn't even until after they'd hooked up, and Steve had messaged him with a 'wow that was great, let's do it again soon,' that they finally exchanged numbers. And that was only because a week had passed since Steve had tried to make contact again, but missed Gerald, who'd logged off only minutes earlier.

Their relationship continued in a very similar vein as it had begun, with Steve being the initiator of things, and Gerald seeing Steve as a presenter of options that Gerald could choose to accept or decline. Steve was basically there when he needed him, but Gerald never really thought it a two-way street. Funny how the power dynamic that a relationship starts with often sets the tone for the relationship going forward.

As Gerald watched Davey and Charlotte grinding in front of him, now simulating anal and howling with laughter, Gerald realised that Steve never really asked for that much anyway. Until the end when he became more demanding, but Gerald couldn't see a future there. Anyone who's happy allowing their career to stagnate in the government system wasn't the type of guy Gerald could see himself with, and although he was only three years younger, Gerald was already doing better than Steve. Gerald reckoned he needed someone with his level of ambition. Now, as it turns out, perhaps having someone less ambitious would have been the exact right thing for him and a potential child. Someone who was prepared to stay at home and do the lion's share of raising him or her – or them. In tender moments, Steve had expressed the desire to be a father, but this had always made Gerald's body stiffen and lead him mentally dissociate from the situation. This would lead Steve to huff in disappointment at Gerald's lack of communication. But Gerald simply couldn't hear it at the time. He was only 26. He had too much to get done. Besides, what if he wasn't a good father? What if he turned into his dad? But no, he wouldn't be. He'd be a great dad. He wasn't Patrick.

Gerald had the sudden realisation that when he and Steve were having such conversations, he had been almost the same age as James was now. James was 27, surely too young to start a family, and too young to even consider it in his future. He could now recognise the pattern of rejection James was offering, the flat-out refusal to discuss it. No wonder he'd been was so upset by James's dismissals. James was using Gerald's own tactics to shut the conversation down. He knew then that the idea of children with James was doomed.

This thought was briefly knocked out of his mind when Davey and Charlotte crash-landed into him like they were two Muppets being manoeuvred by strings on a stage, with Gerald being the out-of-place guest star of the evening. They attacked him from both sides. Each of them dry-humped on one of his legs, their hands molesting him and their heads bobbing up and down. He couldn't join in though, not fully. All around him, everything seemed wrong. The lights in the venue had been dimmed, with flashing, coloured lights now dancing on the ceiling like they were partying in someone's living room during lockdown. It looked more like '70s night at the Metro than the pumping Arq vibes he'd hoped for when he'd ordered these lights. Everyone seemed to be doing their best to get into the spirit, but Gerald wasn't happy.

He knew that anyone watching him would know his energy was all wrong, that he needed to shake off his physical stiffness, to get into the revelry of the night, but his mind was swimming, toggling between regret at his past actions, guilt over his potential future actions, worry of over-reacting, and fear of failing to explore all options when James was being so unreasonable. He couldn't make up his mind whether he was thinking about revenge, thinking with his package, or just thinking with a head full of drugs.

Gerald's phone had started to burn a hole in his tuxedo pants pocket. Surely a message would be there by now. As much as he loved Charlotte, and appreciated her and Davey's attempts to buoy his spirits, he just had to see what his phone screen would be presenting him with right now. Like a gambler's addiction, he needed to keep hitting that button.

Davey was now rubbing his crotch against Gerald's butt while Charlotte grinded against his front parts. He was feeling smothered. It seemed like everyone's eyes were on him, and he felt edgy about the night's interactions: Hannah with her knowing looks, James with his harsh rebuff, even Paul and Benny, who had each been hyper-sexualising the atmosphere in front of his grandmother and James's family. Now Charlie and Davey were clinging to him like they were two pieces of Glad Wrap. The air was stifling. He had to find a way to escape, to figure out whether having children could be on the cards for him. Curiosity got the better of him. He couldn't wait any longer.

'I'm just going to get another drink,' he shouted to them.

'I'll come!' Charlotte yelled.

'Great!' he responded without a hint of the annoyance he felt.

'Sorry, babe!' Charlotte was saying to Davey as Gerald turned his back to them and pulled his phone out of his pocket. 'Hold your breath for me till I get back, okay?'

'Anything for you, sexy,' Davey replied.

Gerald could hear them both giggle naughtily behind his back as he stared at his phone screen.

'Half an hour, okay?' was the response staring back at him.

That was ten minutes ago. Gerald's face flushed as he realised this all sounded more and more like a hook-up. Half an hour was a reasonable amount of time for Steve to "prepare." He pushed the implication aside. That wasn't Gerald's intent.

Thirty minutes gave him enough time for another drink and the ten-minute walk to Steve's place, conveniently up the road on Oxford Street. He responded with a thumbs up, and attempted to swallow through an ever-tightening throat.

They left Davey, who'd already found the next body to interact with, and made their way to the bar. Gerald grabbed a glass of champers and took a dispirited sip. This wasn't the alone time he'd wanted. Charlie's time on the dance floor had obviously sobered her up, so she grabbed a glass for herself, too. Gerald eyed her hand snatching the glass with a silent tsk. He didn't think she needed another one right now, but who was he to say anything? He could barely breathe, tearing himself up between going to Steve's and staying put. He couldn't stop himself, though.

Charlotte had replaced Hannah as Gerald's bestie soon after he'd arrived back from London. Although she was only two years older than Gerald, she'd always been something of an outlandishly cool aunt or nurturing mother figure to him. She'd always been very protective. Gerald liked that feeling usually, but right now the last thing he wanted was a mother figure muscling in on what was an absolute crisis. His stomach was jittery, and his hand was starting to shake as he downed his drink. He knew he shouldn't leave. He told himself not to go.

'Hey, I'm just going to find James,' he lied as casually as he could, then walked onto the dance floor. As soon as he felt he was out of sight of Charlotte, he headed for the exit, walked down the steps, and felt the cold night air as he stepped out onto the street outside.

11 |

Chapter 11

Gerald kept having the same dream, almost like a premonition. It went like this:

He was curled up on the couch, head tucked firmly into his elbows and knees bent up to his ears, trying as best he could to cocoon himself from the world. Tears trickled down the ridge of his nose and onto the sleeves of his blue hoodie. He'd never felt like such a failure as he did at that moment. He was just like his dad, he realised, but he didn't know where this revelation had come from, nor what he could do to stop it. All he knew was that he was blaming himself – he was his father's son. His mother was somehow there too, a look of sorrow coating her angelic features. He thought back to when he was younger, and how he would look around jealousy at all of his friend's families. They seemed to go everywhere together, sit at restaurants, bicker at the dinner table, go on holidays. They all did chores together after dinner. They dressed the same. Gerald remembered promising himself that one day he would make a family like that. But then he found out he was gay, and that having a family would be more problematic than he assumed. He'd left his small commu-

nity of Summer Hill for the big city lights of Darlinghurst to find kindred spirits. And piece by piece, that old dream died, until he was left with the shallow expectation of life as a homosexual—body negativity, promiscuity, and "having a good time"—drugs to hide loneliness, dance parties as community, sex as intimacy, and airing grievances rather than promoting consensus. His first kiss had been magical, but heartbreak after heartbreak meant the pleasure that comes from it had been more and more fleeting.

Then he was sitting balled up on the couch sometime in the future. He and James had been married for some time. He'd thought James would be the one that would make it all stop: the endless search for meaning, the void, the seeking of validation, that he was good enough to have what everyone else had. Now, though, even this was breaking down. He and James were drifting apart, and although his tears suggested otherwise, he wasn't even sure how much he really cared. Perhaps this was the worst thing of all. That he wasn't the kind of person who could really feel love. Maybe the lesson his father taught him all along wasn't that he should try to be a better man, but that love is as fleeting as a wave on the shore. That attempts to force it to stay, to bottle it, simply created a stagnant, salty, and lifeless puddle out of something that was once so dynamic and energising. Gerald felt lifeless. Their love had turned stagnant.

Gerald was no longer on a couch, curled up like a listless blanket. He was now standing on the edge of a beach – somewhere exotic like Mykonos or Ibiza, with gentle waves lapping at the shore. His dress shoes felt weird on the beach, and the stylish and expensive suit he wore was impractical. The moonlight was reflecting off the large expanse that stretched out invitingly before him. All he needed to do was strip his clothes, take the few steps forward, and allow the cool water to envelop him. The possibilities for where he might end up were endless. The suit, his shoes, and his Darlinghurst-centric life would be left in a crumpled heap on the shore, beyond the water's reach. It was time to move on.

***

Gerald's damp shirt stuck to his torso as he moved briskly along Castlereagh Street. The thought of his recurring dream came to his mind in snippets as buildings flashed by, but he pushed any thoughts of it aside. He wouldn't think about that dream anymore. He had to keep moving. His arms were hugging his waist to keep himself warm as he turned onto Liverpool Street. His body was pulsing against the cool air, and his mind was racing, energised, but everything was moving in flashes. Any thought of his conscience was stamped out as soon as it germinated. The thought of what he'd say or do when he arrived at Steve's was snuffed out just as quickly. What could he could possibly say to himself to make this visit appear justified? The thought of his father came and went with a sudden bite. It was around 11pm. The red and green traffic lights meant nothing at this time of night. He watched until the road was free from headlights, then scurried across Elizabeth Street and moved past Museum Station.

Not far from here was where the Mardi Gras Parade starts. Mardi Gras, the night he "officially met" James. Gerald had been immediately love-struck, or lust-struck; one of the two. But who'd have thought it would survive a global pandemic and lead to marriage?

In the distance, Steve's building, the Park Apartments, was coming into view. It was a harsh old utilitarian block that reminded Gerald of the type of construction that might not look out of place in the Soviet bloc. This suited Steve to a tee, Gerald always thought. On the opposite side of the street from the Park Apartments was the Monument Building, where James had been living when Gerald and he had started dating, before they upgraded to Kings Cross. The fact that the two buildings were across the road from each other had provided Gerald with a perfect contrast between the two. One was an old-fashioned and stuffy lump, and the other was sleek, modern, and expensive-looking. Gerald was reminded of this comparison every time he'd gone to meet James during lockdown, and they seemed to provide a reminder to him that he'd traded up, that he was on the right track. Maybe he should have considered there was more to life than appearance and the accumulation of assets, but he'd always had tunnel vision. Besides, those early days had been so exciting.

If only those moments of happiness could last. Right now, Gerald just felt empty. He was like a leaky bucket that just kept needing to be filled. Nothing was never enough. Maybe James just wasn't the one. Maybe it really was children and parenthood he needed in his life. And maybe it was Steve, rather than James, that could give him that.

Gerald mused again about how funny it was that the way a relationship begins informs the way a relationship continues.

Steve had started out as a Grindr hook-up, and here Gerald was again, organising a catch-up that had all the markings of a late-night booty call.

He'd reached the Park Apartments building now. He avoided stepping in someone's fresh Friday night vomit (someone had obviously been hitting the pre-drinks too hard) as he passed a kebab shop, just next to Sydney Sauna. He pushed aside the negative associations he had with Sydney Sauna and the experience he'd had with the daddy, and focussed on the small groups of two or three people that were lining their stomachs for the start of their night out. He realised then that he hadn't eaten. He'd been so busy all day, and with the nerves of hosting duties keeping his stomach in knots, he'd simply ignored the sliders and finger food that were milling around and fed his nose instead. James and he had decided against a formal sit-down dinner. It didn't suit the venue. They made sure they had enough chairs and tables for guests to sit at if they needed to, but the most important thing was that the dance floor remained unencumbered. People could fill up on finger food if they were the type to eat at a party.

Gerald mused that they shouldn't think of their wedding as a party. It was almost like the whole thing was a bit of fun, an interesting concept to participate in, and something that didn't mean their whole life course had just been cemented. What did marriage mean nowadays, anyway? The "till death do us part" stuff had been thrown out the window yonks ago – King Henry and the rise of personalised vows had seen to that. So, was a wedding now just a big party you threw to

show everyone you were deciding to commit to a relationship more than might otherwise be expected for the time being? It was an expensive exercise. All up they'd spent $60,000.
Enough to go towards savings for a house (or at least a one-
bedroom apartment). Actually, this amount would probably
just cover the stamp duty – but still, it was significant.

Gerald once again fondled the ring on his finger. He'd
imagined this piece of jewellery as a symbol, a harbinger of
happiness – something to settle him. But here he was, still
competing with his dad, still looking for something else, still
the same ridiculous figure moving through the night and
committing acts he knew he'd later regret, like Mr Hyde on
a path to destruction, the antidote to his attempt at a respectable Dr Jekyll act.

This night had followed every step of Gerald's self-destruc-
tive cycle. He would always invariably start the night enjoying
company, sober, clean, and innocent, and he'd feel fresh and
fun when the drinks started. Once he was a few drinks in, he'd
want a line, which would make him feel classy and naughty,
like some elegant socialite who could actually afford to waste
three hundred bucks on a bag. He loved this feeling. The first
line or two, just lifting his spirits, adding some MSG to the
night as a small enhancement of their already good time. It
never lasted, though. Inevitably, his inhibitions would leave
him as he got messier and less elegant, by which time that socialite figure was a distant memory. Now he was a sex-starved
stud, looking to be placated. The aftermath would always
bring regret and admonishment, and the promise that he'd
never do it again. And because he felt miserable, he would seek

out something that would make him feel better. A drink or a line. And so the cycle continued.

He was standing out the front of Steve's place. He wondered if it wasn't too late to turn back, but once again, something inside failed to stop him.

He watched his fingers press #1032 and the bell sign on the little silver intercom, and waited while the intercom rang, a little circular light flashing at him ominously. When it picked up and Steve answered, Gerald was surprised by a lump lodging itself in his throat. He swallowed it down and said 'Hey,' and was told to come up. The glass doors slid open silently, the little camera and light of the intercom still watching him, humming as though the building was alive.

As he stepped through the cold concrete foyer, the noise of Oxford Street disappeared, replaced by an ominous silence and the watchful eyes of the empty concierge desk. Gerald's pace quickened as he made his way to the elevator. He felt somehow the concierge desk was judging him, that the walls of the block knew him and were eyeing him suspiciously. Although they'd seen him creeping in with dishevelled clothes and pasty skin so many times in the past, he was usually coming back from somewhere, rather than on his way to trouble. The entire austere apartment block seemed to know he was there with motives not altogether innocent.

In the distance behind him, the door he'd entered through automatically locked shut, so the only noise was Gerald's own guilty footsteps and the silent judgement of elevator making its way down towards him. He'd be able to hear his own breath had he been focussing on that, rather than trying to see in the reflection on the polished steel of the elevator doors just how dishevelled he looked.

He pressed the lift button again loudly to release the tension he was feeling, and stood like a statue to hide his drunkenness, hands cupped around each other, watching the numbers on the lift tick down towards him. What on earth was he doing here?

Chapter 12

It seemed to Gerald that every time he thought he was going to get what he wanted, he found a way to fuck it up. It happened to him at work just a couple of weeks ago. He had a big presentation in front of the big boss. He was nervous. There was a supervisory role that was becoming available in risk assessment, and while this report was about the work his department in credit was doing, it also happened to included risk assessment elements. He wanted to make a good impression. He wanted to apply for the role when Toni, the current occupant of the role, went on maternity leave. He'd done all the preparation, but his nerves were getting the better of him. He decided he needed something, just to take the edge off. He quickly got the lift down to Shelley Street and ducked into the public cubical near CommBank to have a line. The last thing he wanted was for someone at work to hear him sniffling in one of the stalls. He was on his way back when the notification for five minutes till the meeting came up on his phone. *Fuck!* He had to hurry.

He was sweating slightly when he stepped into the conference room and plugged in his laptop. And while it's true that his little bump had taken the edge off his nerves, he failed to realise that he was somewhat more aggressive than he was calmer as a result of his self-medication.

He hammered out point after point during the presentation, and when AJ, the big boss of the department, kept interrupting to ask questions, he couldn't help himself from responding with a slightly impatient and frustrated tone, as these questions were interrupting the flow of the presentation and of his thoughts.

He could see eyes looking startled and jaws dropping around the room as he spoke that way, but he couldn't stop himself. In his view, the boss was asking needless questions, and when stupid questions were being asked, he was responding in kind, regardless of whom he was addressing. Upon reflection, it became clear that the boss was simply testing his knowledge and ability to cope under pressure, which Gerald realised he'd absolutely failed.

He decided that he wouldn't apply for the position, and he'd avoided the big boss since then, keeping his head down and sucking up to his immediate manager to make amends. He would prefer to deal with this latest situation in the same way he deals with many other situations: by pretending it hadn't happened.

He did the same thing when he broke it off with Steve. Even before Steve had suggested they break up, he'd started to pull away. It almost came as a relief when Steve "chose" to break up with him, or brought up the idea at least. There'd been too much arguing over philosophical points of view that Gerald just didn't care about. Gerald wanted more than the boring life Steve seemed set on. How could Steve want children when he was clearly such a layabout? All he saw was a blob that was trying to drag him down, when he just wanted to enjoy his life. So he texted less, was less available, and when he did come over it was only for sex. He could have made it easier and been honest with Steve about how he felt, but that was one of the great sticking points of Gerald's life, and something that he continued to feel victimised by – always upset that no one really knew him, but too afraid to ever open up. And while it was obvious that this was a self-sustaining cycle, how does someone go about breaking it?

Gerald liked to think he was a rock to his friends. Supportive, loyal, caring, always there for them. But he feels they're never there for him when he needs them, mostly because he never lets them know how he feels. It happened earlier tonight – Charlie asked whether he was happy, and he responded like an automaton, not letting any of his feelings out. With Hannah, the same thing. He'd spent so long pushing his feelings down, that when it's time to open up, the skillset just isn't there.

There are rare exceptions, rare occasions where the moment is just right for him to open up, but constantly wondering when it's the right time for it to be his turn is not only egocentric, but absolutely condescending. In his view, his friends are such messes that it never seems like the right time for it to be his turn. Charlie is his best friend, but she's a fruit loop. She's so busy sorting out her demons that Gerald never gets a look in. If he could open up, would that make him happier, or just turn him into another person that's obsessed with talking about themselves?

The elevator dinged. He had no time to think about any of that anymore. The doors opened and he stepped into the cream hallway.

He had to strategise. He wasn't going to do anything rash. He was only going to talk to Steve, see where he was at, what his plans were, see if there was a connection there. He was there to talk, to weigh up options.

He passed rows of doors and had finally arrived at apartment 1032. He knocked. His stomach leapt. He swallowed to push it back down as the door creaked opened.

'Gerry,' said Steve with a flirtatious smile.

'Hey,' was all Gerald could manage.

'Good to see you,' Steve said, smiling, but also looked him over to get a picture of his current state.

Gerald felt exposed. Yes, it had already been a big night. His clothes, his hair, his skin, everything must have been screaming the fact to Steve as he opened the door wider and stepped back to let Gerald in. *It's a booty call* Steve seemed to deduce from the knowing smile that crept over his face. Gerald's face flushed. He stepped inside, and as the door closed behind him, the apartment seemed to envelope him inside it. There was no escape.

From what he could make out, the apartment was just as he'd remembered it: same couch, same TV, same weird artwork on the walls. The apartment was dark, with only the small lamp by the couch lighting the entire space. The contrast between the harsh light of the corridor and the dark apartment made it so that Gerald's eyes took some time to adjust. Steve had not set the mood for conversation; it felt more like he was standing in the corridor of Sydney Sauna than on an errand to sort out his future.

'How are you feeling?' Steve asked him from the darkness, and Gerald felt Steve's hand caress between his shoulder blades. Steve could tell he was "happy," and surely assumed that physical touch wouldn't be unwelcome. Gerald swallowed again, unable to dislodge the lump that remained in his throat.

'I'm okay,' Gerald replied, wondering how glassy his eyes were.

'I bet,' Steve said as he moved in close.

As Steve's face came in for the kiss, Gerald's entire body revolted, tensing against Steve's touch. Steve had both hands around his waist now, gently pulling him towards him. Gerald's head veered to the side and he buried his face in Steve's neck, safely hiding his lips. Pushing Steve away would be rude, but finally the voice of Gerald's conscience was telling him that this was wrong.

Steve's lips and tongue were working in the crook of Gerald's neck as his hands unbuttoned Gerald's shirt. Gerald made the noises of heavy breathing, as though he was into it, while he tried desperately to think how he could pull back gracefully. He'd just wanted to talk. He wanted to gauge the idea of kids. Why the fuck was he here to ask about kids anyway?

Steve's lips had found their way to Gerald's nipples. His tongue was licking and mouth sucking like it was feeding time. Gerald was completely distracted. Everything was happening so fast. All thoughts of strategy went out the window as Steve's hands pushed Gerald's now completely unbuttoned shirt out of the way, allowing his fingers to caress Gerald's waist as they made their way to unclipping his cummerbund. It fell to the floor, and Gerald felt the pressure from Steve's hand on his lower waist, pulling his hips their two ctotches pressed firmly against one another.

Gerald's head rocked back. The problem with an ex-lover is that they know your triggers. Steve seemed to know that Gerald liked to feel as though he was being devoured, that he was being yearned for, that he was deeply wanted. The combination of Steve's lips still locked to his left nipple and the friction around his nether regions weakened Gerald's resolve. He shouldn't have had that last drink at the venue. Pleasure replaced reason; capitulation with Steve's advances now seemed like the right thing to do. Steve could feel the change in Gerald's body language, and his arms tightened around Gerald like a boa constrictor. Gerald found his hand sliding through Steve's hair as his heavy breathing became real.

In the back of his mind, there was still protest. He knew he shouldn't be here. Of all the shitty things he'd done in the past, all the late-night rendezvous and sneaky fucks, this was the worst. Being here with Steve was the step too far he'd been teetering on for too long. He hadn't ever really asked James about kids properly, just a drunken question on the way to the bathroom. Maybe James would eventually say yes. How would Gerald know, if at the first sign of trouble he went running for the back-up plan. This wasn't the right thing to do. Even if it wasn't going to work out and James wasn't the right man, he shouldn't be here on their wedding night. It seemed a little late to finally be having a conscience, but how late was too late? Perhaps there was still time to be not so stupid in actions and thoughts as he was being right now. He could stop where he was, preserving at least some shred of what he might be lost if things kept going. How far was too far?

Steve's hands had reached the button of Gerald's pants. The button was quickly dismissed and his zip pulled open. Before Gerald knew it, his pants were yanked down to his thighs and Steve's mouth, which had been tracing its way down Gerald's abdomen, quickly enveloped the outline Gerald was making in his underwear.

Gerald had his answer. This was far enough. He'd found the line he couldn't cross. His hands quickly moved to Steve's shoulders in protest, which Steve resisted, opening his mouth open wider and take in more of his outline. Gerald could feel the moisture penetrating the fabric of his briefs and Steve's tongue running along the length of the outline. Steve had a way with his mouth; the sensation was amazing. The pressure Gerald was applying to Steve's shoulders lessened, but however much he was tempted to tell himself this wouldn't be so bad, he knew it shouldn't go beyond this point.

Gerald couldn't think. He shouldn't have come. He pushed again on Steve's shoulders, but was again resisted by an increased ferocity. Steve's mouth became like a guppy on a shark that refused to let go. This was so awkward. It mustn't go further. At least for now he was safe; he was protected from complete immorality by the thin piece of fabric that still separated this moment between right and wrong. Steve's tongue and lips worked seductively over the thick outline Gerald was making. This felt so good. But it mustn't go further.

If only moments could be held on to, he thought for a second time that night. The positive energy at the beginning of the day. The euphoria he'd felt after wins at gymnastics tournaments. And this moment where Gerald could possibly still claim some small degree of innocence. These moments ought to be made to last, but they aren't.

As the elastic of his Tommy Hilfiger underwear was being peeled away from his skin, and his hard cock slid along with the fabric, Gerald's whole body awoke like he'd just been zapped by 240 volts. Steve was sliding the waistband down his upper thigh, freeing his tip so it bounced at attention, when Gerald's hands sprang to attention, grabbing the elastic band of his underwear like spring-loaded clasps.

'No,' he said, pulling his underwear back on as his hips drew back and his shoulders rounded to create space between the two of them.

Steve looked with a bemused look on his face, like he was wondering if Gerald was trying to play the prude. Like he was playing the tawdry part of the frigid tart that needs to be lured into the forbidden. Steve would be into that, but this idea quickly gave way to confusion as he realised from Gerald's guilty and pained expression that sexy time was over.

'Are you serious?' he asked.

'Sorry,' Gerald answered, fumbling around with the pants around his ankles.

Steve's confusion soon enough switched to incredulity at this sudden turnaround. After all this time, to be messaged out of the blue with a "you up?" text, and now, when they were in the middle of it, here was Gerald rejecting him yet again, while he was on his knees no less, with Gerald looking down on him. He'd never felt as stupid and vulnerable. He'd taken action, shown Gerald he now understood how to go after what he wanted by throwing caution to the wind and inviting him over, being the sexual instigator, by casting aside his ego and not caring that he was the late-night booty call (though it was only roughly 11 o'clock; Gerald had obviously started early), and all this still wasn't enough. The physicality of the scene only worked to heighten Steve's feeling of humiliation and rejection, though he had no idea what he'd done wrong.

'Why are you even here then?' Steve asked.

'I don't know,' Gerald answered in a huff of self-reproach and confusion, avoiding Steve's gaze sheepishly. 'I shouldn't be.'

That was the final straw. What an ultimate time-waster. What a completely selfish human being. To text someone for a booty call, making him have to douche and wait around for you, only to be fucked off not even halfway through, with some new prudish bullshit attitude, was more than Steve could bare. It brought up all the feelings of how selfish and emotionally aloof he found Gerald when they were dating.

'What's that supposed to mean?' he asked, still not rising up from his knees, but feeling himself growing larger as his temper billowed inside him. 'What the fuck is with you?'

Gerald was occupied with buttoning his pants up.

'Forget about it,' he said, as though relieving Steve of a maths problem he'd asked him to solve.

Steve was incensed. 'Forget about what? You asked to come over and now you wanna leave? Why the fuck tease me like that and then take off?'

'I didn't mean to,' Gerald said, actually meaning every word of it. He didn't want this. He wanted to talk about kids, which was also a stupid idea. It was finally dawning on him how stupid an idea this whole endeavour was, and just how much he needed to get back to the wedding.

'Is that it? Is that all you're going to say? That you didn't mean to?'

'It's my mistake,' Gerald admitted, as though that was the end of it.

'How am I a mistake?'

This was going even worse than Gerald could have imagined. Steve seemed determined to take everything as a personal slight.

'Don't worry about it,' Gerald said, now getting a little annoyed that Steve wouldn't just drop it. He'd done up his cummerbund and was now tucking in his shirt.

'Seriously, you're tucking in your shirt? That's what you're focussing on? I should have known. You never change. I thought you were ready to start again, but of course you're just as incommunicative as ever. Just as fucking uselessly silent. People can only ever guess at what *Gerald's* thinking. Fuck, for someone who hates his dad so much, he sure does act like the spitting image. The apple doesn't fall far, does it?'

'What's that supposed to mean?'

'You figure it out.'

Gerald didn't know where to turn. He knew he wanted to leave, but he didn't know what to make of Steve's attack. He was *nothing* like his father. He walked towards the door, then turned back. 'I really didn't mean to do this,' he said.

'I don't give a shit! You never mean to do anything, you just do it, then you don't explain, and you play the victim, the hurt one who can't possibly open up. Fuck, it's like watching your dad wriggle out of social interactions. You're both the exact same person. Neither of you want to open up, so you both keep hurting people. Keeping everyone at arm's length and making them guess at your motives. Well, I just don't care anymore, just get out. Leave.'

'Hang on.' Gerald was trying to get his head around what Steve was saying, but he had no time.

'Get out!' Steve yelled.

It was done. The conversation was over. Gerald wouldn't get the answers he wanted.

At least Steve had now been cured of his hopeless longing for a past that never really existed. He'd engaged in a misre-membering, of highlighting Gerald's good points, and convincing himself that giving it another go, that changing his behaviour, would make things right. He realised now that they were total incompatible. Gerald really was as selfish as he'd remembered.

Gerald clicked the deadlock back, opened the familiar apartment door and sped out of the room. As he was walked through the brightly lit corridor, the sound of the door slamming behind him encouraged him on his way – Steve had obviously helped it shut with some force. The sound of locks clicking shut, bidding him a final goodbye from apartment 1032, echoed in the distance as he made his way to the elevator. Steve was now a memory. This had been a massive mistake.

Staring blankly at the circle of light emanating from around the G button as the lift carried him away, Gerald wondered what kind of a person accepts a booty call from someone who was in a relationship. Surely it was obvious Gerald wasn't available, so why did Steve say yes to Gerald coming over? Steve was not the person Gerald remembered him always saying he was, always using himself as the example of how society should behave. Who was Steve to stand in judgement of him, and accuse him like that? The real man of morals was Gerald's husband. It was James, the same person Gerald was essentially in the process of cheating on like an absolute asshole. And besides, Gerald was different from his dad precisely *because* he considered other people's feelings and didn't burden them with his problems. This didn't make them the same. The only things he'd inherited from his father were his hair and his eye colour, and he supposed some other physical features. Apart from that, they were nothing alike. Patrick was inconsiderate and dismissive, he stood in the corner and ignored everyone, and besides which, he was absent. Gerald always made sure he was there, physically. Well, except for moments like this. Fuck Steve. How dare he bring up Patrick.

Gerald hated dwelling on the past, but the past was throttling him tonight. His philosophy on ridding yourself of baggage had always been, 'Just ditch it and move on.' He believed that people talked about their feelings too much, and similarly dwelled on bad thoughts, or really good memories, sometimes to the point where it's like, 'Okay, this person hurt you, or you that thing you did was really cool, but how about living in the present?!' *Seriously,* he'd think, *people need to get over things and just not talk about them. Talking about things gives them power, so I'd always rather just move along and not give it a second thought, because welling on it, trying to figure out what went wrong, was a form of obsession. It obviously just wasn't right for you.* Or if there was some fleeting success someone had like five years ago, he hated when they refused to move along, to move on to a new success so everyone could stop being bored by the same old story. It just goes to show that stones that stay still really do get clumped up wth dreary moss. It was one of the reasons he'd broken up with Steve – he was a completely static stone. He'd got his job in comms, then stayed in the same role like a lump while others moved up the chain passed him. He just didn't want to put the extra work in to getting promoted. *What are you doing?* Gerald had asked him in exasperated tones. *And what's with the government? Go make yourself some money, for god's sake!*

Now, though, this philosophy had been tested. Steve had drawn a direct link between Gerald's actions and his issues with his father. And as much as Gerald tried to push back against Steve's attack, by the time the elevator had moved the short distance between level 10 and the ground floor, he had to concede that his actions tonight were a direct result of his unresolved daddy issue, and that ignoring them, moving passed them, was proving impossible. His philosophy had not only been tested, but disproven. He wasn't acting rationally, he knew that. He was acting out directly against Patrick, and it was driving him to destroy himself, or at least to destroy his relationship with James. He realised now that he had to confront his past. He had to stop pushing things aside in his mind. All those issues he was storing away were now stacking up like a messy office full of unlabelled boxes. He was a mess. The elevator walls were closing around him. The space had become tiny. Gerald longed to hear the ding of freedom. Being alone with his thoughts for all of 30 seconds felt like an eternity.

When he finally made it to the street, past the concierge desk that he was sure was still judging him, he let the cool night air course through his lungs. The whole trip down in the lift, he'd felt like he was suffocating, but only once he felt the air sting his throat did he realise he'd been holding his breath the whole time.

He was nothing like his father, he kept telling himself. His dad was an asshole. He was selfish; he'd left him and his mother when he was little. They had to struggle, he never came to visit, his mother had to get a job, he wasn't there. Gerald was nothing like that. He tried to do the right thing. It usually backfired, but that wasn't his fault. It was the circumstances. It just all went wrong sometimes. Besides, when he did the wrong thing, he had the decency to at least feel guilty about it.

If only Patrick had said outright that he never wanted Gerald, instead of letting him guess. Then at least Gerald would know where he stood in the world. He would have a certainty that didn't keep him acting erratically in search of answers.

He had to know. He had to know whether Patrick left Annie because of him. He had to know whether he truly was damaged goods, unwanted, unlovable. It was impossible living like this any longer.

Chapter 13

As he stood on the street clutching himself, his moist shirt clinging to his skin and his eyes glassy inside his pale face, Gerald wondered what his mother would think of him if she could see him now. Would she approve of his lifestyle, of careening from one bad decision to another, or would she be just at least a bit as bewildered as Gerald himself? Would she be concerned – or, worse, feel sorry for him? He didn't want to think about that right now. He never wanted to think about these things.

He pulled his phone out of his pocket and scrolled through till he found Patrick's number, hesitating with his finger over that name, unable to dial just yet. He hadn't dialled Patrick's number since before the funeral. It had only been texts since then. This was bringing back all the pain of his mother's passing, and how he'd ended up where he was now, standing near the corner of Oxford and Pelican, outside his ex's place instead of with his husband at his own wedding.

When his mother, Annie, died eight years ago, Gerald basically ran away from life so he didn't have to deal with his loss at all. She was only 42. It was the greatest pain he'd had ever known, and from that time, his memories of her had slowly morphed into an unreliable mishmash of "best of" moments, deifying her through a highlighting of all her good points (such as her support of him, her unconditional love, her victimhood in the breakdown of his parents' marriage), along with a dimming of other more human qualities she possessed (her snippy temper, her perfectionism, her vanity). She'd become the personification of sainthood. And the representation of the victimised damsel.

Annie had once told Gerald, when they were sitting on the floor making a car out of paper plates, cardboard boxes, and crayons, that when she was young she felt like an afterthought to her parents' fight-then-make-up self-created drama. She never knew where these fights would lead her family, and she never wanted Gerald to feel that way. But Gerald *did* feel that way. He already was an afterthought to their breakup. Or maybe the cause. He didn't say anything. He just kept quietly rubbing the blue crayon against the cardboard box in front of him, letting the moment pass safely. After all, he was never really sure which version of his mother he would be dealing with.

He liked to remember his mother's good qualities, but there were of course hints of the less-positive side of her personality. Times when she'd been snippy with Gerald or workers at the supermarket, and moments where she'd huffed at a minor annoyance and carried all the groceries (or whatever it was that might need shifting) at once, leading to an inevitably more difficult task. There were times where he'd gone to her work after school and seen her martyr herself by taking on all the work of a group project because she felt other people's interference was a nuisance. He'd even witnessed her sending people away who were willing to help her. One day Gerald bravely wondered aloud why she did that, to which his mother snipped out some story about people's offers to help being empty – just something people do without meaning it, otherwise surely she would have accepted them.

'The only person in this life you can rely on is yourself,' she said.

This was one of Annie's many sniper attacks at Patrick, because of whom Annie had to get a part-time job to make ends meet. While she still got Centrelink for being a single mum, she knew Gerald needed money for gymnastics, schoolbooks, and excursions, and she'd expressly told him that her self-sacrifice was because she didn't want Patrick's departure to result in Gerald missing out – hardly the thing a nine-year-old should be having to consider. This, however, had the desired effect of teaching Gerald that the only way to truly be free is through your own work.

'Work is the thing that gives you purpose,' she'd told him. 'It keeps you going even when your life might be falling apart. It's too easy to fall into a lump and just laze around the house feeling sorry for yourself. If you have a routine, though, and you have to get up and do things, then you have no excuse not to succeed. Without money, your life is totally hamstrung. Besides, doing things that have no benefit to you personally helps you forget your own problems and focus on the task at hand.'

It was because of these lessons, on her insistence in the idea that slacking off gets you nowhere, that Gerald was so career-oriented, and so determined to build his wealth. It's why he could afford the lifestyle he has now – a lifestyle he could never have imagined as a child with such humble beginnings. None of that would have been possible without Annie's example. This seemed proof enough of her infallibility.

Of course, what Annie never told quite told Gerald was that it was the chip on her shoulder, and her anger at Patrick, that led her to refuse of any financial help he'd offered. Nor did she tell him that it was her pride that made her stick to that decision when things got tough. She preferred life be a little harder than to back down and admit she needed help. Especially from *him*.

In any case, Gerald credited this fighting spirit with his getting into and making it through university. And yet it was at uni that he'd first done something he knew his mum wouldn't be proud of. She'd always taught him not to cheat, but balancing ambition with honesty is tricky, and on this occasion, ambition won. He was working on a group project with a friend, and while going through her notebook he found the answers to a Finance 1b assignment. As he read through her work, he realised he'd done it all wrong. Rather than going back to his work and figuring the answers out himself, he just copied hers out without really understanding what he'd done wrong. When he got a high distinction for the assignment, it was like he'd eaten ash. He knew he'd done the wrong thing. He tried to avoid such tactics (professionally) from then on.

Yes, if she could see him now, she'd be mortified. But it was kind of her fault, in a way. When she died, she took a large chunk of him with her. It's like she took the good qualities she possessed, the ones she taught him, and left only the underbelly of her teachings. Honesty, integrity, faithfulness. Qualities Gerald tried to emulate on the surface but could never truly live up to.

He remembered the circumstances of her death like it was yesterday. He was in his final semester at uni, with exams coming up. The call came through from his Grandpa Tomlin while he was at work, interning at NAB. He listened to the message on his break.

'Hi, Gerald, it's your granddad here. Your mum's been in an accident. Call me back when you get this message, okay?'

What he hadn't said was that she'd died on the spot. There was no chance for Gerald to go to the hospital, to see her on life support and say goodbye. No chance for closure. Just the rug ripped out from under the future he'd planned. As he'd watched the curtain close on her coffin at the Mannings Funerals in-house chapel, he felt the part of him that longed to be a better person extinguish itself and his whole world go dark.

To fill the void, he finished his degree and fled to England. He hoped that living the Aussie backpacker cliché would help. Instead, he learned what many people learn when they move countries to escape their problems: no matter how far you travel, you're always the same person, with the same baggage.

Thankfully, the move did provide a temporary distraction. Between figuring out the new culture (signing up for the NHS, figuring out the tube, deciphering the British manners that were so different to Aussie ones) and starting a new job at Barclays, he was happily unable to take the time to reflect on his loss, or the guilt he still felt about her death and about all the disagreements they'd ever had. Those feelings could be happily pushed down and ignored as other tasks took precedence.

He'd set himself up in Vauxhall, and he was consistently spending more than his shitty graduate salary from Barclays provide him with. Annie didn't have any savings to leave him, but her super had life insurance. After the funeral costs were taken care of, he received what was left, and this money was bankrolling the extra expenses he was accruing from his new lifestyle, his new wardrobe, and his many weekend jaunts to other European destinations. He thought of his mother with every tap-and-go of his credit card. He and his flatmates either spent their weekends out partying at G.A.Y. or escaping the dreary English weather by travelling Europe, struggling through the Monday and Tuesday come-downs and then doing it all again the following weekend. He, Emily, Darren, and Geoff shared a two-bedroom flat that had four single beds, so any hook-ups had to be done elsewhere – whomever they hooked up with was the host. Gerald kind of liked being the invited participant, the guest star in someone else's search for sexual fulfilment. It made him feel like a stud that was coming in to impregnate a heifer, then extricated once the job was done. He liked this image of himself.

Drugs had, of course, been instrumental in his healing, but after a year and a half of bleeding money and bad weather, Emily and Darren decided to move in with their respective boyfriends, changing the dynamic of the household. Gerald knew it was time to move on. He left London, choosing to do one more backpacking intensive through Europe before returning to Sydney. This would prove disastrous, though.

After successfully exhausting himself with a busy job, a corking social life, and a cramped, action-packed household, he finally found himself alone at various backpackers with nothing to do but sit beside beaches, eat at restaurants, and sleep in the private single bedrooms he'd booked himself as a treat. His brain tried to take advantage of this downtime and process his loss, but Gerald wouldn't have it. Regret, self-blame, and sorrow reared their ugly head. He wished he'd spent more time with Annie. He kicked himself for the various moments he'd let her down. If only he had more time to make it up to her. Gerald decided he still wasn't ready to deal with these issues, and needed to find a distraction.

He was in Nice when these intrusive thoughts started running through his head. Sitting on the rocky beach in a pair of dark-blue swim briefs, peering out of his aviator sunnies at the other bathers all peacocking and watching each other, his mind wandered to his sixteenth birthday. He'd never been popular at school – he was a gymnast, which didn't carry the clout that someone like a runner or footy player would gain for their sport, and his gayness was clearly evident to his classmates. When he was younger, Annie had been instrumental in filling the void left by a lack of social life, and even before

Patrick left, Annie and Gerald had a very close relationship. But as he got older, he viewed this support with teenaged suspicion, deciding she was hindering his social life rather than supplementing it. So when she asked on his sixteenth birthday whether he'd like to go to The Happy Chef, which was his favourite Chinese restaurant, she was taken aback when he rejected the offer and informed her he was going to dinner with his two friends from school, Erika and Ben. He knew he should have offered an alternative date and time, but in the bid to form his own identity, the selfish rebelliousness of youth knew no subtlety.

'Oh, okay,' she'd said. 'That's great.'

There was a kind of hurt in her voice that annoyed Gerald rather than engendering sympathy. He knew he'd hurt his mother's feelings, and while he felt bad about it, he pushed it away and blamed his mother for making *him* feel bad, which only led to him pulling back even more from Annie. Looking back, Gerald understood that his wasn't a unique case of teen rebellion that everyone goes through. The difference is that most people have time to rectify it and get close to their parents again. It gnawed away at him that he never got that chance.

He was so panged by these thoughts as he sat on the pebbled beach, looking out at the calm water of the Nice seaside, that not even the flirty eyes of the beautiful African man bulging out of his white speedos could make him feel any better. He got up, put his shorts on, draped his sheer button-up top over his shoulder, and headed back to his backpackers.

The feeling of his feet locomoting on the cobblestone streets, and the sight of new buildings, of different architecture, and of other tourists interacting with the local businesses, all busying themselves, helped to clear his head. By the time he got back to the hotel, his mood had lifted. He decided that staying still was not good for him. He hopped onto Grindr and found a square that showed a dark-skinned headless torso within his vicinity. After inviting this torso over, he was happy to find his flirty, white-speedoed friend from the beach show up at his door within half an hour. The next few days he spent forgetting his past, turning his attention totally towards the beautiful contrast of Omari's skin writhing between the hostel-issue white bedsheets. In time, the moments of calm silence resting in each other's arms increased, and Gerald's mind once again used this calm to race towards unwelcome topics he didn't want to dwell upon. It was time for him to move on.

Luckily, he was able to pick up someone new easily enough in the next city. His mother taught him the importance of maintaining a flawless physique. She was blonde, blue-eyed, and trim, and once told him the story of why maintaining your appearance was so important to her, and why it counted for so much in life. They'd walked past Donut King in the Burwood Westfield, and Gerald had asked for a Long John, a long donut pastry with pink icing either side and lashes of cream in the middle.

'But you've already had a chocolate-caramel slice today, Gerald,' Annie had said. 'You don't want to have too many sweets or you'll get fat, and all of a sudden you've limited your options for whatever you want to do with your life.'

Gerald had stood perplexed, trying in his eleven-year-old mind to calculate the correlation between donuts and career prospects, but he didn't quite understand the problem.

'When I was young, I wanted to be a dancer,' Annie said. 'When I told my friend Hayley that, she just giggled and said I was too fat. I thought she was a bitch, but she was right. I started looking at dancers, and realised they were all skinny. Then I looked at other successful people and they were all skinny. People are nicer to pretty people; it makes life easier. That's why you don't see me scoffing down donuts like Angela's mum. One sweet per day is enough.'

To say this was a formative lesson for Gerald is an understatement. The scars it left on his perception of body-positivity were long lasting, but it had the desired effect. He now understood why Annie maintained strict control over her diet and daily exercise routine. Rather than acknowledging that this was all just another aspect of her need for control and her desire for safety, she explained away her hyper-vigilance, instilling the importance of physical appearance as one of her main lessons to her son. Her hyper-vigilance was in fact one of the reasons she moved through life like a flustered chicken, but as far as Gerald could see, her erratic physicality was just a reflection of her stress to keep him safe. *She was such a saint.*

Funnily enough, the two people Annie never seemed to snap at were her parents. When Patrick left, they stepped in to help look after Gerald when Annie was at work. She needed them on side, so her snide character assassinations were saved for Patrick and the people at work. If he'd known better, Gerald would have seen what a strained relationship she had with her parents, and the awkward interaction between them every time he changed hands and the adults embarked on small talk. But to him, this was normal. He thought Annie's stilted behaviour was a just show of reverence to the older generation. And maybe that all grandparents just acted differently to their grandkids than they did to their own children. Besides, he liked the idea that Annie maintained a stoicism and respect for her elders. This elevated her respectability in his eyes.

Gerald had such admiration for his mother's struggles that it was a major influence on one of the few areas he and Steve could agree upon when it came to social justice. If taxes went towards anything, Gerald thought, it should be women who find themselves on their own. Mothers or wives trying to escape abusive partners. Women who find themselves alone and unable to support children when their partner dies. These people should have the opportunity to stand on their own feet. Not everyone was as lucky as Gerald, who had grandparents to help. He hated how governments loved to talk the talk about providing support to vulnerable women but never walked the walk. There was no profit in women's shelters and the like. He knew that. But wasn't government there to protect the people? Wasn't it there specifically to help society's most vulnerable when private markets failed? On this subject at least, Gerald and Steve were in complete agreement.

On the subject of how often private markets failed, though, they couldn't agree. This whole topic had been why Gerald was so upset when Steve was able to throw Gerald's past in his face during their disagreement over the Shein shirt. If he was right about that, was he also right about what he'd said tonight?

Damn you, Steve.

As he stood outside Steve's apartment block, Gerald longed for Annie to come and hug him again. The way she used to any time he'd been hurt, even when it was his own fault. He wanted to forget what he'd done tonight. To take it back. To ignore Steve's bullshit. He remembered her arms around him, making him feel like everything was going to be okay. If only she was there right now. He wondered whether she could see him from somewhere – not heaven or anything; he didn't believe in religion; besides, Annie always said religion was crap. But he knew friends who saw ghosts and stuff. Angels. Could she still be out there somewhere, somehow watching over him?

Chapter 14

Although Gerald never quite realised it, Annie did have a life before she became his mother. He'd only ever thought about her life prior to parenthood through the small snippets she'd told him as reasons he either couldn't have something or had to do something. To anyone else who knew her, the idea of Annie being angelic would have at least caused a smirk to cross their face. Bossy, fussy, stubborn, cranky, short-tempered – take your pick of a litany of alternative adjectives that might have better captured Annie's personality. But for Gerald, it was the most natural thing in the world to hold his dead mother in the highest regard.

If someone were to ask Annie, she'd say the trouble really started when she was nine. She distinctly remembered her parents bickering about how to use the new video player. Bickering is something they did frequently and with gusto. The video player was one of those new fancy models that could record the time *and* channel you wanted, even if you weren't at home, by programming a timer and selecting the channel you wanted recorded. This was the forefront of early-'80s home entertainment technology.

'You're just not listening,' her father, Cliff, snapped.

He was trying to explain how to program the 'damned' thing to Mary-Anne, Annie's mother. He'd seemingly forgotten how patiently the salesman at Retravision had been when he explained how it worked to him, and was moving through the steps at a breakneck pace, becoming increasingly frustrated by his wife's plodding comprehension.

'I *am* listening,' she snapped back. 'You're just not explaining anything properly. And you keep skipping steps.'

'What, so now you not being able to keep up is somehow my problem?'

This was purposely inflammatory. Even as a nine-year-old, Annie could see that.

'You are such an arsehole,' her mother said, crossing her arms and becoming obstinate.

'And you're a nitwit,' he replied matter-of-factly, as though saying the sky was blue.

'Seriously, I don't know why I even bother.'

'Neither do I. If I knew it was going to be like this, I would have said don't bother. I would have left you at that alter, by yourself, like you seem to have wanted anyway.'

'You really are a drama queen, you know that.'

They were both fuming, huffing and tsking at one another, bickering in a manner that was absolutely customary of them. This usually continued until one of them walked off. On this occasion, it was her father who stormed off and told her to figure it out for herself. Apparently, being called a drama queen by his wife was a step too far.

'Don't you walk out on me!' Mary-Anne cried after him, following him to their bedroom after saying, 'You stay here, darling,' to Annie, who'd been sitting on the couch watching intently.

The thought that, at any moment, her father really could walk out on her mother filled Annie with dread, and she spent the next half an hour trying desperately to follow the steps he'd been going through. When they came back into the loungeroom looking flushed, she proudly showed them that she'd figured it out, desperately hoping this would make things better. And as it turns out, it did (or seemed to at least), because after showing her parents the different steps she'd followed to get it right, they both told her how smart she was, and said they should celebrate by getting ice cream. On a conscious level, the wrong lesson she'd learned from this interaction was that she could make situations better by doing things by herself, silently completing whatever needed to be done, free of the interference of other people who might just make things worse. It started her on the path to perpetual martyrdom and woe-is-me-ism. The unconsciously wrong lesson she learned was that it was normal for couples to bicker, and that the threat of breaking-up due to such bickering was basically hollow, because what it really meant was that after these little tiffs there would be ice cream (or, in her parents' case, sex, which she only later realised).

In fact, the ice-cream treats her parents would give her after their tiffs were one of the reasons she struggled with her weight so much when she was younger. Ice creams and other sweets symbolised a release of awkward tension or open animosity, and it took years to stop using sweets as a self-soothing mechanism in times of stress and crisis. Eventually, this crutch was replaced with exercise, as part of her bid to shake off the criticisms her friends made regarding her weight and career prospects. First, her friend Hayley quashed her dreams of being a dancer by telling her that you need to have a certain type of physique to be a pro. While this crushed her dream of dancing, her friend Emma later advised her that she was also too fat to be a model. This upset her most of all, since she'd already begun to lose weight after the Hayley conversation.

'Just because you have the perfect body,' Annie argued, scowling at Emma, 'it doesn't mean you're going to photograph well.'

She'd been thinking about her two friends Paula and Jane. They were all in Grade Nine at this point, and Annie's mum had bought her a nice camera. Annie used to take pictures for them both, since they were pretty and wanted to model. Annie even thought maybe she could do some modelling, too. The thing is, Paula always looked so natural and carefree in front of the camera, while poor old Jane looked like an immobile wax figure at Madame Tussauds. Completely plastic. There was more to modelling than looks, this told her, though she had to admit that looks were important. *Mind you*, she considered, *it sucks that no one offers to take pictures of me.* From this conversation with Emma, she guessed that they all thought the same thing: she was too fat to make it. She tried her best to hide how deeply this cut, which wasn't very well.

Her face withdrew and her mouth drooped like a three-day-old balloon.

'It's why sometimes conventional beauties won't make it as models,' she continued. 'You need something interesting, and sometimes that's not even pretty, it's just captivating.'

Emma rolled her eyes, with stung Annie no end with the implication that she was too insignificant to even be argued with. Annie's eyes tightened into tiny slits, and she vowed she would never again be called fat (or 'healthy' or 'jolly,' as her mother—who was the one responsible for buying the ice creams in the first place!—called her).

She started a new diet and exercise regime later that day. While she'd already changed her eating habits to battle the bulge, her newfound hatred of Emma (who remained a toxic part of her friendship circle) increased her motivation. She already felt a need for some kind of control, due to the ever-present fear of her parents breaking up. Emma just added more fuel to the fire. She'd focus her push for control towards an obsession with her weight.

Thankfully, her childhood wasn't all trauma. She was actually able to find some mentors that didn't spend their time fighting in front of her or trying to crush her dreams. Mrs Brown, for example, her Grade Four teacher.

Mrs Brown was her biggest hero when she was ten. She was one of those women who could control the classroom with a look. She never yelled. If needed, she'd just speak slightly louder than her usual speaking voice, but made sure her tone was so emphatically dripping with consequence that the whole class stood still. You could hear a pin drop on the threadbare government-school carpet. Annie admired the gravitas she had, the control over those around her. She wanted desperately to emulate Mrs Brown. It also helped that, when she wasn't being authoritative, Mrs Brown was genuinely supportive of her students. When they got the answer wrong, rather than attacking them, she spent the time to encourage each individual student to think of what the answer might be, and stifled with an oppressive glare any giggles that might have followed from other students. It was the first time in Annie's life where she felt like she was being treated, not like an adult per se, but also not like a stupid kid. More like a soon-to-be-adult. To Annie, there was no difference. Despite the fact that there was still a power dynamic and age difference, she considered herself on par with Mrs Brown. She was so happy not to be treated like some inept plaything – an afterthought in her parents' ongoing dramas, or a distraction from their world of bickering and making up.

In her bid to emulate Mrs Brown, when she wanted to have her say in her friendship group, she'd waited one day, her body stiff and her face expectant in the same way she thought Mrs Brown did it. She sat waiting for her friends to notice it was her turn to speak. They were all sitting in a circle on the grass of the playground, so it should have been obvious to everyone what she was doing. But they went on talking, seemingly oblivious to her wishes, apparently thinking she simply had nothing to contribute. Jessica was sitting directly opposite her, and while she did actually notice Annie's change of attitude, Jessica later told her she thought she was thinking about something else entirely, and left her alone with her thoughts.

As Annie sat there waiting, she could feel herself getting redder and stroppier. Eventually she did away with this approach and instead started speaking over other people. This worked much better as a way of being heard. The fact that the original intention was to emulate Mrs Brown's adept ability to attract attention serenely had totally escaped her in the wake of the overwhelming desire for control over the group dynamics. At any rate, she'd achieved one part of her goal. This strategy had been a victory.

The problem was that this was right around the time she was discovering boys. She quickly learned that bullying them the way she bossed her friends around wasn't going to do her any favours in winning them over. She needed to add some honey to her otherwise vinegarish personality. This was a better way of attracting the opposite sex.

Besides, the last thing she needed was to carry her new forthright and combative personality into her male relationships. She was already too scarred by her parents' ongoing feuds to want to re-live that trauma. She wanted the relationships you saw in the television shows, like *Family Ties*, where couples were nice and respected each other. But without intervention, we are a product of our upbringing. How was she to know that she was speaking disrespectfully to her boyfriends or starting fights from nothing? Unwittingly, she became a human Venus fly trap, ensnaring boys with her newly minted flirtatious and soft personality. Then slowly but surely, as harmless comments were mistaken for personal slights, her temper would ripple and fights would break out. In time, either the boys left once the vinegar started souring the milk, or she'd spit them out after they'd lost their taste. Either way, for reasons unbeknownst to her, she just couldn't make a relationship work.

Everything seemed to change when she met Patrick. She was working as a receptionist at Camperdown Medical Practice at the time. As a twenty-year-old living in a sharehouse in Newtown, she was on the lookout for her next target. Patrick was one of the hot patients she had to greet whenever he came in. After a stalkerish read through his medical file, she found out he was coming in for a sprained ankle—sports injury—so she knew there wasn't anything horribly wrong with him. No weird rash or chronic heart problem. Annie dripped flirtation over every syllable whenever she greeted him, and always made sure she said, 'See you again soon, Mr Davies,' whenever he left, so he'd have to look back at her and remember her "welcoming" smile.

It finally worked. He turned around one day and awkwardly asked her out for a drink, which she agreed to readily. She had another person of interest on the go at that time, but was very happy to trade up. And there were no regrets on her end. While she considered Patrick's personality only partially realised and rather stiff, in the sack he was fully formed. He kept his cards close to his chest, and with his nervy manner, she fantasised that he was almost like a Mr Darcy figure.

She'd always found Mr Darcy hot, especially since he could put up with someone like an Elizabeth Bennet, of whom she considered herself the spitting image. Once again, she'd mistaken her abrasive personality for traits she hoped to emulate – in this case, the quick-witted scepticism of her favourite heroine. *And although Patrick isn't from a rich family,* she would tell herself, caught up in her own fantastical drama, *his bedroom attributes contain all the treasures of Pemberley.* For her part, her insecurities fed her appetite to be desired and irresistible, making her enthusiastic and eager to please, yet her icy reserve made her aloof and mysterious. Far from a Miss Bennet, Patrick considered her more of a Madonna/whore combo.

They'd only been dating six months, and while it was true that not enough time had passed for her full personality to have displayed itself, she had already demonstrated some snappy moments and small frustrated blow-ups – enough to give Patrick a taste of the side she wasn't proud of. Even still, something inside her just clicked. This was destiny, she decided.

Then she discovered she was pregnant. Though it was unexpected, and ultimately led to a lot of unnecessary pain, as soon as she found out, she knew she wanted to keep it. She had no idea how she'd manage if Patrick decided to do a runner. No one ever knew what he was really thinking, nor how much he liked her. Even if keeping it meant she'd have to move back in with her bitch mother and psycho dad after she'd only just escaped, it didn't matter. She just knew that she was all-in from the onset. Whatever else was going on in her life, keeping the baby was the one thing she was absolutely sure about.

Patrick was handsome, and, like her, had a great physique. Both of Patrick's parents were attractive, too. Their kid was destined to have great genes. The problem for Gerald was that his face took on an interesting mix of his parents' features, and his mother's bony structure contrasted with his father's full lips in a way that made him self-conscious rather than conventionally attractive. He was lucky, therefore, that of all the promises and resolutions Annie had made to make life better for herself, her promise to give her child the feeling of being loved really was able to be kept, at least for the most part. She refused to treat him as an afterthought. He would know he was loved. He would know he came first. And while Patrick wasn't the most affectionate post in the yard, if he stuck around, she could envision a world where they weren't arguing all the time in front of their child precisely because he didn't snap back.

You can imagine Annie's excitement then, when Patrick—the cold fish—got down on one knee in the hallway of her sharehouse one night after work and proposed to her. It was two weeks after he'd found out the news. Annie couldn't control herself. Out came a blood-curdling squeal, making Suzette, the only other housemate who'd been home, come running from the kitchen, where she was making herself a veggie lasagne, to see whether Annie had been stabbed.

Patrick shrunk, as though he wanted to disappear into the floor, but Annie couldn't see him. All she could see was her diamond ring and her future playing out in front of her. A wedding, a baby, living together. Patrick's stony reserve would melt away, and Annie would have a baby to think about, so she would make sure to keep her temper in check. Patrick was studying town planning, so her and the baby would be taken care of when he got into whatever job that would lead him into. Possibly private school for the kid, but let's not get ahead of ourselves. Better to take one step at a time. Yes, she was already getting better at being less dramatic; she was planning small. Less frustration when you aim for what your hand could reach.

She put out her hand and splayed her fingers like twigs so Patrick could slip the ring onto her finger. He was still kneeling on the floor, watching Suzette watching them, but looked away self-consciously and slipped on the ring. It was too big. *That's okay,* Annie thought, *easy enough to resize it.* It'd wear well enough at dinner, anyway. She turned away from Patrick and gesticulated wildly at Suzette, who returned the favour. They were both screaming. Patrick got up and took a step back, not knowing what to do. When Annie turned back to him, she thought he looked a little like a spectator to his own proposal. He always seemed to look like a spectator, though, so what else was new? She would help him out of that. Everything would be different now. She'd finally made it.

She realised soon enough how quickly expectations that have been built up so high can come crashing down. Leading up to their wedding day, she'd been having bouts of insecurity that felt different from her usual ones. It all had to do with Patrick's stony reserve. He seemed to be getting worse, rather than better, as a result of the direction they were taking things. This begged the question: did Patrick really want to marry her? He'd proposed, unprompted, so surely that was the answer right there. His actions spoke louder than his words. She'd convinced herself that's just how some men are. Then, at the wedding, after her parents had started their own drama, as usual, she thought Patrick was just shutting down in reaction to them, which was fair enough. After all, he said 'I do' without hesitation, and he cried when Annie came in looking like a blonde bombshell in a meringue, holding her father's arm and a small pink-and-white-rosed bouquet. His speech was all about duty and how much he was looking forward to starting a family, though when she thought back, Annie realised what he'd actually said was how important being a family man was to him. Very different, but she'd heard what she wanted to hear at the time. At the end of the night, they consummated the marriage, so surely there must be love there. But there was something at the back of her mind, niggling at her, questioning whether all of this was real. She put it down to the fact that she didn't really think she deserved love because of the way her parents treated her. She also hypothesised that she was despairing because she wanted to be sure it would all work out, and there was no way of knowing. There never is with love, which is what makes it so all-encompassing. All the questioning, missed signals, false accusation, all in the name of certainty. But his parents were lovely, and all her friends were there, so happy for and jealous of her. That, at least, made her happy.

By the time she realised her fears were justified, it was too late. He admitted, years later, that he'd married her out of obligation. There were signs, of course. She scolded herself that she should have known, but we all want to believe the truth of positive thinking, no matter how much we might know, deep down, that it's a lie. Regardless of how obscene she thought her parents' dynamic was, there was a truth to it. If you love someone, you'll argue and fight – there's a spark there. Patrick would just diffuse any friction and shut down, which was totally fucking annoying. She hated it. He was supposed to fight back. It was weird and unsatisfying. She never was able to calm her temper, but he was likewise unable to open up and be honest. It was lose–lose. When he finally left them after six gruelling years, she wished he'd never wasted either of their time.

She'd always hated liars, but the worst liars were the ones who lie because they think they're doing you a favour. Discovering Patrick was that kind of liar, and that he did it about something as important as saying vows of everlasting love in a church (even though she was an atheist) destroyed her. All those childhood feelings of not being good enough came bubbling back to the surface. The memories of how she'd flaunted her happiness in front of her friends at her wedding and for years afterwards tasted like rotten grapes.

From then on, whenever she thought about relationships of love, she felt like she was spitting dirty rotten grape seeds out of her mouth and onto the ground. She was so angry she couldn't really talk about the breakup with Gerald properly, just saying that his father had faults and they couldn't be a family anymore. A bit weak of an explanation, she knew, but the best she could do at the time. She didn't want to pass that bitterness on to Gerald, but what could she do? Kids have a way of absorbing their parents' biases. She never imagined he would go on to blame himself.

15 ▮

Chapter 15

Annie had a habit of making subtle digs at Patrick, dressing them up as teachable moments for Gerald by admonishing people for their lack of follow-through.

'These people!' she'd cried one day when one of the other parents cancelled a play date because she'd double booked. 'If you know it's beyond your capabilities, or you have no intention of doing it, then don't say yes and apologise later. Just don't even commit in the first place. You're not sparing anyone's feelings by making someone think something's going to be taken care of only so they can be let down and left in the lurch, either having to cope on their own, or beg, borrow and steal for something to get done. I tell you Gerald, it's better for everyone involved to make honesty the best policy. It's usually people who have trouble being honest who commit to things just for the sake of it. What's wrong with saying no? Seriously. I'd rather ask someone for something and receive a straight answer than hearing *Oh, yes, definitely*, then not have anything to show for it. It's a momentary good feeling of being supported only to be let down. Who wants to go through that rollercoaster of emotions? Just be honest and everyone can be happy. Even if that honesty is *I just don't want to*. Better than *Oops! Forgot*.'

Gerald had sat being quietly scarred in the back seat as Annie flicked her always-expressive hands around, waiting for the lights to change. Apparently, it was the height of rudeness to cancel a playdate, or any other date for that matter, and it would just cause unknown grief to the cancellee. This made Gerald wary of making promises, and deathly serious about keeping the promises he did make. This wasn't Annie's intention, of course – she just wanted Gerald not to do to someone else what Patrick had done to her. But children have a way of taking things on board and making life-paths out of them.

Perhaps if she'd been more direct, Gerald would have got the right message. But as it was, with all the secrecy surrounding his parents' divorce, Gerald always felt like he'd done something wrong. Like Patrick had left him, not Annie. He assumed Annie was sparing his feelings, not hers, for refusing to talk about why his father left.

'Those Catholics,' she'd said once, judgement dripping off every word, as a funeral scene was playing on TV in the background while she prepared dinner. One of the characters on *Neighbours* had died and they were making a big fuss about it, but neither Gerald nor Annie liked that character anyway. 'They just can't be honest with themselves for fear of being judged by the rest of the gang, so they all do what they think is right. Steer clear of religion, my boy,' she added. 'Honesty really is the best policy. And don't bury me when I go, for god's sake. I want to be cremated and tossed out to sea.'

Gerald continued to sit on the couch, looking at his homework, but he wasn't able to focus on the numbers on the page. He really didn't want to think about his mum being dead. Where would he go if she did die, with a dad that didn't want him and grandparents who lived out in Woop Woop (Parramatta, really only 20 to 30 minutes away)?

When Gerald reflected back on this scene, he realised that while Annie had been cremated, Gerald had never gotten around to spreading her ashes at sea, even after all the travelling to beautiful beaches he'd done. He'd actually forgotten those particular wishes, as he'd been too overwhelmed by what she'd said directly beforehand.

Funnily enough, the fact that Annie was so open with her feeling—towards Patrick, towards religion, towards everything—was one of the reasons Gerald had such a problem with expressing his own. Despite her best efforts, her son slowly began demonstrating those negative characteristics she saw in Patrick: shutting down, telling half-truths, and people-pleasing. Totally oblivious to her unguarded vitriol for Patrick actually creating these characteristics, she worried that it was genetic, and hoped he could find a nice boy to settle down with who could help him open up a bit. Most of all, she was worried he was starting to want to be a "good boy," a people-pleaser and compliment-chaser. That's where the real danger lies. When actions don't match the intention.

***

'Children should be seen and not heard,' Patrick's mother Cynthia would often say.

Patrick and his four siblings were expected to maintain a quiet repose when in the presence of company. Playing board games without arguing. Drawing. Anything but running around and making noise. Definitely not fighting.

'If you carry on like this,' she'd continue, 'your only friend will be the wooden spoon.'

'Spare the rod, spoil the child,' Cynthia's friend Joan liked to add helpfully, always with a knowing tsk and her nose held higher than it needed to be.

This usually kept Patrick and his siblings in line. But when any of them were in a rebellious mood, Cynthia would count the infringements, each one corresponding with one whack from the wooden spoon once the guests had left. This taught Patrick and his siblings not only to maintain strict control over their behaviours so they were acceptable to others, but it also taught them delayed expectation of punishments if they did step out of line. Sometimes, many hours after their misdemeanours, they were called back to the kitchen and made to assume the position.

'If we don't do the right thing, there will be consequences,' Cynthia informed them before delivering the punishment.

Patrick remembered one time refusing to hug "Aunty Joan" when she arrived for a visit. The time before this, Joan had goaded Cynthia into reprimanding Patrick, even though he hadn't broken any of the rules.

'The way that boy plays with those crayons,' Joan had said, 'you're going to need to buy new ones in no time. Someone ought to teach him how to look after his possessions, or he'll end up without.'

Patrick hated "Aunty Joan" after this. But his attempt to set boundaries on who he'd show affection towards earned him a fresh walloping in front of her. Rather than the usual one-to-one incident-to-punishment ratio, this one act of rebellion resulted in five furious, open-palmed whacks. Cynthia smacked him harder than he ever remembered being smacked. He burst into tears, then was thrust into Joan's arms to make amends.

'Now say sorry,' Cynthia demanded, before sending him on his way.

Patrick would never make that mistake again.

***

'I assume you're going to marry her?' Cynthia asked him.

'Of course.'

Cynthia had made an "impromptu" visit to Patrick's place a few weeks after Annie discovered she was pregnant. Her spies had obviously relayed the "happy" news to her and she was ensuring things be handled in the right way.

At the wedding, Joan had worn her usual knowing expression.

'Something like this was always going to happen with that one,' Patrick had overheard Joan telling his mother at the reception. 'He always wanted to have his cake and eat it too. Why he wouldn't use protection is beyond me. Stupid boy. Instant gratification, that's the problem with this generation.

Never thinking of anyone but themselves. Still. You can only do so much to raise them right. At least he's done the right thing now.'

Cynthia was nodding along sternly. Patrick felt a knot forming in his stomach. *Joan shouldn't even be here!* He felt himself turn pink at this trespass into defiance, and instead stropped away to find a quiet place to be alone. But there was no quiet place. No nooks or corners to hide in, and if he left the venue to sit outside, this would surely result in someone's ire being drawn and some form of punishment being delivered. Instead, he went and sat at the bridal table in full view of everyone. He looked out at Annie. She was holding court, skiting to all her friends. He'd never seen her as long-term. Sure, she was fun, and he was drawn to her larger-than-life personality, but they were just so different. Her with her moods and him with his nerves, it couldn't work.

His mates were all getting drunk on his parents' dime. He enjoyed that thought, at least. Even still, he couldn't help thinking that this was a massive mistake, but he couldn't see any alternative. He'd brought this on himself.

***

When Gerald was born, it was truly the happiest day of Patrick's life. Looking at his own lips reflected back at him, with Annie's eyes, Gerald was the perfect fusion between the two of them. Annie was drugged out on the hospital bed beside him, unable to summon her usual aggression. As he held his baby in his arms, Patrick thought that maybe, just maybe, they would be okay.

He really did stay with them for as long as he could. Coping with Annie's persistent bouts of fury, then her desire, eventually left him too frayed around the edges. He had to get out. Besides, Annie seemed so cross with him the whole time they were together, he assumed she'd be just as relieved as he thought he'd be at his departure.

She wasn't.

The stunned look on Annie's face bewildered him. He'd tried to do the right thing by marrying her, but it seemed to make them both miserable. He'd become more and more distant at home. It wasn't right to Gerald, nor Annie, and it sure as hell wasn't right for Patrick. Trying to do the right thing was tearing them apart. Even someone as out of touch with their emotions as Patrick had to realise that marrying Annie hadn't been the right thing to do. All the TV shows he'd seen had made it clear that women don't like being lied to, that men should be honest. Getting married out of duty was just the kind of fire-and-brimstone stuff that scornful old bitties like Aunty Joan liked to insist upon. So now he was doing what he thought was the actual right thing – letting them all have a fresh start.

To say that this turned out to be even worse was an understatement. Patrick had never seen Annie so quiet. He thought this was better than her usual red-faced shouting, so when she looked intensely at him and she asked him to explain himself, he relaxed a little.

'I guess, I've never really loved you,' he said. 'Maybe we never loved each other. You've seemed as unhappy with me as I've been with you. It's just, when Gerald came, I was trying to do the right thing by you both, and so we got married. I don't know, maybe my parents made me do it. Maybe we would have been happier if we were just separate co-parents? I don't know. What do you think?'

He made sure he said 'maybe' a lot. He'd learned that it usually leads to better reactions if he said 'maybe' in front of a statement. But maybe he'd said 'maybe' too often and it lost its effectiveness. Or maybe Annie saw through his strategy of trying to get her to remain calm by using that word. Somehow, though, it didn't work.

'Hmm, what do I think?' she responded with a frenetic calm. 'I don't know. *Maybe* you're just an asshole. *Maybe* you should go fuck yourself and stop telling *me* what I do and don't feel. Oh, I know, maybe, just *maybe*, you should take a bit of responsibility and stop blaming everyone else for shit *you've* done.'

Patrick looked at her in stunned silence. He knew any false move might be catastrophic. Somehow this silence only seemed to aggravate Annie more.

'You can't seriously be trying to tell me that our whole relationship you've just been doing it out of what, some Catholic guilt? Because *Mummy and Daddy* said so? Are you kidding me? You're trying to tell me my whole marriage to you, what, you NEVER loved me? You think I *trapped* you in this marriage? Tell me you're joking.'

'I didn't say you trapped me.'

'Oh, silly me! I didn't realise we were having a conversation about *semantics* all of a sudden!'

She was getting louder now. Patrick wanted to calm her down. When he'd gone over this conversation in his head, he'd thought being honest would be the best policy.

'What the fuck do you want, then?' was all he could think of saying.

'I want you to get the fuck out of this house!'

Annie had screamed so loudly that Patrick felt like he'd been knocked to the back of the room.

'Where am I supposed to go?'

'I don't give a shit. How about you fuck off back to *Mummy and Daddy's* place?' Annie was stomping around the house in a frenzy now. She was no longer looking at Patrick. She snatched her keys off the kitchen table and stomped back into the living room. Without looking at him she said, 'When I get back, I want your stuff out of this house and I want you gone. I never want to see you again.'

'Can't we talk about this?' he said, desperately.

'Talk about what? There's nothing left to say.'

'What about Gerald?'

Annie stopped in her tracks, her mouth gaping. 'You want to talk about custody? Now?'

Patrick thought this was the obvious time to talk about it, but said nothing.

'My god. I can't even look at you, and you wanna discuss which weekends you'll get to see him? I was going to have this baby with or without you, do you understand me? I didn't need you to get into a fake a relationship with me to have that kid. You haven't done him or many *any* favours.'

'He's still my son.'

'So now you have a voice, do you? Wow. Okay. We can discuss custody later. Through lawyers. I don't want to talk to you. Argh. You're such an asshole, you don't even know how much of a prick you've been. I mean it. I'm leaving. I want you gone when I get back.'

Patrick was trying to think of something to say, but nothing came to mind before Annie stormed through the door and slammed it shut.

Annie was right, he really didn't understand fully what he'd done wrong. He thought he'd done the right thing. He was the one going against his own wishes, so how come he was the bad guy now? All this stuff about being true to yourself and expressing your emotions he'd seen in the new-age TV shows – where was the good of that in this scenario?

Annie refused to answer his texts, and he resisted his parents' calls to sue for custody. They'd done enough damage already. Patrick might not have known much, but he knew better than to drag a kid into the courtroom to answer questions. He would wait for Gerald to reach out to him. When Gerald felt the time was right. He wasn't going to force anyone's hand. He at least wanted to give his child the dignity of making his own choices, a grace never bestowed on him by his parents.

He still got to see Gerald occasionally, but while Patrick felt he no longer needed to step on eggshells for fear of Annie's change in mood, their visits were awkward. Gerald seemed to resent their time together. Patrick felt like an imposition.

'I always try to do the right thing by you, Gerald,' he'd said one afternoon when Gerald was on the couch beside him, moping about something. 'Even if it doesn't always work out for the best, I still try. You can always tell me if anything's troubling you.'

He saw Gerald roll his eyes then go back to staring at the TV. He wouldn't push the point. At least he'd tried, but he wouldn't force Gerald to hang around him if he didn't want to. He'd obviously hurt Gerald as much as he'd hurt Annie. Forcing Gerald to do something he clearly didn't want to do seemed like he was just causing further harm. Patrick stopped demanding Gerald come over on his weekends, and Gerald didn't ask to come, so he just left it.

At least he made sure he called every birthday and Christmas, and sent yearly presents. Plus, he always extended the invitation to spend time together when Gerald was free, if he wanted to. But his son never showed the initiative and reached out, no matter how dearly Patrick hoped he would. He ended up feeling perpetually perturbed and confused by this scenario. He truly believed that doing right by the world would eventually lead the world to do the right thing by him. The problem is knowing what was right. He'd always tried to do the right thing, but it never seemed to work.

Now he had no idea what to do. A therapist or some wise friend might have told him that it was up to the parent to guide interactions, but that would mean opening up about things, and he was so far into his withdrawal-as-restitution strategy that such help was never sought. Over the years, all of this caused him no end of nervousness.

That was until he met Jen.

16 ▍

Chapter 16

'So,' Jen said to him as they walked through the door of their tranquil apartment in the wealthy suburb of Rose Bay, 'today went well, don't you think?'

Jen was kicking off her heels as Patrick fiddled with his tie. Patrick was rather handsome for his age, and despite still having a thick head of dark hair, tanned skin, thick lips, and still no gut, he failed to exude confidence.

'Very well,' he replied thoughtfully. 'I think that maybe we've moved beyond the mistakes of the past. I think maybe this is the first step.'

'I think so, too,' Jen said with a twinkle.

He met her five years ago at a friend's 50th in Dee Why. Terri, the friend in question, was rotten as a chop. She'd grabbed Patrick by the button of his open shirt and slurred the words, 'Come here.' The other hand's index finger coaxed him suggestively as she dragged him halfway across the living room. Impressively, she'd avoided stumbling over her wobbly legs as they manoeuvred backwards. Her eyelids were so heavy that the seductive look she was trying to maintain made it look like she was half asleep. She'd gyrated sloppily to the music while Patrick inwardly cringed at the thought of being the evening's *Dirty Dancing* spectacle. He couldn't let the birthday girl down, though. He dutifully held her waist (mainly to avoid her falling onto the glass coffee table nearby) and they both slithered together. Terri flopped this way and that, living out her main character fantasy.

Jennifer had been watching from behind one of the sofas, and was surprised at how well Patrick could move, considering he'd been standing in the corner like a stiff-kneed robot most of the night.

'Nice moves,' she said after Patrick had allowed Terri to careen into the couch, huffing and puffing from exertion and giggling like a schoolgirl. He'd participated in the dancing part of the evening for a polite number of minutes by that stage, then made his escape. The howls and hoots of party onlookers were still ringing in his ears as he tried to figure out whether Jennifer was flirting or making fun of him. In any case, he thanked her, wishing to God he'd been able to escape further from the centre of the room than he was at that moment. They spent the rest of the party together. Jennifer carried the conversation, for which Patrick was extremely grateful.

Terri was a friend of his from work, and Patrick had been spiralling about how awkward Monday morning might be as he left the "dance floor," but Jennifer's stunning features and easy conversation were pushing those thoughts out of his mind. He couldn't believe that such a woman would be interested in him, so he assumed her conversation was temporary sympathy for the embarrassment he'd felt from his chivalrous turn. That's why, when he left without offering to exchange numbers, he was flabbergasted to get a text from Jen two days later, chastising him: 'Hey there stranger. Jen here. Can't believe you made me get your number from Terri. Someone likes to play hard to get huh? Naughty!'

Patrick barely knew how to respond. He did respond, however. And over the course of their correspondence, Jen was always assured and direct in her answers. She was obviously a go-getter – probably what some would call a 'ball-breaker,' but Patrick didn't mind. He felt safe with her. He could hide in the corner while she filled the space. This worked at home as well as it did at social gatherings. She drove their conversations, and questioned his decisions when he was thinking of committing to something he didn't want to do, saying things like, 'Are you sure you're not just saying yes because you don't want to let people down? I thought we'd talked about this.'

He was in awe of her. After all, she was the whole package. She was the life of the party, took the weight off him at social occasions, earned more than he did, and made him feel like he was home when they were together. She completed him. She also treated him like a piece of meat in the bedroom, which Patrick very much enjoyed. He'd never been interested in being the alpha. If only other aspects of life were so simple.

Jen was also a proverbial shoulder to cry on when it came to Patrick's relationship with Gerald. He had no idea what to do. How could he get Gerald to see things from his perspective, to forgive him for all the pain he'd caused? From the impression Patrick got from Gerald's online activity, he actually thought Gerald would like him if he gave him a chance. They both cared about social issues: wealth disparity, income inequality, our increasing reliance on online interaction, the impact these issues were having on our sense of community. (Gerald actually didn't seem to care that much about the last of these, but it was important to Patrick, so he included it in his discussions with Jen.)

'Patrick, dear, don't you think it just a little ironic that you espouse these views from the Eastern Suburbs of Sydney, one of the premier regions of wealth in Australia?' Jen asked in response to his diatribe one day. 'And aren't your views usually spread online via Facebook, a wealthy multinational conglomerate that's been instrumental in increasing antisocial behaviour?'

Patrick thought that statement was below the belt. She was the one with a property port-folio. He couldn't help his personal circumstances. She must have seen that Patrick was upset by her, because she immediately stopped smiling and never brought it up again. She attempted to make up for it by booking him in with her therapist, just to help him 'order his thoughts a little more' and strategise.

'I know you say you're terrified of bringing the past back up,' Angela the psychologist had said, almost exasperated at Patrick's placid attitude. 'But how can forgiveness come to pass if you don't bring it up? How can Gerald forgive you if you don't make the first move? You need to confront these things head-on. You can't just sit and hope the past is forgotten, that it'll somehow be replaced by some fairy-tale version of the present you're imagining. You're the parent. You need to take action.'

Patrick never went back.

Instead, he turned to self-help books to work his way through his issues. One of the books, *Functional Habits*, focussed on the importance of routine, and he followed the routine laid out in that book to a tee. When he woke up in the morning, he started his day with affirmations to build up a positive outlook. The next thing he did was put his sneakers on and went for a walk. He'd read that morning walks draw oxygen into the body, gets blood pumping, and promotes mental activity. He used to sometimes do it on the treadmill, but he'd also read somewhere that the brain needs things passing by the eyes to stay engaged. This must have been true, because when he stared blankly at the wall, his mind went into the negative feedback loops and he focussed back in on his faults. The frenetic outdoors was much more effective for giving Patrick that outward-looking, optimistic feeling. After the walk, it was time for the water with lemon juice to rehydrate. He squeezed half a lemon per glass of water, which was supposed to kick-start his metabolism. This was another thing he'd read about, although he'd also read that it was a placebo, so he wasn't sure what to believe. He was almost going to cut the lemon juice out until he saw something on Facebook about how such routines are more important for the 'holistic outcomes they promote than the chemical reaction they produce.' This was of course backed up by the "science" discussed in *Functional Habits*, so the juice avoided the chop. Then he showered, brushed his teeth, and dressed for work.

While *Functional Habits* hadn't solved the problem he'd gone to the therapist to deal with, this early morning routine did help him cope with the days a lot better. It was much more preferable than the psychology appointment – and at $35 for the entire book, it was a lot cheaper.

He told himself that being tucked away beneath Town Hall, working for the City of Sydney, was ideal for him. He liked to believe his work as a town planner allowed him to contribute to society in some way. He could do his small part towards helping young people with the housing market (a problem Jennifer's property portfolio contributed to). And he was an active online social justice warrior for the marriage equality plebiscite. He liked to be seen to be making a difference, but he knew that all of this was a band-aid for the real issue. He understood deep down that he was trying to make amends in some small way for the pain he'd caused in the lives of people he knew. People he was supposed to be there for. But that was all so long ago. What could be done about it now? He was tired. Tired of blaming himself. Tired of being blamed. Although he wanted to be forgiven, he couldn't see a way of mending things.

That's why he'd been so surprised when he received the invite to Gerald's wedding. This gave him hope. Despite psychologist Angela's insistence that his hope for things to magically turn around was unrealistic, it seemed as though the unthinkable had happened. This might potentially be a new chapter, a new lease on their relationship. Gerald had finally forgiven him. He'd no longer need to act so solemnly around him, with all the undercurrents of silent apologies.

True, he hadn't been asked to give a speech as the father of the groom, but that wasn't important. Baby steps. It was enough to be invited. Plus, Patrick hated giving speeches. He was glad not to give a speech.

'Oh, no one was supposed to give a speech!' Geoffrey had told him at the ceremony, even though he'd just given a 20-minute master class in public speaking. People laughed, cried, and sighed, and all the while Patrick wriggled in his seat at the prospect that he may be expected to go next. 'Yeah, I just grabbed the microphone and started talking. They weren't gonna stop me talking at my own son's wedding, I don't care how unconventional they think they are. Fuck, even Charlie had a go,' Geoffrey went on, referring to Charlie grabbing the microphone after his speech and slurring her way through one long, meandering thought about what a beautiful couple they made and how much she loved them. 'Not sure how much sense she made, the poor dear, but her heart was in it.'

'She got the boys up to the mic, so you gotta give her that,' James's brother Andrew said.

Patrick remembered the boys expertly hugging her, taking the mic, and then thanking everyone for coming as Charlie stumbled off towards the bar.

The night had been such fun. And on a personal note, Patrick considered the night a massive success. He'd finally been jovial, and he loved getting to know James's family. Gerald paid him *lots* of attention, he'd noticed. Always looking his way. Patrick had even been able to allude to past mistakes in an off-hand and easy manner. And he'd been gracious, wishing Gerald more success and happiness than he'd experienced in his life.

Yes, as Patrick moved to his lounge room to make himself a nightcap, he patted himself on the back for what a roaring success the evening had been.

'I think we've finally turned over a new leaf,' he said to Jennifer.

'You were wonderful, darling,' she said supportively.

Patrick swelled. He *was* wonderful. He'd overcome his shyness, and had a normal conversation with his estranged son. All the tension from years of animosity felt like it had melted away. It was a new dawn; he looked forward to more of such occasions to come. Maybe he'd even invite Gerald to his next event, who knows.

The important thing was that he'd been forgiven. Maybe one day he might be called Dad instead of just Patrick. Maybe one day he and his son might say 'I love you' to one another. Yes, that would be something.

Patrick sat at their dining table with his shirt unbuttoned, revealing the slender physique of which he was so proud. He sipped on his gin and tonic while Jennifer was in the bedroom getting out of her gown (why women's fashion was so uncomfortable, he would never understand). He had his drink in one hand and his phone in the other, scrolling through photos of the wedding. Photos of Jennifer next to a rose bush, of the beautiful reception and all the people there, of a snap he'd taken with the whole family – James, his parents, Gerald, Jennifer and him. He felt a wave wash over him. He scrolled back to a picture of James and Gerald, and imagined that at this moment, those two love birds would be having the time of their lives.

The years of turmoil were over. Patrick was happy.

Chapter 17

Oxford Street was a blur. Gerald was still standing on the side of the road looking like a strung-out clothesline. His jaw was tight and his body shivered, but not from the cooling night air. His arms were crossed, shielding him from the world, and the phone he'd been playing with moments earlier was now tucked firmly under his arm, the locked screen hiding Patrick's contact details from him. He couldn't deal with that just yet.

People walking past must have thought him completely tragic, but he didn't care. He was still reeling from the altercation he'd had with Steve. The accusations Steve had made about him and his father, and the fact that he'd nearly capitulated to Steve's advances, were playing over in his mind. He felt sick. He knew he shouldn't be here; his body was physically revolting against his actions this evening. He still had his baggie in his pocket, but there was nowhere nearby to go to give himself a little lift. Instead, he turned his thoughts back to Patrick – if he couldn't self-soothe through chemical assistance, he could at least divert his sorrows towards more constructive emotions like blame and anger.

The hints had all been there that his father had never liked him. Even though Annie never outright blamed Gerald, it was so obvious. Patrick never came to his gymnastics tournaments. *Too gay*, Gerald had reasoned, especially considering how much the kids at school teased him for it. Patrick never really said goodbye, either. And when Gerald had seen him on rare occasions after the separation, he was so distant it was clear to Gerald that he was only doing it because the court must have mandated it or something. Perhaps even Annie forced him into it. Gerald had noticed the way Patrick looked at him, like he was alien, some weird child he had no idea what to do with. Gerald had already been teased enough at school for his obvious sexuality without being uncomfortably aware that his father had a problem with it, too. He hated those catch-ups.

He learned not to care, though. He chose to embrace his sexuality, the thing his father seemingly had such a massive problem with. Not only were his mannerisms maximised, but when he realised that everyone had been right about him, that he really was the fag they'd all said he was, he embraced that part of his sexuality, too. He wouldn't be shamed into changing just because a bunch of bullies thought they could intimidate him. Not when it was they who all had something wrong with them.

'Everyone's an individual. We're all different, and everyone has problems,' Annie said once. He'd asked her what 'gay' meant, because they were calling him that at school. The kids had been talking about Savage Garden, saying the lead singer was gay, and that Gerald looked just like him.

'Gerald is the gay guy from Savage Garden's mini-me!' Derek had cried out to the laughter and sneering of the rest of his little buddies.

Rather than take the bait and fight or cry, Gerald learned that pithy retorts, a witty comeback pinpointing some of their flaws, usually worked best to counter these attacks. Getting emotional only served the bully's needs. Bullies want you to get angry. It was safer for Gerald to stay level-headed and cool. But this strategy of removing emotions from any situation to avoid being hurt was so effective that it became his main coping strategy, eventually leaving him feeling detached. Lacking intimacy.

Is it any wonder he used his sexuality like a weapon, seeking out emotional sustenance though physical means? He didn't mean to, but perhaps if Patrick had shown even the smallest amount of guilt about the way things had gone and the harm he'd inflicted on Gerald's upbringing, things might be different. As much as he tried to tell himself his intentions weren't as sinister as that, he knew Steve would try to have sex with him, and that the rejection from James is what really prompted him to act out. He'd felt scorned emotionally, and he once again turned to the strategy of using his flesh as a magnetic conductor, drawing in a willing partner and burning them as soon as they'd given him the attention he wanted. He didn't know anything different, though. He wanted to be loved – he needed it. He craved the feeling of being wanted, in a way he'd never been by Patrick. He'd been rejected, cast aside, deemed unlovable, like he was faulty merchandise. That's why he tried so hard to be good.

Everything on paper told him how "good" he was: a banker, a loyal shoulder for his friends, successful, always listening to others' problems without burdening them with his (would they even want to listen?), the fun party boy, aesthetically pleasing gym body, an all-round package. But they were just traits. Traits he collated in his search to feel loved. The problem was that the well could never be filled. The void always needed more feeding, because deep down he knew he couldn't be loved: his mum was dead, his father didn't want him, and even his friend didn't know who he was (because he never opened up, but that's besides the point). They didn't know how insecure he was, that he was a cheater, that he churned through things – drugs, alcohol, random men – not because he was a fun party boy, but because he craved something to fill the void, like some garbage disposal that constantly needs more junk to devour. He hated it. He wanted to stop. He had to stop. He worried that, one day, he'd finally be shown for what he was – a pariah, undeserving of love. That couldn't happen.

He realised that he was fighting something of a Dr. Jeckell and Mr Hyde battle for his soul. All his late-night outings, sneaking away to saunas (or bathhouses, as the Americans say), or random guy's places for a quick hit of love (or admiration), then feeling like shit afterwards. It had to stop. The Hyde side of his personality – the one that made him do things confirmed how horrible he was, how truly undeserving of love – needed to be tamed. But this couldn't be done without dealing with the root cause. It was just his father leaving that gave the Mr Hyde side so much power. His mother's death was the moment that deepened his belief that he wasn't deserving of love. His mother, who'd always been there. And Gerald, so repulsively selfish.

People always say that everybody deserves love, and Gerald believed it until his mother died, then he knew then that it wasn't true. He'd never told a soul what happened. He was too ashamed, but he was thinking of it now.

She'd called him the day she died, but he never picked up the phone. He was too busy hanging with friends, so he'd just let it ring out. He'd worked a half day at his internship with NAB on Wednesdays, and he'd wanted to be as unbothered as possible during his downtime. *I'll call her back later, whatever.* But there was no later. He never knew what she was calling about, or, had he answered the call, if that day might have gone differently. Maybe she would have been held up. Maybe she wouldn't have ended up where she was on that day, at that specific intersection, where that specific truck ran the red. Maybe her whole day, her whole life, could have been changed if he'd answered that call. But he'll never know.

He'd tried to admit it—to Charlie, to James—but every time he thought about finally coming clean, the words clogged up his throat and refused to come out. *Thank God the words refused to emerge,* he'd think to himself after such episodes of almost opening up. He really did love those two. The last thing he needed was for them to turn away from him once they'd truly seen him for the selfish person he was. Too self-involved to talk to the one person who was always there for him. The type of person who would actually watch the name flashing on the screen of the only person who'd always been there for you and pretend not to see it. No, that part of himself needed to stay hidden. The consequence was the acting out, the impulsive nights, the trips to saunas or random men's apartments when no one was looking. Then he could be the dependable rock for the people who needed him, the strongman.

He pulled his phone out of from under his armpit and unlocked the screen. Patrick's name stared ominously up at him. He didn't hesitate this time. He pressed the button and put the phone to his ear. It was dialling. Gerald felt like his whole life had been leading towards this confrontation. Throughout the night, thoughts, memories, and unresolved trauma had been impregnating his consciousness, but he'd terminated them without any ultrasound to assess his mind's machinations. Not even a split-second investigation into these thoughts was being conducted, just purposeful ignorance. Maybe it was late, but it was time.

The sound of two girls in heels stepping out from the apartments behind him and giggling made him turn his head. They looked fresh, like they were waiting for their Uber to take them to the Cross or the Sheaf. A few drinks under the belt, pre-loading to save money, obviously still students with fast-fashion outfits from the Iconic and heels that didn't really match the belts and bags; too cheap to afford better at that age. They gave Gerald a look; he knew he looked like shit, but this was the least of his concerns. The phone was on its second ring. He realised only now that he needed privacy. He needed to feel free to speak his mind. He would finally find out the truth. This was when all his fears would be confirmed. He didn't know where he could turn. He needed somewhere dark, out of sight. After considering moving to a little alley across the road, he realised there was a quiet alcove down the steps of Riley Street, not 100 metres away. He was scuttering away from the women in heels when the ringing suddenly cut off.

'Hello?' Patrick's voice came over the line, catching Gerald off guard by how soon he'd answered. He also had a jovial tone, which was not setting the tone for the conversation Gerald was intent on having at all.

'Hi,' he said briskly, his breath catching as his steps quickened.

'Did I forget something?'

It was almost perfect that Patrick would say something so incredulous. Couldn't Gerald be calling to chat? Why would it need to be because he'd forgot something, like that's the only reason to warrant a son calling a father.

'What did you mean when you said I'm sure you'll make a better go of it than I did?'

'What?'

Gerald had just blurted it out, emboldened by the obtuse reception Patrick had greeted him with.

If he wanted to play obtuse then Gerald would be direct. 'You said James and I would make a better go of it than you and mum did. Is that because we won't have kids?'

'What are you talking about?'

'Is that why you left mum, because you had kids? Or was it just me?' Gerald was still talking calmly, but he could feel the thunder rumbling inside. He could feel a lump starting to choke him, and tears well up, as he waited for the answer. In the lingering silence, he felt himself turning pale, as the horror of what he'd spent his whole life avoiding was finally here. 'Was it because I'm gay?' he asked to fill the space and dig himself in deeper. There was no way out now – Patrick had to answer the question.

'Gerald,' came the answer, 'I think we should talk about this properly in person.'

'What, it's too hard to say over the phone?!'

He couldn't hear his voice ringing off the walls surrounding him in the small alleyway he'd snuck into. He couldn't hear the rhythm of the footsteps passing by falter, either. All he could hear was the beating of blood through his temples and the pin-drop silence of his useless, good-for-nothing excuse of a father finally confirming what he'd always suspected.

Gerald was standing bolt-still in the middle of the alleyway of the tiny Norman Street, his phone pressed to his ear, his shoulders around his chin and his knees shaking. A second seemed like an hour while he waited to hear Patrick finally man up and say those words – that he didn't love him, either because he could tell early on that he was gay, or because he never wanted kids. Every sense was heightened waiting for whatever blow was about to come. He hadn't felt so ready for a fight with since his dad deigned to come up to him at Annie's funeral and say, 'Now it's just us two, I hope you know you can always count on me,' which got his blood boiling. It was such bullshit. It engendered a rare moment of emotional authenticity from Gerald when he told him to 'Fuck off.'

He'd found the statement had been absolutely galling. He'd never been able to count on Mr. Johnny-Come-Lately – what had changed? He could only imagine that his father had finally wanted to have a relationship with him because of guilt, or because Gerald was a grown-up. That Patrick didn't like kids. It seemed to confirm what he'd felt as a child, which increased the swirling rage in Gerald's stomach. Having someone of age relying on you was much less effort that someone who actually *needs* something from you like children do. The repugnant emptiness of this statement, at his mother's funeral of all places, was unconscionable, especially since Patrick was ultimately unnecessary in any way whatsoever. Gerald had aunts, uncles and grandparents. The last thing he needed was someone who thought they were changing the world as a town planner, tucked away beneath Town Hall, living his life doing the equivalent of playing a strategy game for the local government, the most useless bureaucracy of them all. 'Fuck off' had been all Gerald could think of to say to that statement. It had been all he'd managed to get out before turning and walking to another side of the funeral parlour where his grandparents were sitting. He later wished he'd said it with more venom, but he'd been taken off guard, with a red face and bloodshot, watery eyes. He consoled himself with the fact that he'd at least managed to say something.

He always told himself that he'd never been good at displaying emotions, but that wasn't quite true. He'd only become good at hiding them after his parents split up, then he became even better at ignoring them after his mother passed away. Yet he was always good at standing up for himself, and standing up to bullies. He remembered one night when he was nineteen and had just finished a study session with his friends Benny, Jack, and Anita. They'd gone to Shark Bar in the city to celebrate their studying for a whole two hours straight, and some arseholes had walked past and whispered 'Poofs' under their breaths. Gerald assumed they were from the west and were just looking to start a fight, and he'd already learned to use dismissive tones with bullies on the playground in primary school to deny them the opportunity to escalate tensions, so he simply responded with a 'Lolz.'

This wasn't the playground, though, and one of them sauntered up to Gerald and said, 'What did you say to me, cunt?'

With the Westie staring him down, waiting for him to fight back, Gerald replied as nonchalantly as possible, 'I said "Lolz."'

'Fucking fag,' the Westie said, obviously rueing the lack of real resistance, then waited, daring some further response. When there hadn't been, he strutted off like he'd won.

It might not have been a Westie, Gerald realised after the fact. It could have been anyone, but in Gerald's biased memory that's how it had been. His friends had thought it was well played that he gave the guy nothing *further* to attack them on, but why he even needed to respond in the first place was beyond them. But Gerald always responded to homophobia. It cut close to the bone, since it was one of the possible reasons for his dad leaving. Perhaps that's why he felt like he was ready to confront his dad now. His wedding, his dad's statement, his continual feelings of inferiority because of the way people viewed gay people – it was all bubbling inside him, and maybe he was finally confronting his dad on his homophobic tendencies.

All that is to sat that now, on the phone to Patrick with a deafening silence burning in his ear, he was once again ready to stand up to his father and his weaponised passivity. He waited.

Patrick blurted out, 'I didn't leave because of you. I stayed because of you.'

Gerald was struck dumb. This boggled the mind. It was so different from anything he'd been expecting that he was once again caught completely off-guard. What on earth could that even mean?! He didn't stay. *He left*.

'Huh?' was all Gerald could manage.

'Your mum and I were basically over, but when she found out she was pregnant, I stayed.'

'So you *didn't* want me.' Gerald could see it all now. Right from day one, Patrick had resented him for trapping him with his mum. Of course. He'd felt it growing up. How could he not? Patrick was always so distant. 'Well, that answers that.'

'Of course I wanted you,' Patrick countered, 'that's why I stayed. But your mother and I were incompatible. Don't you get that?'

Wait, so I'm the stupid one? Gerald thought. 'What is it I'm not getting, then?' he asked, his voice coming out like an angry bark.

'I wanted you and I loved you, enough for your mum and I to stay in a loveless relationship and get married.'

'Mum loved you!' Gerald shot back.

Patrick was finally living his fantasy. He was still holding his gin and tonic, and somehow he held on to that feeling, that lightness that came with the idea that he could be forgiven. This was the moment he'd been dreaming of, where he would have that conversation with Gerald. It was finally happening.

'I thought marrying her was the right thing to do,' he said. 'By you, by our families, by her. But it wasn't. I did what was expected to do, but it wasn't right for me and it wasn't right for anyone else. I had to start being honest. I had to stop doing what I thought was expected of me. I just kept doing what I thought other people wanted, but it always backfired.'

This was like a stake through Gerald's heart. What did he mean he did what he thought people wanted him to do. That's bullshit – Gerald wanted him to do heaps of stuff when he was young—*like staying!*—but he didn't. Steve's words shot into his head like a bullet – *The apple doesn't fall far, does it?* But Gerald did what he did because of trauma, because of Patrick. Steve had to be wrong. It couldn't be possible that Gerald was just like Patrick – careening from one self-created drama to another because he couldn't be honest about what he wanted. Patrick was aloof. Patrick was heartless. Patrick was emotionally distant because he didn't like Gerald. It can't have just been in Gerald's head. He couldn't think. He felt the lump in his throat chocking him again.

'If you wanted me so badly, why'd you just fuck off and ignore me for the rest of my life, then?' He wasn't going to let Patrick get away with placations. He would get the explanations he needed no matter how much it hurt.

'I didn't do everything right, Gerald. It wasn't right to marry your mother when I didn't love her. I know it was weird for you having a dad that couldn't express himself. And when I left, I thought I was doing what was best for you. Removing myself. Letting you have space. I didn't want to. But I know I hurt your mum. I know she loved me, and I tried to pretend I loved her back. To make a happy family. But I just couldn't do it anymore. Too many secrets and lies.'

Gerald winced.

Patrick continued. 'I knew I should have done everything differently. I had to live honestly.' His voice was stammering; he swallowed before pushing forward. 'That doesn't mean I wanted to give you up, but I didn't think you needed a dad in your life that reminded you of the pain I'd inflicted on your mum and you when I left. I do it all the time – I try to anticipate what I think people would prefer me to do and do it, and it almost always backfires. That's why I said I thought you and James would make a better go of it than I did. You seem to really love each other. And at least neither of you are approaching it from a second-guessing point of view.'

This was yet another gut-punch. The walls of the alley started to close in on him. Secrets. Lies. Pretending to be someone to please others. Gerald was guilty of all of it. And this rendezvous with Steve, all for what? His eyes darted around the alley. He felt exposed, but no one was watching him.

Patrick worked to fill the uncomfortable silence, something he'd never dreamed himself capable of before. 'I really didn't want to leave you, Gerald,' he said. 'I do love you, and I thought I was making the sacrifice by letting you and your mother be. I thought if you wanted to, you'd come to me. I didn't realise that allowing you to come to me would make it seem like I didn't want you. I really thought I was doing the right thing. I'm really sorry. I tried to talk to you at your mother's funeral, but I know it wasn't the right time.'

He'd had said it. He'd said, 'I love you.' Patrick he felt a wave of relief wash over him. Jennifer, who'd been watching him from the bedroom door, had made her way over to the table and now slumped herself down in the chair opposite him. She put her hand on the table and Patrick took it without looking at her. Their hands closed together.

Gerald, on the other hand, could feel tears dropping off his cheeks and onto his shirt collar. He wiped his eyes roughly, but uncrossing his arm from its tight grip on his ribcage made him actually break down into silent sobs. He'd secretly dreamt of hearing his father say these things, but never, ever believed they would come. Rather, he'd believed and prepared himself for the opposite, building a wall of tension around himself, like an armour, one that now felt like every bit of the strain it was.

His mind was racing. He'd spent a lifetime convincing himself that he didn't deserve to be loved, that he was the reason Patrick left, that not answering his mother's call the day she died was the proof in the pudding that he somehow wasn't right. The actions he took— cheating on James, partying, the money-grubbing selfishness in his career aspirations—all worked deep down to reinforce this belief, while at the same time he would convince himself that these very things—sexual prowess, his ability to acquire capital, and his party-boy image—proved that he shouldn't have been abandoned – that he was worthy of love. He wanted Patrick to see that tonight: that he was loved by James, who had an amazing family and was hot and sexy; that he was loved by his friends; that he could afford the venue, catering, and free-flowing booze. That this would all prove to his father that he was worth loving. It proved he was better than Patrick. He'd anticipated feeling relief when it all came off, when he'd defeated his father by showing him how much better he was than him, when he'd see it in his eyes, his father breaking, and Gerald would know he'd won, and Patrick would know what a miserable fool he'd been. All the hatred and anger broiling inside him would disappear in a cloud of smoke. That all should have happened tonight, but it didn't.

That's what had been missing. Patrick hadn't crumbled. Instead, he'd made some pithy remark and smiled. It had been wrong. Gerald had even agreed to James's assertion that they should have a traditionally themed wedding with black and white tuxes, when it would be much more modern to have pastel pinks and blues and khakis, but he thought this would be a better show of respectability to stab at his father. Not even that had worked.

But now everything had changed. Gerald had been given what he never thought was possible – his father had said he loved him, that he was wanted. What did that mean for him? For all the shit he'd ever told himself in the past? It didn't change his pain, his abandonment, but could it change the way he thought about it? The way he thought about himself? He couldn't process. He needed this to be over now. This isn't what he expected. 'I've got to go,' he said.

'Okay, I love you. Sorry.'

Fuck! Gerald threw his hands to his head and circled the alley, clutching his hair in tufts. He could feel his hands pressing his phone into his skull awkwardly, but he didn't care. Twice in one night he'd heard his father say it, I love you, after a lifetime of believing the opposite to be true.

Gerald's hands were now on his hips and his movement had stopped. He was thinking about the worst day of his life – the day that his mother sat him down and told him Patrick was leaving. He remembered not understanding why he cared so much – Patrick had always been absent. He figured this was just the next step, that he'd failed at being a good son, as though trying to fix whatever it was that was wrong with him was worth it. As though Gerald wasn't worth it.

Only later did he realise that this was the germination of the thought that he wasn't worthy of love, but even at the time he'd hated his dad for how it made him feel. He'd been angry with his mum, too, either because she'd been the messenger or because she'd been the reason Patrick had left. Or maybe she hadn't been honest about why his dad left – that he couldn't stand Gerald, or he was ashamed of him. In. any case, he hadn't been able to figure out whether it was her or him that made Patrick leave, but as children so often do, he suspected it was him. True, Annie did say it wasn't because of Gerald, but he'd already realised that everyone lied, whether it to protect someone's feelings or avoid unnecessary drama, or to stop from getting in trouble when you've done the wrong thing. It was just a part of life. So, he just assumed Annie had been lying, but there had been no way for him to know. It's typical of life: you can never really know the truth of any situation when everyone is telling their own version of the truth, and misrepresenting themselves to make you like them more? Anyway, he felt like he was damaged goods – like he was so annoying that Patrick just had to leave. He'd learnt a lesson that day that he needed to make sure people liked him, otherwise they might leave.

And now here he was as an adult, struggling with the fact that no one really knew him because he was so busy trying to guess what they'd like him to be, and then be that for them, invariably letting them down by acting out when he could have just been himself from the start and avoided all the heartache. *The apple doesn't fall far, does it?* Steve's words again. Everything inside him contracted tightly.

Whether it be tonight's ill-conceived catch-up with Steve, his liaison with the daddy in the sauna, or his ludicrous absence from his own wedding, for Gerald there was always the promise of something. He'd present as though he could be something great to someone if they wanted him badly enough, but what always followed was him retreating then leaving a bad taste in the other party's mouth. He was constantly reliving a situational ambition to reel someone in and them make them mourn his absence. It was a compulsion – to hurt someone else the way his father had hurt him. It made him feel bad, so why did he do it? And why did he spend so much time people-pleasing in other aspects of his life? He had great friends who never understood what he was going through because he was so happy to play the shoulder to cry on. On the rare occasions he had tried to open up, either he got defensive that they weren't as attentive as he thought they should be, or he'd get halfway though the story, chicken out, and abandon ship. Apart from with Charlotte, who was a total mess herself but still gave time for Gerald. And while Charlie took up the lion's share of their drama club, she was there for him and a lot of fun.

What would Charlie say about Gerald's actions tonight? She'd definitely be pissed. There was never usually any judgement, but what he'd done was so obviously the wrong thing.

He had to get back to the party. He wiped his face again. His nose was snotty, his eyes probably red from all the shit running down his cheeks and nose. He must have looked like death. But there was no time to clean up. He knew that if he thought even Charlie would say he was a piece of shit for leaving the wedding to sort out secondary options, he'd clearly fucked up.

Chapter 18

Charlie was what older gays, like Paul, would call a 'glamour girl,' and what even older gays (possibly also like Paul, depending on his real age) might call a 'fag hag.' She adored her gays, and they loved her. There was a camaraderie there that wasn't just about mutual love of dick, self-expressionism, and liberation from social constraints. There was mutual respect – they understood each other, and refused to judge each other. Aside from that, they made each other feel safe. Charlie realised that straight men acted differently towards gay men when women were around to look bad in front of – they were less likely to act aggressively or show their homophobia. By the same token, Charlie felt safer with gay men. Funnily enough, straight men were less likely view women as targets of conquest with a gay man present – it was almost like you couldn't cut another man's grass, even when they were a gay man. Whatever the reason, Charlie appreciated her ability to let loose when she was in her gay friends' company.

Gerald remembered her telling him about the moment she'd realised how unsafe a night alone could be for a girl when she made the wrong choices. She'd run out of money on a night out and didn't have a way to get home. It was late and all the trains had stopped. She decided she didn't have any other options (with her other friends either asleep, or drunk as well and unable to give her a lift), so she went up to an older gentleman (40–45, which was terribly old to her young mind) at the bar, stood next to him as though she was waiting to order a drink, gave him a look, then casually said, 'Hey', as though she was only being polite. As cunning as she thought she was being, the older guy, Frank, knew this game, and played along, asking how her night was going. She flirtatiously said that she'd probably just get one more drink then head home, leading to the inevitable question, 'So where's home?' The response (Rushcutters Bay) wasn't important. The important question from him came next: 'Feel like some company?'

'Sure,' she'd responded casually, glad that her feminine wiles had worked.

As the small talk continued in the taxi Frank had gotten them, she'd started to feel awkward. He didn't seem like a serial killer – he was dressed in a suit without a tie, with only a small paunch of a stomach, so he obviously kept himself somewhat fit for his age; his thinning dark brown hair was brushed to the side, allowing his tanned face to be clearly visible, and his smile seemed genuine, though of course creepy, since he was flirting, which she thought always made people look weird when they're old.

When they hopped out at the front of her place, the sound of the taxi doors slamming back shut and the soft hum of its engine were the only noise punctuating the night air, Charlie's heart started racing. This wasn't the smartest move, she realised. The taxi drove away. She stuck her hand into her bag, wondering why she'd done this, chastising herself for not having thought of simply walking home, but then decided that she might have been picked up and murdered on the walk home. Thinking quickly, Charlie fumbled with her keys and dropped them.

'Oops!'

Frank bent over to pick them up, as she'd hoped, at which point Charlie shoved her fingers down her throat and vomited all over the pavement.

'Oh god, I'm really sorry,' she cried. 'I'm not feeling well. I'm sorry, I have to go.'

She stumbled away on purpose, doing a little more than she needed to and betraying just how drunk she actually was, then ran to her front door and slammed it shut.

'So, nothing happened,' she'd told Gerald. 'But the point I reminded myself of was that something could have happened. We make stupid decisions when we're drunk. Imagine if that guy had come after me anyway? I'd have been fucked. Literally. It was really stupid.'

She made sure to never to do that again, to never get so messy when she was out alone without one of her boys, and certainly not to use her sexuality as a bargaining chip. She'd always been proud of her sexual liberation. She was loud, with an uncouth and raspy voice that carried across a pub like a galah screeching from a powerline, and believed that all women should be allowed to be as uncouth as men without repercussions, or fear of being "slut-shamed," and shouldn't be made to accept their apparent place. Her presence shouldn't make her a target, and she celebrated her freedom to be the way she was. And while she'd made sex a big part of her personality—an embracing of things that had traditionally been considered unladylike traits—she knew she was not defined by her sexuality. This all led her to struggle with internal conflicts about whether she actually enjoyed sex that much or whether she had simply made it an almost integral part of her personality out of protest.

Either way, she wore it like a badge, while recognising it was a two-way street – that she couldn't claim sexual liberation on one hand then use it as a bargaining chip like it was a prize being dangle about with the other. Dangling it in front of that man for a free ride home was not part of her politics, and she deemed that she would do better. Her mantra regarding sex was that her body was free, but that she was free to consent or otherwise.

'I'm a dolphin,' she'd once told Gerald when they were talking about spirit animals – one of those conversations that were rather shallow but seemed deep at the time. 'Dolphins enjoy sex; why can't we?'

'The problem is' Charlie told Gerald, slurring her worlds over a glass of prosecco as they sat on her lounge late one late evening, 'that society keeps propagating this whole concept that a woman should fix a man's problems.' She believed a relationship should allow two people to complement each other, not to solve an underlying problem. It was insulting to her that women were always put up as having the social role of being the nameless support for their man and the family unit. 'It's bullshit.'

She couldn't stand gender roles, but she feared she'd never find someone to settle down with who fit the bill, and that she would ultimately compromise, which she knew could lead to violence when power struggles occurred.

She'd confessed once to Gerald that she was unsure as to whether the big feature she made of sex in her personality was a good thing or a bad thing.

'Like, have I made too big a thing of promiscuity as a protest, or is thinking that thought actually a version of internal slut-shaming?' She couldn't decide whether she was merely fighting against the prejudices that existed in society. These difficult-to-answer questions would keep her up at night if she didn't adopt the attitude of *Fuck it, who cares.*

To Charlie, it was better to have lost innocence than to stay naïve.

'Innocence is absolute bullshit,' she'd say.

Innocence would mean she'd still be getting let down, used, discarded, and treated like a man's object. It would mean accepting toxic behaviours based on people's explanations, instead of assessing how she felt in real time to decide whether such behaviour was acceptable. It would mean compromising more and more with her partners, giving over her safety and her agency. It would mean losing herself for someone else to prey on her weakness.

No, Charlotte had agency. It was just that it was hard to find a straight guy who accepted her for the strong bitch she was. The type of bitch who didn't accept being treated second best, and was able to push back against anything she didn't think was appropriate without fear of blowback.

Gerald wished he could say he was a dolphin too, but he considered himself more like a German shepherd, one of those pets who loved getting pats when the owners were there, but when they were out of sight would sneak treats they knew they weren't allowed to have, or take food off the bench when the owners' backs were turned.

'Me too,' he'd said regardless, not able to own up to how lowly he really viewed his relationship with sexual freedom. He thought he'd seen Charlie give him a sideways look as she'd acknowledged his answer with a 'Mmhmm,' but he couldn't be sure. She'd always considered his spirit animal a hyena, because he seemed to view sex as a sneaky pleasure that he didn't want others to know about, rather than something that could be openly acknowledged. Plus, he did care about being part of a friendship group, so he was clearly a loyal pack animal. She chose to say nothing, though, and let him believe he was a dolphin if it was that important to him.

Gerald had never been able to hide things from Charlie. She was the most observant person he'd ever met. They'd met at Macquarie Bank when Gerald moved back from London. After a year and a half of work experience and partying overseas, he'd shed his old skin, his old lifestyle, and his old friendships. She was two years older than him, and hadn't taken a year and a half out of her career to live abroad, so she was in a more senior financial analyst position to him. They'd stood next to each other at the CFO's presentation about the innovation revolution under way at Mac Bank, and it was giving cult-leader-energising-the-followers vibes. It was Gerald's second week at the company, and he was desperate to make a good impression, to knuckle down and propel his career forward, so he stood to attention with his hands clasped in front of him like he was a waiter at a restaurant, nodding and laughing when expected.

Charlie, on the other hand, fanned herself with a random sheet of paper she'd picked up from the printer on the way to the stale meeting room. She'd tried to give Gerald a sceptical look when Greg, the CFO, said, 'We're so excited about the work that's happening right now that will put us on the front foot to being market leaders' (this must be one of the main phrases in the CFO handbook), but Gerald flicked his eyes back to the front and refused to be seen to be anything but loyal to the company. This amused Charlie to no end; she thought it was the cutest thing ever. Beneath her smirk, she looked him up and down and decided there and then that she was going to take this uppity little gay boy under her wing. For Charlie, it was love at first sight. She'd never seen anyone give such adorably camp "pick me" vibes in a corporate setting. She needed to know who this guy was.

For Gerald's part, his stress levels went up as they walked away from the 'Future Aspecting' presentation (whatever those words meant), and the bad influence beside him said, 'Well, that was something wasn't it?', watching for his reaction.

Gerald's eyes darted to her, then around at which managerial personalities might be spying on him, and said, 'Yeah, it was pretty interesting.'

Charlie fell even more deeply in love, as though he was a little puppy trying to jump up steps that were too big for him. It was too cute. This suck-up strategy showed that he was ambitious to get ahead in his career, but he'd obviously never been educated on what really matters in a business sense. This was a waste of his energy; he was clearly crying out for mentorship.

'Okay, so we're doing lunch. See you at twelve?'

Gerald's bewilderment was clear from the way his eyes bugged and his head twitched side-to-side, as though he was one of those motorised clowns at the fair.

'Great,' she said, regardless of Gerald's silence. 'See you then.'

At 11:55, Charlie turned up at Gerald's desk and escorted him out of the building. She talked to him about careers, asked about his goals, and played the mentor assessment role, all of which got Gerald opening up and talking. Then they talked personal things, personal politics, things like that. She told him that as a woman in business, the five traits she valued most for herself were strength, resilience, determination, charm, and a forthright nature. Probably the most important of these traits was the charm aspect, she'd said, because without it, she felt like it would be too easy for society to pigeonhole her as the angry, bossy, or bitchy woman, the career gal with no friends who everyone bitched about and secretly or outwardly hated. But because of her charm, she could disarm some of this thinking, making it easier for her to portray her strength with humour, her resilience with warmth, her determination with compassion, and her forthright nature with the feeling that she was doing what was best. To her, charm meant that you could be honest and likeable, and it was a skill that needs development.

'Look at any of the CEOs or CFOs, or people in senior management,' she said, 'and what they have is an ability to disarm while giving feedback. This empowers people. Playing the uptight yes-man will get you somewhere, but it's not where you ultimately want to get to. Okay?'

Gerald was in awe. He'd never thought about it like that. While he sat there, allowing his brain to tick over what she'd said, Charlie lit up a ciggie and asked, 'So, what do you do for fun, Gerald?'

Gerald gave some pithy answer about going out, gym, etcetera – very PC.

'London, huh? Quite the party city, isn't it? I loved my time over there.'

The twinkle in her eyes and the cheeky grin on her face let Gerald know he was in safe company. The floodgates opened. They talked about the party scene, shared wild night stories, body-issue stuff, the difference between being a gay man in the workplace and being a woman, and how Charlie viewed her role within the corporate sphere.

'It's not fair that the world needs to view strong women through certain prisms,' she'd said. 'But it is what it is.'

Only by succeeding in life, she believed, could she pave the way for women who would come after her, just as other women paved the way so she could flourish in hers. She talked about how there was a secret sense of shame—programming from her upbringing—that came with her success, one that went along with the false narrative that women needed to choose between motherhood and careers, being nurturing or bossy, all the shit men don't have to think about. By being an example to younger women, though, she wanted to enact change, to be a beacon for people who wanted to succeed regardless of the category society wanted to place them in.

Since this first interaction, aside from the fact that she was such a beautiful person, Gerald admired her, and even looked up to her as someone to emulate. Even though there was only a two-year age gap, he'd never met anyone so impressive, so unashamedly honest and vulnerable while at the same time so kick-arse, so political yet fun, so immaculately dressed and able to hold her own without being aggressive. She was everything Gerald wasn't.

She loved Gerald just the same. Sure, he was young for his age, emotionally speaking, but he had an energy and a way about him that was adorable. Even when he was being a piece of plywood in a conference room, he had an air that was fun, unassuming, and that wanted to be earnest. There were too many fakers in finance, Eastern Suburbs boys whose parents had got them the job and who couldn't care less about how they acted in a work environment because they knew they had it made. This was one of the reasons she retained her Westie drawl – as a protest to the boy's club mentality. She would succeed and be charming even with her bogan upbringing. At least Gerald was just so obvious. Without meaning to, he wore his truth like a sign around his neck. That's what really drew her to him – her ability to see through him. He aimed high, he was respectful, and he was obviously impressed, rather than intimidated, by her as a strong woman, which Charlie felt demonstrated the right mindset. Too many people had underlying and unconscious suspicions of powerful women. Even when he was playing the "I'm such a good employee" persona, Gerald was so obvious about what he really wanted that he couldn't be taken seriously. She could see over the course of their first conversation that he truly wanted to be the best version of himself he could be, and she was here for it. From then on, they were inseparable. They were supportive of each other's mistakes, problem-solved solutions, and laughed about what train wrecks they both were.

Out on the street, Gerald wondered how long it would be before he and Charlie could both laugh at his actions tonight, or whether this was a bridge too far for someone to even be friends with him. Had he thrown away everything he'd worked so hard for on one stupid mistake? He quickly pushed the thought out of his mind. No point. He'd know his fate soon enough.

Chapter 19

Gerald strode onto Liverpool Street as fast as his legs could carry him, adrenaline pulsing though his body. He could feel himself sobering up, and wondered if he'd manage to get back to the venue before anyone noticed he'd been gone. How long had it been? It felt like forever, but when he looked at his phone, it was only 11:30pm. When had he left? The message from Steve came through at 10:30. He'd left at 10:50. So he'd left 40 minutes ago, 50 by the time he got back. Was that a long time? It wasn't that long to be missing on a regular night out, but what about a wedding – your wedding? What would James say? What would he say to James? *What could he say?* Fuck. This was bad. He was usually much more careful about going off half cocked, and usually the only people who got hurt were strangers, so the consequences weren't too dire. Perhaps he was just becoming more daring, the way any addict does when they seek their thrill. James was the last person he'd want to hurt like this.

He kept going back to that same question: had he married James for the wrong reasons? Surely it wasn't just because he thought it was the right thing to do. James had never mentioned it, and no one was placing the future of the gay world upon Gerald's slutty shoulders to set an example. No, he wanted this. Of that much he was certain. When he thought about being free, he pictured James. James made Gerald understand what people meant when they said 'love can be freeing.' He felt freer with James than he ever had. It was hard for him to say, even to himself, because he was more of an analytical person, but yes, he would say that he loved James, and that he felt freer because of him. But not totally free. He supposed that when you were in a relationship, you needed to moderate yourself just a little bit – always teetering on the edge of what would or wouldn't affect your partner negatively, so you could never truly be 100 percent yourself like you could with your friends. Was the trade-off between his partner's needs and his needs the reason he kept sabotaging things? Was he actually trying to free himself from his relationship with James? But James was freedom. Gerald was just trying to push his luck, he supposed. But to what end? To see what would happen if he got caught? But he didn't want to know what would happen. That would be almost unthinkable . . .

The fall-out would be so messy. Gerald's legs kept powering him forwards as he hoped against hope that shaving a minute or so off his return journey might make all the difference. He didn't want his relationship with James to end. Funny how the thought of losing something made you realise whether you really wanted it or not. Gerald could see himself losing James, and it filled him with dread. That begged the question: was this just plain, old loss-aversion like he'd studied at uni – the kind of dread that comes with losing a toy or some other possession you once had and you're upset that you no longer have it? Or was it real dread, like you're about to lose something you actually care about? He didn't know.

We all go through life according to our understanding of how life works. On his eighth birthday, Gerald was in his room and heard his parents arguing about something. When he'd got up and went out to the living room, they'd plastered broad smiles on their face, with bugging fake eyes, and had said in a sing-song voice, 'Happy birthday!'

He'd known something was off about it, but had been happy for them not to be fighting. When he'd opened his present and it was a Pikachu teddy, he'd swallowed his disappointment and said how much he liked it, which had satisfied his parents. He liked seeing them happy for a change. Submerging negative emotions and replacing them with surface pleasantness was a good way of controlling the things around you, and it had seen him in good stead. Did Gerald even know what he wanted, or was he just so used to trying to make people happy that he had no idea who he even was? All he knew was that he felt like a hollow being – shiny and sleek on the outside, but empty on the inside, lumbering through life, devouring praise and affection. Always looking for some magic trick to make him feel whole.

His heart was beating at the top of his chest as he turned the corner to Castlereagh Street. He would soon learn how badly noticed his absence had been, and would need to come up with some excuse as damage control. He should have stopped at the City Convenience store and got some gum, then at least he'd have a reason for having left the venue. As it was, he was empty-handed, and his mind was racing trying to come up with an excuse for why he absolutely needed to be a momentary absentee groom. As he kept powering along the footpath, the sight of a silhouette made him freeze in his tracks.

'Charlie?' he called out.

Charlotte's yellow, strapless, floral dress was rustling around her purple heels as she flicked the ash off the end of her cigarette.

'Where the fuck have you been?' she said, her arms crossed in a motherly pose as she stomped her way up to him.

Gerald's sheepish lack of an answer spoke volumes as Charlie's heels filled the silence, clip-clopping sternly over to him.

'What the fuck Gerry? What did you do?'

'It was my dad. I thought he was making fun of me for not being able to have kids. Then James said he didn't want kids. So I went and caught up with Steve.'

Charlie's face distorted itself into a grotesque shape, like someone had just taken the lid off a container of rotting fish. 'Steve? Your ex Steve, from three years ago?!'

'Yep.'

'Oh my fucking god.' Charlie waited for the explanation that could have made it okay, but none came. 'I thought he hated you.'

Gerald was silent. *Apparently not* was the look he gave her.

Charlie shook her head in disbelief. 'This is the worst thing you've ever done, you hear me? It is not okay.'

'We didn't sleep together. Steve wanted to but I said no.'

'Who gives a shit?!' she snapped back at this ludicrous venture into semantics. 'And by the way, James didn't say he didn't want kids, he said "Not right now," right? That's what he told me when he asked if I knew where you were, and I had to suddenly sober up when I couldn't see you. I had to lie for you. As per fucking usual.'

'What did you say?'

'What do you think? I said you were going to meet your dealer 'cause we were out of coke.'

Gerald was stunned. This was actually a good excuse, especially at the drop of the hat. Charlie was amazing at thinking on her feet, and Gerald sunk a little bit at the thought that he'd made it her unhappy responsibility to protect him from himself.

Guilt panged somewhere else in his stomach, too. He knew why she was so upset. He currently had what she ultimately wanted for herself: someone to settle down with and start a family, someone who would treat her as an equal and not as a submissive appendage, all which was so difficult for her to find – for anyone to find. She saw that Gerald had that in James, so why would Gerald so actively be seeking to destroy that chance at happiness?

Gerald knew it. He was completely out of line. He stood there like a chastised schoolboy, avoiding Charlie's gaze as she stood, statuesque in billowing floral, smoke spewing from her stern lips and eyes locked on him in judgement. The Botox she used to keep the lines at bay meant her squint, rather than her brow, expressed her upset and disappointment, and she was giving off major favourite-teacher-whose-student-had-let-her-down vibes. For his part, Gerald was playing the part of a pupil who wasn't offering up any further details on his bad behaviour, which meant Charlie had to maintain her role of the stern inquisitor.

'So, why Steve? Because he wanted kids, right? What, you have one brain fart, and your relationship with James can be replaced for someone you were totally incompatible with? You're drunk and high, so I can almost understand your thinking, but that's just so fucked up that it forbids comprehension.' Charlie took another drag of her cigarette and blew the air into the sky, looking like a glamorous chimney. 'So, tell me – we've spent all this money on this wedding, right? Is that because you actually love James, or what, you're just going through the motions? I mean, I don't give a shit that you can't keep it in your pants. And I don't think James does either, honestly, but you know this is different, right? You actually explored an alternative to *being* with James. *On* your wedding night.'

Just going through the motions? No, he'd thought about that possibility earlier in the night. He remembered his excitement when he was getting ready to propose to James. When he'd heard James's keys jingle in the door, he ran to stand in front of it, got down on one knee, and saw James's face light up as he opened the door to find a ring box thrust in his face. He remembered their first breakfast at Lumier, after their first Mardi Gras, and his first meeting with James's parents, when he'd tried his hardest to make a good impression. He even thought about the fights he'd had with James – about James leaving his shit over the apartment, James calling him obsessive–compulsive and Gerald calling him a grub who didn't consider anyone else's feelings, the silent treatment, the apologies, and then the make-up sex, all followed by lying on the couch watching shit on Netflix like nothing had happened. Yes, he truly loved James. So why had he done what he did? Sneaking around as though he wanted to get caught. Perhaps he did want to get caught. He wanted to be found out, for James to realise what Gerald thought he knew deep down: that he didn't deserve love. But what tonight had shown him is that he was wrong. His whole life was a lie. His dad did want him. It was lack of communication, his mum keeping her cards too close to her chest, that allowed Gerald's negative feelings and self-blame to go unchecked, and build up piece upon piece for so long. By leaving things unsaid, by letting a young mind fill in the blanks, and by letting her pain influence the feelings of her child, Annie had created a negative energy that engendered Gerald's negative feedback loop surrounding his parents' separation. It had been Patrick's acting against his own self-interests, staying in a marriage where his nerves were frayed by Annie's hot moods, that had made him an aloof father figure, which all stemmed from his people-pleasing behaviour – a behaviour Gerald could recognise in himself. Patrick's unsure presence only served to amplify Gerald's feelings of unwantedness, of not being good enough. He'd convinced himself he wasn't deserving of love.

The penny had finally dropped. It's why his mother had been so concerned about him becoming a "good boy," someone who sought out that compliment, always ready to put others first, always ready to ignore his own desires, to devalue his needs in reverence to others. The people-pleasing. He sought out the compliments, stroking his ego. He knew he did this, that he'd chased affection, and then once he'd obtained it, when it hadn't healed him, moved on to the next rush. He'd done it with the daddy in the sauna, with Steve tonight, and even with James. It hadn't fixed him. He'd always felt bad about it, but didn't understand why he did it. He saw it now, though. He was chasing acceptance from someone he'd always despised for never loving him. How could anyone who loved him, someone undeserving of love, be good enough? There must be something wrong with them if they wanted him. It's what he'd always told himself. He finally understood why.

But what did it matter? Could he honestly change how he felt and how he interacted with the world just by knowing something different? He felt trapped, like he was sinking into a despairing world that he knew he shouldn't be in, but that he had no mechanism for pulling himself out of. He felt like there would always be a void, some part of him that wouldn't allow himself to feel these moments of happiness without trying to destroy them, without trying to tear apart the thing that was causing these moments, without telling himself that his actions had ulterior motives. He'd done it countless time. He'd even done it tonight. He'd stupidly convinced himself that maybe he'd been confused, that maybe he didn't actually love James and he was merely bowing to social pressure to get married. The mind is such a powerful tool. It can convince you of any reality it chooses, and rearrange your thoughts to fit the picture it's trying to create. How could Gerald resist such a strong force? Even when the proof of the opposite was there: all those people had come to celebrate a love that they'd witnessed first-hand, but Gerald's mind just had to spin it the wrong way, to second guess, to sabotage . . .

Charlotte had waited long enough for an answer. She'd asked him whether he loved James or not – she hadn't asked him to calculate an algebraic equation. 'Hello?!' she yelled, arms flailing and eyes bulging at him impatiently. 'It's not that hard a fucking question!'

'Yes, of course I do!' Gerald blurted out.

'Okay! Great!' She took another drag to simmer down. 'So, what happened? Tell me everything.'

Gerald relayed his awkward interaction with Steve, then his conversation with his dad, while Charlie finished off her ciggie and stomped it out with her purple pump. She waited till he finished and said, 'So, that's big.'

'Yeah.'

'So you know this whole daddy thing is something you're going to have to unpack, right? A lot of your baggage is tied up in all that.'

'Yeah, I've known it for ages, but I don't know what I'm supposed to do about it.'

'Well, that's for another time. Right now you've gotta get back in there and fix this.'

'How am I gonna tell him I've been gone all this time and still didn't get anything from my dealer?'

'Don't be such a fucking moron. I have a spare bag I was gonna give you guys for the end of the night when you went back to your hotel room.'

Gerald was dumbstruck as Charlie rummaged through her bag.

'Oh, thank you,' he said.

'Well, God knows I've had enough of your bag, so it was the least I could do.' She pulled a folded-up tissue out of the side pocket and handed it to Gerald. 'I'm getting some of that one now too, though,' she said sternly. 'That's not waiting till the hotel room anymore. You owe me big time.'

'Okay,' Gerald said, a smile cheating its way onto his face.

'By the way, one of the reasons you broke up with Steve was because he wanted kids. And now here you are starting drama by springing it on James without giving him any time to process. So you just need to decide whether this was all a big fuck you to your father, or something you actually want.'

Charlie gave Gerald only a second or two to let what she'd said sink in. 'Come on,' she said. 'I need a drink.'

They took two steps towards the stairs, then Charlie stopped and turned back, looking sternly at him with her finger in his face. 'And don't you ever do this to me again. I'm not your keeper. I won't be party to this again. Okay?'

'Yup.'

'Okay.'

As they climbed the steps into the venue, Gerald couldn't believe how lucky he was to have such a tour-de-force of a best friend. She really would make a great mother. She was right to have already frozen her eggs, her risk analysis being applied to her personal life once again providing a template for better decision-making than Gerald was capable of for his life.

She was right about everything, of course. This was the worst thing Gerald had ever done. All the little deceits from the past were just physical infractions, but this time he'd actually sought an alternative. And he truly did love James – how could it be possible that this bitter rivalry he'd created with his father could be stronger than love? His heart sank again at the thought that he was so broken, and that he might have ruined things forever.

Yet again, as the music pumping from the speakers inside got louder and louder with each stair they climbed, he felt his mood spiralling back into the hole Charlie had just pulled him out of.

They turned the corner at the top of the stairs to find a shirtless Benny now being molested by Paul against the wall. Seeing Benny's athletic body that he'd spent months perfecting for this night grinding against Paul's pudgier and more-seasoned frame made Gerald wonder whether he should step in to stop any potential morning-after regrets. He realised, on closer inspection, that Benny was clearly enjoying being devoured by someone who truly appreciated how hot he was, and both of them needed the tactile feedback from each other, so he moved along. *Molly's a funny little mistress* he mused, then returned to focussing on his own problems.

20

Chapter 20

The house lights in the venue were off. The large warehouse space was now being lit by flashing strobe lights that Gerald had forgotten they'd ordered and pulsating coloured disco lights, giving the impression of a mini underground rave. It looked much better now. Bodies were grinding against each other and the floor was peppered with smiles, chewing, laughing, and even some droopy eyelids on bodies that were swaying like zombies to the beats blasting through the speakers.

Gerald scanned the room for some sign of James, but frustratingly couldn't see him. He wondered if it was this annoying for James when Gerald went missing?

'Congratulations, babe!'

It was Ellis, one of James's straight workmates, careening in for the hug. He was one of those people who wore his allyship like a badge, which was nice in a way, but Gerald liked his straight people to behave like bookish prudes, and was confused by such overt ease with their sexuality.

'Thanks, Ellis,' Gerald replied with a stiff smile as his eyes darted around the room for an exit.

'Beautiful ceremony,' Ellis continued. 'You and James looked immaculate. Very sexy. It's been such a great night.'

Ellis was always extremely earnest. His hand was on Gerald's shoulder, his head leaning in, and his eyes looking so deeply into Gerald's that it was like he was trying to see through to his retinas. Gerald considered it possible that Ellis, with such clingy hands and laser-sharp eye contact, had been brought up Christian. If only Gerald could untether himself from his physical form and go in search of James, leaving his body where it was to deal with Ellis's persistent engagement.

'You're off to South America soon, right?' Ellis said.

'Yeah, should be a great time. Neither of us have been before.'

'It's amazing. You guys are going to have such a good time.'

There was a subtle wink in Ellis's voice, but Gerald couldn't figure it out. Did he mean they'd like the culture and landscapes of South America, or the men, or the drugs – or some combination of all three possible options? How much did Ellis know about their relationship? Or was he taking an educated guess? It's always so hard with allies to know just how much they understand when you're sharing details of a homosexual lifestyle.

Gerald decided to play it safe, and simply answered, 'Yeah, we can't wait.'

'I'll be doing James's work while he's gone, so I'll be wishing you a wonderful but speedy journey.'

Fuck! Who cares? Gerald thought to himself, but instead laughed in reciprocity with Ellis's laugh. *How was that even a joke?*

'Where in SA are you guys going?'

If Ellis's eyes weren't still locked onto Gerald's so tightly, he'd have rolled his eyes at this point then scanned the room in desperate search of his husband. Instead, he raised his eyebrows and rattled off some locations automatically: Machu Picchu, Rio, Bogota, Buenos Aires, whatever. Where else do Aussies go when they first go to South America? Such a stupid question, but Gerald couldn't figure out any polite escape route from this conversation yet.

'Oh, you'll love Bogota,' Ellis replied, and Gerald wondered whether he did indeed know they were cokeheads, until Ellis added, 'I met my Maria there.'

Oh, Jesus! Gerald tried to remind himself that if he wasn't in such a hurry to placate his own conscience, this might actually be a great opportunity to mine Ellis for advice on their upcoming honeymoon, and that this was the opportunity Ellis was purposely providing him with. But he couldn't help feeling more and more like a cat wearing a leash, furiously trying to fling off the oppressive constraint and regain his freedom.

'Wow,' he said a little too excitedly, deciding the only way to safely transition out of this discussion was to become proactive. 'I didn't know you guys met there. Is she here tonight?'

'Yeah, she's in the bathroom – she'll be back in a moment.'

Bathroom . . . So they did do coke? Or just drank too much water. Alcohol? Who cares . . .

'Oh, awesome. Actually, have you seen James at all?'

'Not recently, no,' Ellis answered, for the first time breaking eye contact with Gerald to look around the room. Gerald thought it no surprise that he hadn't seen him, since he seemed to spend his whole life using his eyes like magnifying glasses, oblivious to the space around him.

'I need to chat to him about something. I'll be back in just a minute,' he lied.

'Okay!'

Argh, he's really just so earnest, Gerald thought, as he turned his back and waded through the crowd, nodding at guests who patted him or gave him a wave. He'd just passed Emily and Graeme, work friends from his old job at ANZ, when he saw James standing at the bar with Prue, James's best girlfriend. She'd been there the night James and Gerald met at the Ivy, where she'd worn a purple bikini and her short jet-black hair slicked back so severely she looked like something out of *The Matrix*, with the frigid personality to match. She'd been with them ever since, though there'd always been a frosty glaze over Gerald and Prue's relationship. Gerald knew that she knew he wasn't everything he pretended to be, and that she was looking out for her friend, but he hated that about her. James was a big boy and could make his own decisions. He didn't need some bossy mother figure glaring over his shoulder his whole life, especially when James's own mother was so loving and trusting.

Gerald always admired that about James's family. It was so easy to second-guess things, to look for the negative and expect the worst (another thing Annie had taught him, he just realised). It was so much harder to see something for its potential while at the same time accepting its inherent flaws, whether it be with people, situations, or physical things. Perhaps that was what made Gerald love James so much – James's example gave him something to aspire to, even though his own repugnant flaws left him falling horribly short and feeling like shit in the process. The pit of Gerald's stomach had the grace to sink at the thought of the advantage he took of James's nature. He had to pry him away from Prue so he could make things right. Should he confess? Or play along with Charlie's excuse for why he hadn't been there? Gerald couldn't decide which would be worse.

He inched towards them reluctantly, as though resisting invisible hands pushing him forwards with every step he took.

'Gerald!' James cried out when he saw him. He held his arms out and leant back on the bar.

Gerald was startled and unprepared, even though he was only a metre from them and had plenty of time to think of what he was going to do. Prue gave him a look. She'd actually been nice earlier in the evening, at the ceremony and during the posing for all the photos, but now she was back to her stroppy best. Gerald half expected her to say something like, "I hear you've been busy tonight," or, "Wow, you're back," but no such remark reared its sarcastic head. Gerald supposed she would allow James to at least have this night of happiness before she started undermining things, which he was actually extremely grateful for at that moment.

'Hey, guys,' Gerald said. Prue had the good grace to respond with a wince of acknowledgement at his greeting.

'Umm, Prue, do you mind if I borrow my husband for a moment?'

'Of course,' she said with a derisive smirk.

Fuck she's a bitch!

'Did you get the stuff?' James whispered in his ear as they walked away from the bar, and from Prue, whose eyes Gerald could feel watching them. He could sense her brooding, as though she was calculating how long she'd need to wait before she could start causing trouble. She was patiently biding her time. Or was that just his conscience?

'Let's go this way,' Gerald said, and led James towards the melting cheese table. No one was around. Beside them, the lonely bunch of lilacs lay slumped in their clear glass, tired from the night's proceedings. They'd be able to talk here without their voices echoing like they had in the bathroom. They could also avoid other people overhearing them if things happened to get loud.

Gerald looked James in the eyes and said, 'Actually, Charlie got it.'

He couldn't believe he was doing this.

21

Chapter 21

Ever since this night began, Gerald had done everything wrong. How on earth could he come clean with the whole truth now? How far back would he have to go? James would realise there was no way tonight had just been a one-off. Gerald had been way too casual about taking off in the middle of an event to meet another man for it not to be habitual. Owning up now would mean completely stripping himself bare and allowing James to see how fucked-up he really was. Then again, after everything tonight had shown him, he surely couldn't think that continuing to hide the truth was a good idea. Lack of communication and half-truths are the very thing that had allowed him to harbour a lie for his entire life.

He looked around at the lights, the smiles, the decorations, the flowers that had stayed out well past their bedtime. Tonight was supposed to be the happiest night of his and James's lives, the celebration of everything they'd worked for together, but Gerald realised it could also be their last.

Of course, all of Gerald's concerns just went to show how little you could actually know about someone when you've closed yourself off. The problem is, when you're so busy thinking about what you're hiding it's impossible to notice what the person in front of you is letting you see of them. He knew James wasn't stupid, regardless of the clown show he put on for his friends, but he kept being surprised by James precisely because James was so good at playing the zany, slightly ditsy, good-time-gal type of guy.

'Hung,' for instance, was James's typical answer to the question of what he was looking for in a man, which had the virtue of both being funny, shallow, and substance free, while also holding a grain of truth. James would say he didn't care what people thought of him – that this was why he used pithy comedic statements to diffuse deep conversations and keep people at arm's length, but this wasn't particularly the case.

If James were to cast his mind back to Grade Two, he would have remembered that his persona started its development when his classmates, tired of him putting his hand up when the Mr Lim asked a question, started calling him 'TP' (short for Teacher's Pet) for seemingly being such a suck-up. The nickname didn't really bother James, because he thought the teacher asking questions was just the same game his parents used to play with his family at the dinner table or in the car, him asking them questions and encouraging them to give a considered response, then going through the steps of how to find the right answer. Everything was a teachable moment to James's parents, and James found "the game" fun, firstly because he didn't know any better, and secondly because his parents made it exciting with their playfulness. James would allow his imagination to run away with him in trying to figure out the answer. No one else thought answering the teacher's questions were fun.

Things changed when Mr Lim asked, 'Does anyone but Master Sanders know the answer?' due to James's hand once again shooting up. This seemed to indicate that even adults, even his teacher, thought it was weird or annoying to always try to show you knew the answer. He wasn't going to be always met with cheers and congratulations like he did with his parents – he would instead be singled out as being "too keen" or "too smart." After that, he wouldn't put his hand up again, instead opting for playing stupid, which worked much better as a tactic to making friends. When he chose to max that character out, this also brought laughs, which made him even more popular. He realised he could use his intelligence to craft humour out of everyday scenarios and avoid derision. It was win–win.

That's why he'd prefer to say things like, 'I've always been a size queen, that's how I know I've found "the one,"' when people asked him why he liked Gerald so much. No one would be interested in the real reasons, anyway. *Ergh, boring.*

'People needed a laugh,' he told Gerald once. 'There's already too much seriousness in the gay community as it is: the plebiscite, trans rights, talk of power dynamics in activist circles, the right pronouns to call someone – so much political correctness. People don't want to feel intimidated by the need to speak intelligently about these things. Laughter has the power to bring people together. You need to keep things light, even in hard times. Being rabid is a much less effective tool for getting your opponents on side than humour. Being funny lets them see you as a person, a likeable person. Angry yelling just makes you the other, the enemy. Besides, I hate direct confrontations. Humour can help you side-step aggressions and avoid betrayal.'

Betrayal was the big one. This, he failed to realise, was the other reason he cared what people thought, enough to use humour as a defence mechanism. He'd need to cast his mind back to when he was in Grade Nine to realise when he'd started to put walls up around his personal life. Betrayal had come in the form of Arthur, a friend who wasn't one of his closest friends, but close enough, who he'd told that he figured out how to wank, and he'd wanked on the toilet. They'd been sitting in the playground sometime after this, discussing the 'Teenage Dream' film clip by Katy Perry, when Brendan, one of the kids from the people-who-thought-they-were-cool group came over to pick a fight.

'What are you losers talking about?' he'd asked with that little-prick inflection bullies liked to use.

Three of Brendan's friends were standing just far enough away to watch and provide an imposing sense of backup to Brendan's aggression. Such a tough guy.

'Katy Perry, she's got a new song out,' James had said quietly, defiant and cautious while his friend Arthur's eyes darted to and fro.

'Who listens to Katy Perry? What, you wank each other, too?'

It wasn't totally clear what the correlation was for Brendan to ask such a question, but he really didn't need a correlation. Brendan knew people don't like to be called gay, so it was enough that one sentence followed the other. To those who met James when he was young, they couldn't be sure whether he was simply a clown, or whether he was both a clown and gay, but this didn't matter. Being called gay usually had the desired effect; whether someone was gay or not, they'd always arc up. In the background, the three stooges flagging Brendan started cooing 'gay, gay, gay' at them, which James was happy ignore. He was already cool, since he was so liked by the rest of the class, so he didn't need to fight. Plus, he didn't want to spread his business everywhere when it didn't need to be. The chant changed from 'gay' to 'wankers' when the first insult had no effect, which was enough to send Arthur over the edge.

'No I'm not,' he snapped, the taunting all being too much for his nervy disposition, 'but James said he wanked on the toilet last week!'

James eyes locked on Arthur's. Arthur's finger was pointed directly at him. In the corner of his eye, he could see Brendan's head rocking back in laugher and the idiots behind him contorting their faces with mirth.

'Toilet Tugger' was what they called James for the rest of high school. To say he was pissed off was an understatement. Arthur was dropped as a friend like the albatross he was, and while James was considered the victim in the affair at school, the damage had been done. When he told his parents what had happened, they rightly focussed on the betrayal of Arthur as the point of contention.

'Don't worry about those dickheads,' his dad told him. 'Everyone wanks. And when you're young, you tend to do it everywhere: in bed, on the toilet. It's just part of growing up and getting to know your body. If those kids in your class aren't doing it yet, they'll soon start. It's just that they probably feel shame about their sexuality and can't talk about it, so they think it's something to tease someone else about admitting. It's just like this – when people feel guilty about something, they'll try to make other people feel badly about it, too.'

Once again, everything was a teachable moment with James's parents. As comforting as this was, it still wasn't nice to be singled out as a sexual deviant, regardless of how hypocritical it was. As is often the case, James had two choices: to shrink from this criticism, or to embrace it. He learned to see the notion of sexual hypocrisy—the idea that people publicly scorned sexual admissions while engaging in the same behaviours themselves—as another funny social convention. This is why James thought his joke about being a size queen as an explanation to why he liked Gerald was so funny. First of all, there shouldn't be so much frigidness in the discussion of sex, so he was using a slightly shocking statement to push against convention. It was also self-deprecating, making it look like James had a one-track mind, which was also frowned upon as a way someone should represent themselves, so it was a double protest against stupid conventions. Plus, it really did make people laugh, whether they understood the underlying politics behind it or not.

Poor Gerald, though. James's little joke only reinforced Gerald's belief that no one could love him for anything but his physical attributes. Gerald once imagined his epitaph to read, 'Here lies a cold fish who never opened himself up and never felt anything, but at least he was honest with his opinions, loyal and supportive to his friends.' The idea of this long epitaph sucked, of course, but what could he do? He would've liked it to have read, 'Here lies a sexy stud, and we're all fucking heartbroken. He was so smart and fuckable that he was absolutely loved by his friends, loyal, helpful, like a rock, and an up-and-comer at work, and even his clients loved him.' This wasn't much better, but it showed what he placed so much importance on. No mention of emotional availability, no mention of honesty, just that he could complete tasks that endeared him to others.

Everyone needs to accentuate and take pride in their good qualities, but hiding from his emotions for so long had given him a false sense of what was important. As such, whenever James made his little joke about only wanting Gerald because of his physical attributes, which he'd once again alluded to in his vows at the wedding that day, Gerald would usually be left laughing awkwardly with the group, and thanking his lucky stars that someone like James at least liked that about him.

Even early on in their relationship, he'd wondered what James had seen in him. He thought that, at any moment, James might realise he could do better. He'd see Gerald's massive flaws and red flags and drop him.

One vivid memory was a day when they'd been on one of their long lock-down walks. They'd chosen a particularly long route – the loop around Centennial Park, a two-hour round trip from their respective homes in Darlinghurst. If the authorities had any way of keeping track on exactly how long you'd been out for, they would have been worried about exceeding their one-hour limit for outside activities. But they were confident they wouldn't be found out.

As they passed a drinking fountain, they stopped for James to fill his water bottle. To one side of them was a large toilet block, and to the other side was an abandoned oval sports field.

'Who was your first crush?' James asked Gerald as he put the lid back onto their bottle.

'Umm, a guy named Daniel.'

'Daniel, huh? When was that?'

'When I was sixteen. So, I guess twelve years ago.'

'Mmhmm. And where'd you know him from?'

'Oh, he was this guy from gymnastics.'

'Okay.'

James's voice had inflected upwards as though waiting for further details. Gerald realised it was his turn to share. He wasn't as comfortable rabbiting on about himself as everyone else seemed to be, but he bravely pushed forwards.

'He was a rich kid from the city. He was really cute. I went to the gymnastics school in Summer Hill, umm, because we lived in Ashfield. But I met him at a tournament. He had both of his parents there. He did his routine and I went up to him and complimented him on it. Actually, that was the second time we'd competed together. The first time was when I was fifteen. That was state championships. I did a triple summersault on the beam and won my division. I saw Daniel and thought he was really hot, but I also really wanted to beat him. I don't know why.' Gerald's cheeks flushed slightly at this lie. He knew why: he wanted to impress him, but didn't want to say it. 'I know I had to hide my woody from him at one point, though.'

'Young Gerald busting out of his leotard, I would have liked to see that. Hmm.'

'Haha. Yeah. But then I focussed on the competition and it went away. I had to get my body in the zone. I did a really good job. I nailed every landing and my angles were really good. When I finished, the judges lost it. And it felt great, standing there and watching their faces. But mum took me out to celebrate and all I could think about was Daniel. How I wished I'd flirted with him a little.'

'Ok so you're a competitive kind of guy.'

Gerald felt his face flush.

'It was the state championships. It's supposed to be competitive.'

'Hmm. Maybe competitive is the wrong word. But you definitely gushed when you talked about the judges. And you did choose to focus on demonstrating your talents rather than using your words. Maybe Gerald's the kind of guy who likes positive feedback?'

'The point of that story was that I was too scared to talk to the boy I liked, so I focussed on trying to impress him with my routine.'

'Hmmm, okay. So, you're a shy boy, that's your take away,' James said as though trying to be convinced. 'I guess we all just interpret things from different angles, don't we?'

'Yeah.'

Gerald's face was burning. He didn't quite know whether James was admitting to fault in his interpretation or trying to insinuate that Gerald was wrong, but he powered forward to make his point.

'Anyway, the second time, I remember watching his routine and going up to him. And this time I complimented him on it. I actually didn't know whether he was straight or gay, but he *was* really good at gymnastics. I was just better. And that meant I could complement him without him thinking, "who the hell are you?" and he wouldn't think I was trying to get into his pants if he was straight. Anyway, it worked. We spent the rest of the competition together. I won that year as well in the end, by the way.'

'Wow. You must be very good at gymnastics.'

Gerald tried not to beam too brightly at this compliment. He was under the distinct impression that James was trying to prove a point.

'I used to be,' he said, attempting modestly.

'I bet you could still straddle that beam nicely.'

'I'd give it a run for its money.'

Gerald felt more comfortable with this type of innuendo than telling simple stories about his past so people can interpret him and analyse his character. *The past is the past,* after all!

'So, what happened with little Daniel?'

'Oh, you know, we caught up with each other on the weekends mostly. Sometimes outside of school on the weekdays. Kissed a little. A bit of wanking, that's about it though. It never went any further.'

'Okay so he was gay. You need to work on your story telling, by the way.'

Gerald smiled at this. 'Yeah, I guess. Anyway, it didn't last long. In the end, it lasted six months, I think. He got a job and started working on the weekends. We kind of tried to keep seeing each other but we only really had gymnastics and mutual attraction in common and it was just too hard, really.'

'Oh, that's a shame.'

'I didn't mind. It was my first crush and he liked me back. It's kind of a good luck story.'

'So, who stopped texting who?'

'It was kind of mutual.'

'But mostly you right? I mean, it didn't sound like you were the one who was upset by the ending of texts.'

Gerald's face flushed. James seemed intent on taking the wrong moral from his stories. 'So anyway, that's the story of my first crush.'

'So, Daniel was a rich kid huh? Would you say you have a type?'

'I like them cute.' Gerald corrected him. This is why Gerald hated telling stories. While it's true that he somehow gravitates towards people who are "well set up," James had obviously missed the part of the story where he said Daniel was hot.

'Hmm, good answer.' James's shoulder bumped Gerald's playfully. 'Well, speaking of mutual masturbation, I asked about your first crush because you see that toilet block back there? The one where I was filling my water bottle up?'

'Yeah.'

'That's where I blew my first crush.'

If Gerald was drinking water, he would have spat it out. 'How is that mutual masturbation?'

'Well, it's not *real* sex. Oral is mutual masturbation but just with a mouth involved. Anyway, his name was Elliot. He was pretty good at sports, like your handsome self, and he'd obviously seen me checking him out for a while. For some reason, our school was using that oval back there to do Friday sports. I guess something was happening to our field and they couldn't use it. Either way, I'd gone to the toilet to pee, and all of a sudden, Elliot walks in and says, "It's cool being away from school, huh, Jimmy?" And I was like, "Yeah." And he just said, like, out of the blue, "Come here a second, I wanna show you something."'

'Umm.'

'I know. It was so sus. He walks towards the toilets and of course I follow him. Then he walks into one of the stalls and says, "In here." So, of course, I followed him. And in this cramped, gross, wet toilet block, he pulls out his dick and says, "What do you think?"'

'Woah.'

'I know. So anyway, I did what any respectable young boy would do and said, "It's nice," and he was like, "Want a taste?" I got on my knees and took it in my mouth.'

'Oh my god.'

'It was really awkward. He was all sweaty and musky down there so it was kind of gross. I didn't know any better at that age, though. And to this day, I reckon he was straight and just trying to see whether he could get blown. But yeah, that was my first time.'

'How old were you?'

'Like, fifteen.'

'That's not even legal!'

'Oh, come on, we were the same age.'

Gerald's mouth curled itself into a tight grimace.

'Oh my god, you're such a prude. That's too funny. You do know it's common, right?'

Gerald said nothing while he considered James's accusation. Prudish? That was a new one. Especially since he often worried he was *too* sex focussed.

'Look, if it makes you feel any better,' James continued, 'we were in grade ten. So, he was sixteen and I was fifteen and, what, eight months I guess at that time.'

'You know,' Gerald said, moving passed the idea that he was a prude, 'your story with the toilet block kind of reminds me a bit of how we met. At the Ivy Pool Party.'

'Yeah, I guess so, except that I was the one instigating that time.'

'So, is this some formative memory? Like you're trying to recreate it with different people?'

'Oh my god, Gerald, I love this pop-psychology!' James was laughing, but Gerald couldn't see the joke. 'Aww. That is too good. Yes babe, I'm recreating patterns. That's my one and only Modis Operandi.'

'So what is it, then? Some guy gets you to suck his dick when you're young and it has no effect?'

'Gerald, it was the same age as you were when you were playing around with little Daniel.'

'But that wasn't in a public bathroom with no foreplay.'

'Judgemental, much?! What was I gonna do, let the chance pass me by? People had already sexualised me at school, so I didn't care about the kind of slut-shaming I'm copping right now. Plus, I liked him. What if I never got the opportunity again? I don't have hang-ups about sex, Gerald, even though *some* people do. We were always open about it in my family. It's why I joke about being a slut so much. People think they're ok with it and then I say something slutty and they're shocked, like they've just heard something unspeakable.'

Gerald was trying not to turn crimson. He'd just been accused of 'slut-shaming' his – what were they, boyfriend? Person of interest? In any case, James was right, he had been judgemental and prudish. He'd let the different circumstances – the toilet block, out in public, straight into it without foreplay – colour his judgement. He had a sneaking suspicion James had purposely set it up that way to make it shocking. If this was a test, Gerald had definitely failed.

'Anyway,' James continued, 'sorry, I shouldn't have laughed. By trying to analyse me, I know you were trying to show concern for my wellbeing. So, thank you.'

Gerald's face had barely stopped burning the entire walk. He bristled with the condescension of that last comment, and wondered what on earth they were doing this for. James clearly didn't think Gerald had much to offer apart from sex. Gerald considered himself quite an analytical person, and since he still believed his analysis had merit, he didn't appreciate being laughed at for it.

In fact, Gerald's analytical abilities were one of the strongest parts of his personality, in his opinion. He'd obviously hit a raw nerve with James, who didn't want to acknowledge that there might be the slightest amount of trauma associated with his experiences at school. Or was Gerald merely pushing his morals onto someone else? James didn't seem all that tortured by it. Perhaps James was right to snicker. Gerald couldn't tell. All Gerald knew was that this walk had been a complete disaster. He'd shown how sub-par his conversation skills were. He'd offended James by being a judgemental prude. He'd been defensive throughout. And to top it off, the terse look he wore on the way home can't have been a good look.

By the time he pushed the large iron gate to his apartment block, he'd convinced himself that this would probably be their last walk. Surely, he'd be ghosted after this. Somehow, though, he survived the chopping block. Whether it was the dearth of options James had available to him during Covid or some other miracle, he still received a 'Good night' text with a kissy emoji from James that evening. Something had saved him.

'They say you should find the person that completes you,' James had said at the wedding ceremony as part of his vows. 'Gerald, you definitely fill my slot and make me whole.'

To this, an eruption of laughter ensued. And while it didn't seem to Gerald like the most promising thing to have built a relationship upon, and it meant that their relationship could crumble depending on James's sexual appetite, Gerald would happily accept James's partnership regardless of what drove his affections.

Had James known the level of his new husband's insecurities, perhaps he might have spent more time building him up, but this would have required Gerald being vulnerable, and vulnerability could lead to people seeing you for who you are and leaving you. Again, with the daddy issues . . .

'You have to invite him!' James had said, bewildered as he watched Gerald's face sink behind an invisible rain cloud. 'You can't not invite your dad.'

James couldn't understand how Gerald could not want to invite family. He thought that if he could convince Gerald to reach out his hand, he could have what James had with Geoffrey.

'I love my dad,' James had said one day when they were on another one of the Covid-lockdown walks.

They'd been dating for just over two months. The Covid infection numbers had been starting to fall, and the government was making noises about the end of lockdown being in sight if everyone kept being good little lemmings. They'd tried to choose a different walk each day, and rather than heading towards a park, they'd chosen to walk along George Street, one of the main thoroughfares of Sydney City, and head to Circular Quay. The usually busy street had been eerily deserted, and made it feel like they had their own private concrete playground. This seemed to trigger James's thoughts of his parents and childhood.

'He's a great role model on how to treat your partner. He calls himself a SNAG – a sensitive new-aged guy. No gender-role tussles around housework. It's just who wants to do what, and if neither of them like it, it came down to whose turn it is. And he's really patient. Whenever I'm in trouble, I can just call up and ask him for help. When I was young, they took me to an ice-skating rink out west. They hired skates, and when I stepped into the rink, I was holding on to the bar so tightly I thought I wouldn't be able to let go without falling through the ice and freezing. Dad was there every step of the way while I tried to figure it out. It took two hours before I could finally kind of skate a little. The most important thing was for me to let go of my fear of falling, then my upper body relaxed and I could move smoothly. That wouldn't have happened without patience. That's dad down to a tee. I'll never forget that. It's where I get my patience from.'

Gerald had wondered at this last statement. They were walking past the Apple store, and Gerald had to turn away to hide a smirk. While James was a lovely guy, 'patient' wasn't one of the first words he'd use to describe him. *Assertive* was a better way to describe him, Gerald thought, or *Quick to form and enact a private agenda*, but he said nothing, and let James continue his trip down memory lane.

'I got that from him, because he told me he doesn't see what the rush is for people to want others to do something or get something that's new to them so quickly. Dad would tell me to do something, and when I didn't get it right, instead of saying "You're not listening!" he was like, "Oh, you don't understand what I'm asking you. Look, when I say move your foot to the side, you're doing this, but you need to do is this, you see? It's a different angle, and that's what helps you propel you forwards and still keep your balance." That's how I learned that if the message isn't getting through, it's not because people choose not to listen to you when you ask them or tell them something most of the time – it's that they don't understand how to process what you're telling them. Most people don't see the world that way, but it's so obvious that that's how the world works. Dad's who I came out to first. It was so smooth and easy. Mum had no problem with it either, of course, but she's always been more of an assertive figure than Dad, so even though I like that she's got that strong female vibe, it's more comfortable with Dad because he's a bit softer.'

Gerald was putting two and two together. So, it was Maureen that James really got his personality from, although James considered himself a mini-me of his dad. It was cute that James was just a little delusional.

'Mum gets a bit more bored by explanations,' James had continued, 'but Dad would just sit there when I asked a question and tell me as much as he knew. Then if it was obvious he didn't know the answer, he'd look it up for himself, then explain it as well as he could. He kind of taught me it's okay not to know something. It's why I don't mind being a ditz. Mum, on the other hand, she likes to know stuff and likes to be seen as formidable. Lucky, too – otherwise if I was too soft, I wouldn't have dealt with coming out to the rest of the world as I did. You kind of need a mix of both parents, I think.'

James had come to the end of his soliloquy, and by then they'd reached Circular Quay. They'd looked out over Sydney Harbour. The Sydney Opera House sat resplendent as the glimmering water surrounding it reflected light onto its white tiles. The Harbour Bridge on the other side was looking ominously at them, its impressive size made even larger without cars passing over its roads. Gerald couldn't help but think how small he was as James had relayed his feelings about his upbringing. It was so foreign, like a trip to Oz, where everything's fairy dust and lemon drops. It certainly had no relevance Gerald could see as it pertained to his relationship to Patrick. And yet it was a comment Gerald had made about not liking his dad much that had spurred James into this diatribe.

'Mmm,' Gerald said rather succinctly, eyes glazed over and consciousness ejected, and while they'd moved to other topics for the walk back to Darlinghurst, Gerald thought how crazy it was that people's upbringings could be so different.

He eventually submitted to James's advocacy to invite *all* family members, including his horrid dad. Anything to keep James happy. He was obviously the better, less-fucked-up half of the relationship.

If Gerald had thought more about the discussions they'd had regarding the planning of the wedding, he could have saved himself a lot of hassle. James had demonstrated his decision-making process time and again during this period. He'd refused to react aggressively when pressure was being put on him to either accept a proposal or to consider it quickly. He would make sure to allow himself time and space to decide which way he wanted to go.

They'd had a disagreement about the chairs, of all things, and it had gotten heated. By this time, Gerald had acquiesced to inviting his father along, and now secretly wanted to make the wedding a showcase of how much better he was than Patrick. He'd decided that he desperately needed these chairs, whose cost was three times as much as the second-best option, because they looked so much better. James was worried about the cost blow-out (which continued to rise), and neither of them were budging. Gerald was getting upset that decisions were taking way too long to make.

'They're ugly!' he'd said, 'We can't have people sit on those shitty clear chairs with just a tacky sash as the only thing that makes them look like they weren't borrowed from a two-bit office meeting room.'

'Gerald, I said I need to think about it. I'm not making a decision now.'

'It's always about you, isn't it?' Gerald cried, exasperated. He thought this was a neat trick, turning a boundary into form of selfishness, but unfortunately it didn't work.

'No, it's about cost-benefit analysis. You should know about that.'

Gerald was too impressed by how sharp a retort that was to argue, and while he'd worn a sulky expression when he replied with, 'Wow, okay,' James could see it had been appreciated. Gerald ended up getting the chairs he wanted, because upon consideration, James thought the other ones looked less sturdy, and they had grandparents to think about. But the main thing was that he'd refused to be pressured or rushed.

Gerald and James were still standing just next to the heaping lilacs and the melting cheese table. They were hidden at an isolated part of their wedding reception. Gerald was realising what a fool he'd been. They were right back in that same sad location as Gerald had been earlier tonight when he and Charlotte had been looking for James, only now Gerald noticed two of the aforementioned chairs were sat looking up at him, taunting him for what an idiot he'd been.

Charlie was right. James hadn't said no, he'd said not now. It was just like the chairs, like everything else they'd made decisions about. Gerald was always impatient, and James would always put the brakes on. James was just refusing to be pressured again. He wouldn't give Gerald white lies and placations, so of course Gerald didn't get the immediate 'Yes' he'd hoped for, nor the 'That's a good idea, but let's talk about it later,' and Gerald didn't like the response he got. The whole night had been an episode in Gerald creating his own drama.

The insides of Gerald's cheeks were closing in on themselves as he stood there sullenly reprimanding himself for what an idiot he'd been.

You dipshit, he told himself. *You deserve everything you get.*

Chapter 22

James's clothes were dangling from him. His drooping shirt matched the soggy tablecloths from the neglected table they were standing beside. Only a few of the guests had dared graze from it all evening; most of the gays had been intent on watching their figures or nibbling on sliders. Now the cheeses looked soft and flat, the spring rolls were damp, and the crackers looked limp. Even the poor watermelon had started its transition from vibrant purple to dry eggplant-coloured. Next to the neglected food table was the safest place to be right now.

'So where were you, then?' James asked. His tone was direct, a hint of pre-annoyance laying beneath it, and a look of defiance in his eyes. This put Gerald on the back foot. He guessed he was channelling his mum right now, because this wasn't the soft James he hoped he'd be dealing with. But Gerald's honesty in denying Charlotte's lie meant he wasn't being the usual Gerald that James was used to dealing with, either.

Gerald pushed on regardless. 'Well, you know how I wanted to talk to you about kids earlier?'

'Yes.'

'So when you said you didn't want to talk about it, I figured you didn't want kids.' This resulted in an involuntary harrumph erupting from James's stiff figure, but Gerald continued, 'So I texted Steve, my ex.'

'Okay, so after you fucked me, you went and fucked him.'

'No, we didn't fuck.'

'But you went to.'

Gerald wanted to say no. In his mind, he'd gone to Steve's to discuss having kids. But deep down, he'd known Steve would try to have sex with him. He'd framed his text as a hook-up. He'd had no plan of how he'd broach the subject, or what he'd do if he were to ask Steve about kids. He'd clearly gone to gain immediate gratification that would come with Steve wanting him back. Only Steve had been too full-on. It hadn't gone as planned, and Gerald aborted it. He didn't want to sleep with him, but he had basically gone as a hook-up.

'Yes,' he answered.

'So what do I care?'

Gerald could feel his eyes bug out like a guppy. His mouth opened and closed just as silently. James shrugged a little and waited for the response.

'Well, I wasn't here at our wedding,' Gerald said, unable to keep the incredulous mansplaining out of his voice. *Why do you think you should you care?*

James eyes rolled so far into the back of his head that Gerald thought he surely must have seen the wall behind him.

'Oh my god, Gerald, you're always stepping out to do god-knows-what. I found your PrEP pills and put two and two together ages ago. It's not a big deal. Why should our wedding night be any different?'

'Because this night is supposed to be special,' he said in an argumentative tone, as though standing up for their relationship. But he was actually standing up for himself. This means James knew that when he went missing, he was fucking other people. Yet he married him anyway. Did James even care about him at all, or did he really not give a shit about Gerald personally, just so long as he fucked him as well? What did that say about all those insecurities Gerald had, that told him that no one actually loved his personality, and that people could only love him for his physical attributes?

'Okay, but it's not like you're suddenly going to change because we have a big party and get a new piece of bling.'

Gerald was reeling. He always thought people wanted others to be better, but James seemed to be saying Gerald was never going to change. That he was incapable of change. He was just so matter-of-fact about it, sledging Gerald's character and this situation. This is not how he thought the conversation would go. James was supposed to be upset. He was supposed to give him ultimatums, to give him a reason to be a better man. It wasn't meant to be a fatalistic assassination of Gerald's abilities to be better. He wanted to be pushed to be good. He felt exposed, and worse, he felt dismissed.

'What, so you don't think I can change?'

Even as drunk as he was, James was always quick to size up a situation. As Gerald stood before him like some kindergartener surprised that the flower they'd found half rotting on the ground and given to you hadn't made you jump for joy, he realised Gerald was trying to give him something, something he'd never asked for. He took a breath. This really was a waste of their time, James thought, and he wouldn't hide that he felt that way. It was time to nip this in the bud.

'Gerald, I don't care if you do change. I didn't marry you so you could be someone else, I married you because you make me happy. If fucking randoms makes you feel good, then what do I care?'

'But it doesn't make me feel good, I feel bad about it!'

'Of course it makes you feel good, because you keep doing it.'

Gerald wondered whether James was taking this tone to punish him and make him feel worse. It had to be. It wasn't fair, though. He was being honest, and James was picking him apart. He rallied, and insisted, 'No, it doesn't. I don't know why I keep doing it, but I always feel bad.'

'What are you looking for, Gerald? I've given you absolution, but you don't seem satisfied, so what do you want me to do? Should I be more upset?'

'Yes. What I did was wrong.'

'I see. And then what – I get so upset that I say we should break up? If after this party, you realised you don't wanna be with me, you should just come out and say it instead of making me do the work. It's not that hard to be honest about what you want.'

Gerald had no response that was intelligible.

'No . . .' was all Gerald could manage in response to the idea that he was trying to force James's hand to break up with him. But how else could he explain his actions?

Honesty can sometimes feel like a weapon, and Gerald was feeling attacked. He didn't want to break up, he knew that. But James was right – he was looking for something from James. He wanted James to show Gerald that the thought of him being with someone else filled James with spasms of envy. He wanted him to be to be upset and so jealous that he would lash out in unpredictable ways. He didn't like the idea that James felt so little possession over him that he would be happy sharing him around like a piece of meat, like some soggy Sao biscuit that everyone had a turn on but no one wanted to eat at the end of the session. How was that love? Gerald had never felt as small as he did right now, shrinking under the ambivalence James was showing towards him.

'So you don't care what I do,' he said sulkily, as though the lack of upset on James's part was clearly the problem they were having right now.

James had had enough of Gerald's absolute self-indulgence. The disappointment coating Gerald's angular features was more than he could take. *The gall of someone confessing their sins just so they could keep wallowing in their own filth.*

'If you want me to be upset by something,' James said, 'how about we make it that you think so little of me that you think I don't know who you are and who I chose to marry. Do you think I'm an idiot? That I don't see you sneak off every now and then, only to come back sheepishly? You think I have no idea what it means? I was happy when Charlie told me you'd gone to get coke because I thought you were doing it for me, or at least for us – plus she used most of our bag anyway. She shouldn't have needed to lie to me, especially when

I'm the one marrying you, not her. How about we get upset about you both thinking I'm stupid and can be managed?'

'That's not ...' was again all Gerald could manage. He could tell he was frowning defensively, but he couldn't help himself. For god's sake, he'd admitted he was wrong, and now he was getting yelled at for something completely different. None of this was fair. 'I don't think you're stupid, I just—'

'Well, you do, actually,' James said, refusing to let Gerald finish the rest of his thought, 'because otherwise you both wouldn't conspire against me and keep me in the dark instead of trusting me and being honest with me.'

There was nothing else to say. Gerald stood diminished, shrinking and uncertain of what to do next. James was so pissed off. He didn't look drunk anymore. He still looked like a mess, but a cranky mess. Gerald allowed what James had said to sink in. He never thought James was an idiot. He never even talked about James being dumb; that wasn't Gerald's issue at all. It was that he'd lied to James, that he was a cheater, that he was never happy. This night was supposed to be special, but he couldn't keep even that free from turning into something sordid.

'I'm sorry,' he said. 'I don't mean to keep hurting you.'

James stifled a chuckle. It was actually kinda cute that Gerald was acting so forlorn.

'Gerald, you don't think I know you have issues? You're an emotional clam, you run around behind my back because you think everyone's as incapable of having emotional honesty as you are, and you definitely have a problem with being told "No," but I don't give a shit. Because you make me happy.

You make me laugh, you don't judge me, and you make me feel appreciated. I normally need to be the class clown, but I never feel like I need to be "on" with you. Sure, I know you go off every now and then, but I've told you I don't have sexual hang-ups. You always come back, and at least have the decency to look sheepish about it, which is kind of sweet, even though it's dishonest. But it lets me know you love me. I mean, for someone who's so emotionally frigid, you actually wear your emotions on your face quite distinctly. You make me feel special. Times when we're lying on the couch watching Netflix and you're playing with my hair, or when we're on our walks. Even when we're fighting about plans or getting ready to go out partying. So what if you need to blow off steam every now and then? That doesn't mean I don't feel loved. It doesn't take away from the little things. And those are the things I love about us. Seriously, I don't care about that other stuff. I just want you. Why do you think I married you if I didn't love you, warts and all?'

Gerald's heart swelled. His package swelled. He knew it was a kind of inappropriate moment to be getting hard, but he couldn't help it. James had never been sexier than he was right now. He just told Gerald that he loved him for everything he was, even the slutty side. Even the horrible, shitty personality side, the one that went behind people's backs and sneaked around in the dark, doing what he knew he shouldn't. James had accounted for everything and still loved him. Besides which, he hadn't mentioned Gerald's physical endowments once. Unlike the empty vows James had said earlier in the evening, the ones that were made for effect and for laughs, Gerald knew James loved him for him. For the second time this evening, Gerald's eyes became hot, and stung a little. He flinched and looked at the floor, trying to stop tears from becoming visible.

'You big baby,' James said to him. 'Come here.'

James took Gerald's hand and drew him towards him. Their arms wrapped around each other, their bodies pressed together, and Gerald rested his head against James's shoulder. No wonder that gnawing, empty feeling had started to settle in sometime after the vows. Without knowing it, James's comedic vows had drudged up all the insecurities Gerald had about his inability to be loved. His guilt about his mum, his father leaving, his self-sabotaging ways, all that proof that he wasn't deserving, that no one could possibly love him if they knew the real him. But it was all out in the open now. He couldn't be happier.

'I'm sorry I didn't tell you,' he said quietly, wiping his eyes on James's crinkled and moist shirt.

'That's okay,' was James's response. 'You will in future, though, right?'

Gerald pulled him closer, pressing his crotch against him as his answer. Gerald wanted to make James feel how happy he'd made him. Clearly it would take some time for him to even begin to unpack his connection between sex and love.

'Okay, so we're done with this pity party now, are we?' James asked, grabbing Gerald's butt.

'Mmmhmm.'

'Good. Now, I don't expect miracles, but we're going to have more moments like this where you open up, aren't we?'

'Okay.'

Gerald sighed as he melted into James's arms. Earlier that evening, he thought he'd understand what people meant when they said 'Love can be freeing,' but he had no idea how far off the mark he'd been. He felt James kiss the back of his neck, and he thought of how Julie, their celebrant, had read out that annoying poem people quoted at weddings all the time: 'Love is patient and kind,' she'd said. 'It does not insist on its own way.' It had all sounded so foreign, like a Hallmark card, like the Disney version of love everyone said was out there but no one really lived up to. But he thought of his mum, his biggest cheerleader, and how she would fight with Patrick—often over nothing—but also how she would fight for Gerald. She'd loved him. And he thought of poor Patrick, choosing the absolute wrong way to go about things, waiting patiently for Gerald to reach out, consistently prompting his engagement but never insisting he should reach out to him. Regardless of how idiotic Patrick's actions were in the attempt to show love, he'd said he really did love Gerald. And then there was James. He'd capitulated on many things leading up to the wedding: the chairs, the catering, even the choice of venue, but when he had said no to discussing Gerald's whims, it wasn't just so he could get his own way, but because he really thought it best to wait. Of course, he was right. Gerald was the one incapable of patience. He knew now that he didn't always need his own way.

'It does not rejoice at wrongdoing,' Julie had continued while James smiled at him and Gerald had internally rolled his eyes at the prosaic verses, 'but rejoices at truth . . .' This last part made Gerald's eye-roll stop in its tracks and his stomach sink. He thought he could never be fully honest. In his view, this would of course lead to an end to every relationship he had – friends, family, work, and James. He hid something from nearly all of them, maintaining a cold, metallic exterior that calculated just how much he'd reveal to different people. But now here he was, in his husband's arms after confessing his sins, and he felt closer to anybody than he ever had. Honesty really could make things better, rather than destroy them.

'Love . . . hopes all things.' Another tear trickled down Gerald's face as he kept thinking about Julie's words, and he discreetly wiped his cheek on James's shirt again. Had he known that this "annoying poem" was actually a Bible verse, or who the Corinthians were, he'd have been mortified that something religious had touched him like this. Being guided by "the Word" was so lame, in his view. It was for sheep who couldn't think for themselves. As it was, though, he was blissfully ignorant. He was finally hopeful for the future, for his future with James, for what he might be without the cover-ups and second-guessing of himself. Gerald didn't even know who he was, let alone believe that James knew who he was. But James did know him. He knew Gerald better than Gerald knew himself. So he felt settled. This was the first step towards being a better man.

He could feel the chip on his shoulder slowly melting away as he melted into James's arms. Katy Perry's 'Dark Horse' was playing. They shuffled along to the music like it was an old-fashioned waltz. The party was raging on all around them, but unlike usual, the frenetic energy of the party wasn't making him skittish. It wasn't driving him to think about the next hit, about what else might be needed to fill the space inside. The music didn't echo through him like he was a hollow man made of tin. Instead, it pumped deep into his chest. The screaming void inside him had been quietened. He felt grounded; he felt full. This Tin Man finally felt his heart, and realised that, even with his flaws, he could be loved. He was whole.

Coda

Gerald and James sat on the edge of a catamaran their friends had hired to cruise the harbour. It was one of those four-hour deals where they pick you up at Sydney's Woolloomooloo wharf and take you to some bay, park for a couple of hours to let you drink and take a dip, then drop you back where you came from, looking much less crisp than when you hopped on. The boat had taken them to Cremorne Reserve, close to Taronga Zoo, and everyone was already in their speedos or swim shorts. The onboard speakers were blasting dance music, and their friends were all getting messy, but Gerald and James sat quietly with their sunnies on, looking down at the canister Gerald was holding. James placed his hand on Gerald's shirtless back, reminding him they were doing this together.

His mum had always said she wanted her ashes scattered at sea. Gerald had considered taking the ashes on their honeymoon and spreading them in Columbia or Argentina, but she'd never mentioned South America. Annie had always lived in Sydney, and they'd gone to Taronga Zoo once when

Gerald was a child, so he thought this would be more appropriate. He'd actually forgotten she'd wanted her ashes scattered at sea until he found the canister sitting in a box with all his junk when he'd returned from his time in London, and after that he'd made sure the canister was hidden out of sight, either under his bed or on the top of his wardrobe, because he didn't want to think about it. The guilt he'd felt when he blamed himself for ignoring his mother's call the day she died still burned too hot for him to even think about it. Out of sight was the safest place for it to be. But now he was ready.

Gerald took off his sunglasses and put them beside his thigh. He and James, both dressed only in a pair of speedos, felt the sun beat down on their skin as they conspicuously overlooked the harbour. The air was still today, and the water was crystal clear. James removed his hand from Gerald's back to give him his moment.

'Goodbye, Mum,' he said quietly, over the shouts and squeals of his friends revelling in the party-boat atmosphere behind them, then he pried the canister open and leant over the boat to gently relieve it of its contents. His almost-naked body glistened in the sun, giving him the look of a neoclassical statue.

James took off his sunglasses now, too, watching Annie's ashes tip in clumps into the sea. He thought it would look more serene, like sand sliding out of a bucket. He also assumed the overall effect when the clumps hit the water would be that they'd dissolve beautifully into the ocean like sugar into water. Instead, it was messy and awkward, more like flour than sugar.

Gerald had hoped it would look more beautiful, too. He hated the way his unsteady hand refused to figure out the best angle to tip the contents out smoothly, and he hated the clumps. Perhaps the canister had been locked up too long, he thought. It wasn't going the way he wanted it to, but nothing in the way the canister's contents emptied itself into the salty sea hid death's reality, its randomness and disappointment.

When all the contents had slipped out, and Gerald shook the canister to make sure it was empty, they both sat watching Annie's ashes either sink below the surface or float away. Gerald could hear splashes nearby, and turned to see friends swimming and others bomb-diving off the boat. He sorely hoped they wouldn't get any of the remains on them. James's arm wrapped around him and he was taken out of this concern, turning his attention back to the task at hand.

For years, he'd held on to a lie that had kept him trapped. He'd run away from addressing all the blaming he'd been doing of himself, assuaging his guilt by trying to achieve milestones. A certain amount of money saved. Achievements at work. Accumulating a certain number of stocks. The regard of his friends. He thought that if he looked the part and acted a certain way, if he could make people like him more, he'd fool them into believing he was worthy. Or he'd fool himself. Instead, his endless endeavours towards his achievement lifestyle had left him empty. He remembered his premonition, the dream he'd been having where he took his clothes off and waded into the water. He understood it now. Watching Annie's ashes sink beneath the gentle waves made by the swimmers nearby, he felt as though he wasn't only saying goodbye to her, but to himself. His old self. The part of himself that needed approval, and sought it at any cost. He'd stripped himself of the need for the external embodiments he used to clothe himself in to make him feel good enough. He was already enough.

James kissed his cheek gently, and Gerald tilted his head onto James's shoulder.

'Are you okay?' James asked him.

'I'm fine,' he said. 'Thank you.'

They sat for some time on the edge of the boat, looking out over the harbour, listening to the tiny speakers work their hardest to get the other fifteen people on board amped up. Gerald felt James's hand running across his back and lifted his head.

'I'm proud of you,' James said.

'I couldn't have done it without you,' Gerald replied honestly.

They looked into each other's eyes, and Gerald felt a weight lift from his shoulders. It was done.

Then all of a sudden, as so often happens, the moment was over. Gerald looked over his shoulder. There were bottles of soft drinks, juice, and vodka out on the table beneath the canopy, and a few untouched dips and nibblie plates that were only there because the organisers said, 'You should bring food.' Everyone knew this was to stop people getting too drunk too fast on empty stomachs, but no one listened.

Prue and Charlie were chatting to each other up on the front of the boat, and a few of the boys were pulsating to the rhythm, making sure their movements were kept to a minimum to ensure peak faux-masculinity. It amused Gerald that gay people so often mistake "straight acting" for placid and boring. All the activity made him want to get in amongst it. It was time to move.

'Shall we go inside?' he said to James.

'Yeah,' James said. 'Let's go have a line.'

Acknowledgements

This book started as a project at uni, so I first have to thank Michelle, even if I didn't strictly follow all of your advice.

To Cleo, the very first reader of this work – thank you for your editing prowess and encouragement.

To Annette, Christian, and "the long-suffering" John: thank you for all your support, corrections and suggestions.

JP enjoys using humour to explore queer issues and how queerness impacts upon the way we navigate ourselves within the world. He grew up on a farm in Queensland, Australia, before moving to the bright lights of Sydney, where he attained a Bachelor of Arts (Creative Writing). *Tin Man Nuptials* is his first novel.